PRAISE FOR

Arsenic and Adobo

"I love to read a well-written and quirky cozy mystery. Manansala has created just that with her debut novel, a tale full of eccentric characters, humorous situations, and an oh-so-tricky mystery. Check this one out for the poetic prose and the mouthwatering recipes that are integral to the plot."
—*The Washington Post*

"This book hits the exact right spot. . . . Mia P. Manansala manages to create a murder mystery where nothing is too horrifying and you know everything will be okay in the end. . . . I've heard it described as a 'cozy mystery' and that's exactly what it is, a perfectly cozy puzzle to solve."
—Taylor Jenkins Reid, *New York Times* bestselling author of *Carrie Soto Is Back*

"This breeze-right-through-it mystery follows baker Lila Macapagal as she investigates the murder of her ex-boyfriend, the town's too-mean food critic, after he dies over a meal in her aunt's flailing Filipino restaurant. Finding out whether or not Lila can solve the crime and save the restaurant is as satisfying as it is climactic, with just the right amount of drama."
—*Bon Appétit*

"[An] enjoyable and endearing debut cozy . . . Manansala peppers the narrative with enough red herrings to keep readers from guessing the killer, but the strength of the novel is how family, food, and love intertwine in meaningful and complex ways."
—*The New York Times Book Review*

"Mouthwatering dishes and a funny, smart amateur sleuth make *Arsenic and Adobo* by Mia P. Manansala my favorite new culinary cozy mystery series."

—Lynn Cahoon, *New York Times* bestselling author of
the Kitchen Witch Mysteries

"You will be rooting for Lila Macapagal to save the family restaurant and keep herself out of jail while interacting with her interfering yet well-meaning relatives. The first in a lip-smacking series!"

—Naomi Hirahara, Edgar Award–winning author of *An Eternal Lei*

PRAISE FOR
Homicide and Halo-Halo

"While the follow-up to *Arsenic and Adobo* is a cozy mystery, it's darker, dealing with PTSD, predatory behavior, dismissive attitudes toward mental health, and other issues. Filipino American food and culture, as well as family and community, remain essential elements in the story."
—*Library Journal* (starred review)

"An enjoyable series worth reading."
—DailyWaffle

"Another fantastic book in the Tita Rosie's Kitchen Mystery series! This cozy mystery was just as wonderful as the first book in the series!"
—She Just Loves Books

"A delightful small-town mystery with fun characters and an easy-to-read story. It will also make you hungry, and at the end of the book are a lot of recipes to make what you read about."
—Red Carpet Crash

Blackmail

and

Bibingka

Mia P. Manansala

BERKLEY PRIME CRIME
NEW YORK

BERKLEY PRIME CRIME
Published by Berkley
An imprint of Penguin Random House LLC
penguinrandomhouse.com

Library of Congress Cataloging-in-Publication Data

Names: Manansala, Mia P., author.
Title: Blackmail and bibingka / Mia P. Manansala.
Description: First edition. | New York: Berkley Prime Crime, 2022. |
Series: Tita Rosie's Kitchen Mysteries
Identifiers: LCCN 2022008060 (print) | LCCN 2022008061 (ebook) |
ISBN 9780593201718 (trade paperback) | ISBN 9780593201725 (ebook)
Classification: LCC PS3613.A5268 B53 2022 (print) |
LCC PS3613.A5268 (ebook) | DDC 813/.6—dc23
LC record available at https://lccn.loc.gov/2022008060
LC ebook record available at https://lccn.loc.gov/2022008061

First Edition: October 2022

Printed in the United States of America
1st Printing

Book design by Kristin del Rosario

To James,

Your love and support have meant everything to me.
For that, I'll let you be the funny one in this relationship (for now).
Let's grab some steamed hams later. Love you 3,000 😘

Author's Note

Thank you so much for picking up *Blackmail and Bibingka*! Lila (and I) are in much better places than we were in Book 2, but this is still a crime fiction series and I touch on some topics that can be rather troubling.

As usual, I'd like to give my readers a heads-up for potentially triggering content, which I'll list below. If you'd like to avoid possible spoilers, feel free to skip ahead.

CONTENT WARNING:

substance abuse, gambling addiction, infidelity, emotional abuse, police corruption, family abandonment, physical violence, mentions of suicide

---

Glossary and Pronunciation Guide

HONORIFICS/FAMILY
(THE "O" USUALLY HAS A SHORT, SOFT SOUND)

Anak (ah-nahk)—Offspring/son/daughter

Ate (ah-teh)—Older sister/female cousin/girl of the same generation as you

Kuya (koo-yah)—Older brother/male cousin/boy of the same generation as you

Lola (loh-lah)/Lolo (loh-loh)—Grandmother/Grandfather

Ninang (nee-nahng)/Ninong (nee-nohng)—Godmother/Godfather

Tita (tee-tah)/Tito (tee-toh)—Aunt/Uncle

FOOD

Adobo (uh-doh-boh)—Considered the Philippines' national dish, it's any food cooked with soy sauce, vinegar, garlic, and black peppercorns (though there are many regional and personal variations)

Bibingka (bih-bing-kah)—Lightly sweetened rice cake, commonly consumed around Christmas. There are many varieties, but the most common is baked or grilled in a banana leaf–lined mold and topped with sliced salted duck eggs, butter, sugar, and/or coconut.

Buko (boo-koh)—Young coconut

Champorado (chahm-puh-rah-doh)—Sweet chocolate rice porridge

Lambanog (lahm-bah-nohg)—Filipino coconut liquor

Lumpia (loom-pyah)—Filipino spring rolls (many variations)

Matamis na bao (mah-tah-mees nah bah-oh)—Coconut jam (also known as minatamis na bao)

Pandan (pahn-dahn)—Tropical plant whose fragrant leaves are commonly used as a flavoring in Southeast Asia. Often described as a grassy vanilla flavor with a hint of coconut.

Pandesal (pahn deh sahl)—Lightly sweetened Filipino rolls topped with breadcrumbs (also written pan de sal)

Patis (pah-tees)—Fish sauce

Pinipig (pih-nee-pig)—Young glutinous rice that's been pounded flat, then toasted. Looks similar to Rice Krispies.

Salabat (sah-lah-baht)—Filipino ginger tea

Tuyo (too-yoh)—Dried, salted fish (usually herring)

Ube (oo-beh)—Purple yam

OTHER

Bruha (broo-ha)—Witch (from the Spanish "bruja")

Macapagal (Mah-cah-pah-gahl)—A Filipino surname

Mayabang (mah-yah-bahng)—This term has several meanings depending on context, but here it's being used to mean "show-off"

Noche Buena (noh-che bwe-nah)—Christmas Eve. From Spanish, it literally translates to "good night."

Oh my gulay—This is Taglish (Tagalog-English) slang, used when people don't want to say the "God" part of OMG. "Gulay" (goolie) literally means "vegetable," so this phrase shouldn't be translated.

Parol (pah-roll)—Star lanterns commonly used as Christmas decorations in the Philippines

Simbang Gabi (sim-bahng gah-bih)—Nine-day series of Catholic masses before Christmas (literally translates to "nine nights")

Tsismis (chees-mees)—Gossip

Blackmail and Bibingka

Chapter One

"Adeena, can you *please* shut that off? If I have to listen to that Mariah Carey song one more time . . ."

I scratched out the third mistake I'd made while trying to finalize the menu for the annual Shady Palms Winter Bash. It tied with the Founder's Day Celebration as the biggest event in my tiny town of Shady Palms, Illinois (population: 18,751), and this was the first year my business—my *dream*—the Brew-ha Cafe, would be participating. Considering what a mess the Founder's Day Celebration had turned out to be, I really needed to wow at this party. Despite obsessing over it for the past month, I had less than two weeks till the big bash and hadn't finalized anything.

My best friend and business partner, Adeena Awan, turned the cafe's speaker system down to a decibel that didn't make my ears bleed. "Way to be a humbug, Lila. Ms. Mariah cannot and will not be silenced. Her lambs will make sure of it."

"Hon, you don't even celebrate Christmas. Why do you have all of these?" Elena Torres, Adeena's girlfriend and the third and final member of the Brew-ha Cafe crew (aka our voice of reason), scrolled through the cafe's playlist on Adeena's laptop. It currently had no fewer than ten Christmas music compilations that she'd had on repeat since December 1. It was only December 4, and I was ready to ban her from programming the shop's playlists ever again.

Elena raised her eyebrows at the mix of both religious and secular Christmas songs. "Were you secretly raised in an intensely Catholic family like Lila and me? Because this is a *lot*."

Adeena laughed and handed Elena her morning cup of yerba buena tea. "No, I just like the music. It started as me being rebellious as a kid. Well, as rebellious as you could be in my house. You didn't grow up here, but Shady Palms has a pretty big Muslim and Jewish population, so it was easy to keep Christmas out of schools. But there were still all the commercials and Christmas specials on TV, so I got kind of obsessed with the holiday. I'm mostly over it now, but I still love the music and movies. And also the parties because Lila's family goes *all in* on the holiday."

Despite my "humbug" response, as Adeena put it, I really did love the holidays. The food, the parties, the gifts, the karaoke, the fantastically cheesy and comfortingly predictable holiday romance movies . . . what wasn't to love? I mean, I wasn't like the rest of my family, who used to put up Christmas decorations in September (something about the Christmas season starting in the -ber months) until I convinced them to at least wait till the day after Thanksgiving, but I already had a Google spreadsheet prepared for all the holiday movies the Brew-has and I were going to watch, and had no fewer than ten cookie recipes I wanted to test. There's a reason it was taking me so long to finalize things for the winter bash.

However, I was finding it hard to get into the holiday spirit ever since my long-lost cousin Ronnie came back into our lives a few days ago. Fifteen years of nothing, only for the prodigal son to show up on our doorstep like nothing had happened, saying he'd bought a winery just outside of town and would be staying in Shady Palms for the fore-seeable future.

"Overjoyed" would be an understatement regarding Tita Rosie's reaction to seeing her only child for the first time in over a decade. If she wasn't filling his plate with third and fourth helpings, she was touching his face and fighting off tears, as if she couldn't believe he was real.

I couldn't believe it, either.

Considering everything he put her through, the kindest thing he did for our family was leave, just like his father had before him.

"Let them go," Lola Flor had muttered when I was a kid, as we watched first Tito Jeff and then (a few years later) Ronnie abandon us, Tita Rosie sobbing alone in her room each time. "The Macapagal women will do just fine without them."

My grandmother had been right. Maybe it had taken a while, but the Macapagal women thrived without them. Tita Rosie's Kitchen, our family restaurant, sat right next door to the Brew-ha Cafe and was now doing so well that people from all over the Midwest came down to Shady Palms just to enjoy my family's food. That's right, our hole-in-the-wall restaurant was now a tourist destination. Thanks to that, we finally had enough money to hire outside help and, get this, my aunt and grandmother could actually take a *whole entire day* off.

My beloved Brew-ha Cafe wasn't quite there yet, but it was still on track to turn a profit within the next year or so. We had a rough start back in the summer, but thanks to Adeena's barista skills, my baking wizardry, and Elena's plant witchery, we'd started to establish our-selves as the hang-out spot for the below-forty crowd. We also appealed to anyone who appreciated quality drinks, Filipino-inspired baked goods, and an array of plants and organic bath and beauty products.

As I doodled in the edges of my notebook, trying to figure out what was easy to bake in bulk yet still had enough pizzazz to draw a crowd among the twenty or so tables and stalls that would be at the winter bash, Adeena came over with a tray holding three small cups filled with a creamy concoction dusted with cinnamon.

"Tasting time!" she said. "This is the atole recipe I plan on serving at the big bash. Elena's mom gave me the recipe and I added my own tweaks. What do you think?"

I picked up a cup and took a big sniff, little curls of steam enveloping my face. Along with the cinnamon, I detected a touch of vanilla and a faint scent that I couldn't immediately place until I took a small sip.

"Corn! Is this thickened with masa harina?" I asked.

Elena nodded. "Yup! It's pretty typical for breakfast, especially around Christmastime. I'd asked Adeena to make champurrado, the chocolate version, but she said there was also a Filipino dish called champorado that was rice-based, and we didn't want the customers to get confused."

"Aww, that's sweet. And a good idea, since I think my family will be serving champorado at the big bash. I love this, Adeena! Are we all set with the beverages?"

"Think so. There's Elena's atole, my chai, and of course the house blend with bags of my hand-roasted coffee beans to sell alongside it. You sure you don't want to include one of your drinks?"

"Three is plenty. Our table's kind of small, so I want to make sure we have enough space for everything." I looked down at my winter bash planning list and scribbled down Adeena's contribution before checking her off my list. "What about you, Elena?"

She was reeling off the inventory of potted plants, herbs, and other products she'd set aside for the party when the bells above the door tinkled, announcing our visitor: my cousin Ronnie. He was below average height and had a slight build, but the way he held himself made it seem like he filled the entryway. That air of confidence, plus his carefully styled wavy black hair, golden brown skin, and cocky grin had led to more than one Shady Palms mom showing up on our doorstep, screaming at Tita Rosie because he'd broken another girl's heart—most notably my cousin Bernadette (not a blood relation, don't worry, just a very close family friend). If I was annoyed by Ronnie's return, Bernadette was *livid*. She hadn't stopped by the restaurant or cafe since he'd arrived, and I missed her.

That coupled with the old feelings of resentment that always bubbled at the surface whenever I thought of him, and my anxiety about preparing for the holiday party made my voice come out sharper than I'd meant. "What are you doing here?"

The grin didn't leave his face. He was way too smiley for seven in the morning—I didn't trust anyone who smiled that much before the sun had fully risen yet.

"Good morning to you too, Cuz. And to you, Adeena." He nodded at her before turning his attention to Elena. "Sorry, we haven't met yet. I'm Ronnie Flores, Lila's cousin."

Elena shook his hand. "I thought you were Auntie Rosie's son? Your last names are different."

His smile flickered for a moment before going back to its usual brilliance. "Yeah, it's my dad's last name. My mom went back to her maiden name after he left. Can't blame her."

"Ronnie, what do you want? If you haven't noticed, we were in the middle of a meeting."

He had the grace to glance guiltily at the table strewn with our meeting notes. "Sorry about that. Lola Flor sent me. She said it's breakfast time and you all need to come over. Plus I have something for you all."

"What is it?" Not that I wanted anything from him. But the idea of him giving us something when all he'd ever done was take roused my curiosity.

"Guess you'll have to join us for breakfast to find out." He winked at the girls, who gave him grudging smiles.

I couldn't ignore a breakfast summons from our grandmother, but something held me in place. Since he'd arrived, I'd done my best to avoid him. I'd had more than my share of trouble this year, and being around Ronnie would increase the chances of more drama a billion times over.

He noticed my hesitation. "Mommy would love it if you could all eat with us."

I sighed. This man was playing dirty and he knew it. You couldn't say no to anything that would make Tita Rosie happy. Not unless you were a monster, anyway. *It's just breakfast*, I told myself. Nothing bad ever happened over breakfast, right?

Chapter Two

"Taste this."

Lola Flor shoved a tray of freshly baked bibingka toward me, the charred banana leaves wrapped around the grilled rice cakes releasing an indescribably intoxicating aroma. There were four different topping choices: the usual butter, sugar, and cheese, plus butter, sugar, and coconut, in addition to the more unusual varieties of salted duck eggs and the works (which was basically all of the above). Tita Rosie cut the bibingka into slivers so we could sample them all while Lola Flor poured us mugs of tsokolate to accompany them.

We crowded around the table and took our time tasting each one. Bibingka had a soft and spongy texture, like a chiffon cake, but with a flavor all its own. Modern bibingka was simply baked in an oven, but it's traditionally grilled using charcoal. Lola Flor had a grill behind the restaurant that she used for occasions like this, and her bibingka was miles ahead of any other version I'd tried. My sweet tooth preferred the simplicity of the sugar-topped ones, but the complexity of the salted duck eggs against the other ingredients made me keep reaching for another piece.

"If you're trying to decide which ones to serve this weekend, I'd say combine the sugar, cheese, and coconut toppings for a sweet version and have the salted duck eggs with cheese to tempt our more adventurous eaters," I said.

Lola Flor gave a curt nod, as if I'd passed a test. "What do the rest of you think?"

"The sweet version definitely gets my vote," Adeena said, picking up another piece and dunking it in her hot chocolate. "What do you think, babe?"

Elena had also grabbed another piece, but she chose the salted duck egg. "I think Lila's right about combining the sweet versions, but you should also add coconut to the duck egg and cheese. That hint of sweetness with the salty ingredients is really something."

Lola Flor actually cracked a smile at that. Huh. Couldn't remember the last time she'd smiled so approvingly at me. I glanced at Ronnie out of the corner of my eye and saw him studying Lola Flor's expression with a frown. At least she grudgingly approved of me. She never bothered hiding her dislike of Ronnie.

"Lola, I think—" Ronnie didn't get a chance to finish his sentence because our grandmother turned away while he was talking and walked back to the kitchen.

For just a moment, he let the façade slip and his face crumpled at Lola Flor's rejection. I instinctively moved toward him to . . . what? Comfort him? Why would I bother?

But he must've sensed that small movement, so before I could decide what I wanted to do, he wiped the expression off his face and went back to his practiced nonchalance. "Hey Mommy, what else are you preparing for the weekend?"

She touched his cheek and went into the kitchen without saying anything. The four of us left in the room stood around awkwardly until Ronnie broke the silence.

"They really upgraded the place. It looks way better than I remember. My mom said you had a big hand in it."

I'd been home for almost a year now, and in that time the restaurant had transformed completely. The walls gleamed with a lovely warm terracotta shade instead of the dingy white they'd been my whole life. The art prints, fans, and large wooden spoon and fork set hanging on the walls as well as the woven table runners added a distinct Filipino flair, while the carefully cultivated monstera plants scattered around the room added a lushness and freshness we never would've achieved without Elena's skillful hands. We'd been able to replace the mismatched and scratched-up chairs and tables a few months ago and were starting to acquire new tableware as well. Elena's mom was a skilled ceramicist, just one of her many talents, and we'd hired her to create special dishware for the restaurant. The only things that hadn't changed were the large painting of the Last Supper hung above the table in the party area and the karaoke machine tucked in the corner.

"She wouldn't get rid of that painting, huh?" Ronnie asked, smiling knowingly.

I fought the urge to smile back and failed. "Tita Rosie can be surprisingly stubborn when she wants to be. Considering she let me change everything else and get rid of the Santo Niño statue, it wasn't worth fighting about."

He nodded, a contemplative look crossing his face as he stared at the familiar painting. "Look, Lila. I—"

"Hoy, come help your mother with the dishes," Lola Flor said, interrupting whatever Ronnie was about to say.

He obeyed without a word, a first for him, and with his help the table was laid out. Not with the typical meat, fried egg, and garlic rice we'd usually have for breakfast, but what I can only assume were the dishes they'd planned for the winter bash. They chose dishes that were easy to portion out and still tasted OK when cold: the typical pancit and lumpia (vegetarian and with meat) that you'd see at any fiesta, along with two kinds of siopao, Filipino fruit salad, and champorado.

While we helped ourselves to a little bit of everything (Adeena and Elena sticking to the vegetarian dishes), Lola Flor and Ronnie were locked in another battle, with my grandmother trying to make him eat tuyo with his champorado and Ronnie absolutely refusing:

"These go together."

"I don't like tuyo."

"You're supposed to eat them together."

"Why would I eat dried fish with chocolate porridge? It doesn't make sense!"

"It is traditional! Salty goes with sweet, just eat it!"

This went on for a while before I interrupted their childishness.

"You said you had something for us, Ronnie?" I glanced at the time on my phone to show that we were on a tight schedule.

"Oh yeah! Hold on a sec." He got up and grabbed a tote bag that was over by the hanging coatrack. "I wanted you to try this. It's a few bottles of our signature cabernet sauvignon as well as the lambanog I've developed with our vintner. I know you have a liquor license, so I thought I'd offer you free samples to see if you'd like to stock it at your cafe."

"Lambanog? How're you making coconut wine in Shady Palms?"

The traditional Filipino coconut liquor was popular, especially around Christmas, but since my aunt and grandmother didn't drink, I'd only tried it a few times with friends in Chicago.

Ronnie launched into a long story about how he'd met a master lambanog maker in Florida (what had Ronnie been doing in Florida?)

and had brought everything he'd learned to Shady Palms so he could introduce the Midwest to the wonders of Filipino-made wine. He also explained, step by tedious step, the process of making lambanog—something about collecting coconut sap from flowers. I'd zoned out a few minutes into the explanation; the only thing I could focus on was Ronnie's obvious passion for his subject. I'd never seen him care about anything so much, and that included his own family.

Tita Rosie, meanwhile, was hanging on his every word, smiling and nodding as if she cared about the laborious distilling process and Ronnie's grand plans to put Shady Palms on the map as a purveyor of delicious and unique wines. Which she probably did, since she was nothing if not supportive and loving toward those of us who didn't deserve her.

"—anyway, I was hoping you had time to tour the winery with me later today. Mommy's been wanting to see it and I'd love to introduce you all to the Shady Palms Winery team. Our investors are in town and I was hoping we could all show them a good time."

I hadn't realized how much I'd spaced out till I caught the last half of Ronnie's sentence and couldn't for the life of me figure out how we got from me tasting his wine to all of us entertaining his business investors.

"Sorry, can't. We're finalizing the winter bash menu today and then I'm going into full production mode. Tell them to stop by the cafe though. I'm sure Adeena and I can set something aside for them."

He frowned. "You sure you can't free up an hour or two? I really talked up how our whole family are successful entrepreneurs, and they'd love to meet you. I also bragged about the karaoke parties we have and they really wanted to attend one. I was hoping we could have one tonight."

My aunt froze. "Oh anak, why didn't you say something sooner? I have time to visit your business, but we're also busy preparing for the party and serving our usual customers. We can't just shut down the restaurant at the last minute to accommodate your party."

I flinched at Tita Rosie's use of the word "anak" for someone who wasn't me. OK, so Ronnie was truly her anak since it means offspring, but she'd been using it to refer to me and only me for over a decade. I didn't appreciate sharing that term of endearment with anyone, especially not someone who left us fifteen years ago and was now glaring at my aunt as if she were the one being entirely unreasonable.

"These are my main investors. Without them, I wouldn't even have this business or be back in this town. I owe them everything." Realization at what he had just admitted swept over his face, and he clapped his hand over his mouth like a little kid who accidentally said a bad word. "No, Mommy, I didn't mean it like that! I just, of course I would've come back eventually! It's just that I didn't want to return with nothing to show for it, you know? I, uh . . ."

He stammered on like that, trying to backtrack and make it seem like he hadn't accidentally let his true motivation slip, but the damage was done. Both Lola Flor and I stood up and walked to Tita Rosie's side, who was staring at her son as if he'd just insulted her food. The ultimate betrayal.

"If you want to impress your investors, tell them to stop by our table at the winter bash. Now get out of here. Don't you have work to do?" Lola Flor pulled Tita Rosie up and marched her to the kitchen, not allowing her to stop or say anything.

Elena cleared her throat. "Um, it was nice meeting you, Ronnie. Thanks for the wine." She met Adeena's eyes and the two of them left together. I should've followed them, but I had one last thing to tell my dear cousin.

"If you've turned up after all these years just to break Tita Rosie's heart again, I'll kill you. I'm serious. And Ate Bernie will help me hide the body," I said, bringing up his ex-girlfriend and my cousin/friend.

"So you better not mess up this time. Tita Rosie may be all forgiving, but Lola Flor and I aren't."

Tita Rosie hurried over with a bag full of takeout boxes, interrupting my threats. "Oh anak, I'm sorry we can't host your business partners tonight, but please take this for their lunch. Let them know they're welcome here any time as customers, and I look forward to meeting them later. Maybe tomorrow after the lunch rush?"

She held out the bag as a peace offering, and Ronnie met my eyes before taking it and thanking his mom. She smiled before hustling back to the kitchen.

Ronnie watched her, his expression unreadable. "I swear to you, Lila, I'd rather die than hurt her again. I'm back for good and my business *will* be a success and nothing's going to stop me from proving to my mom that I'm not the screwup I was when I left." His eyes hardened. "I refuse to let anything get in my way again."

Chapter Three

"Your cousin may be a jerk, Lila, but the man knows his wine."

Sana Williams, the Brew-ha Cafe's business coach and our good friend, gazed at the crimson liquid in her glass appreciatively before taking another sip.

As bougie as I was about coffee, tea, and food in general, I didn't know much about wine. My snobby ex-fiancé, Sam, used to mock me about that—to me, wine was either red or white, sweet or bitter, bubbly or not. Also, I could not tell the difference between a five-dollar and sixty-dollar bottle, which was strange because I prided myself on my palate. I mean, I could pick out all the notes. Hints of melon, aged in oak, all that good stuff. But for some reason, I couldn't keep all the varieties straight in my head and was annoyed by my ex's insistence that price was synonymous with quality. He'd wanted me to be his sommelier, but when he realized I wouldn't try to convince people to splurge for the most expensive bottles, he bumped me to back of house. Which was fine with me since that's what I'd been going to school for anyway.

All that to say, I liked wine but wasn't entirely knowledgeable on what made a wine "good." So Adeena, Elena, and I had invited Sana and our friend Yuki Sato (another restauranteur) for a tasting party at the Brew-ha Cafe. Sana had an elegance I could only aspire to, so I trusted her after she tasted the red again and said, "A little dry, but not so much it makes my mouth pucker. The hint of berry makes it pleasant to drink on its own, but I bet it'd be great in my sangria slushies, too." She took another sip, savoring it, and a slow smile of pleasure spread across her face. "The Shady Palms Winery, huh? I might have to visit soon. I'd love to pick up a few bottles for the open house I'm hosting at the studio."

"Then you think we should serve it here at the cafe?" Adeena asked.

"If the rest of their wine is as good as this sample, I'd say it's a worthwhile investment. I'm surprised you need my opinion though. Wine tasting shares a lot of similarities with coffee tasting, and both you and Lila excel at that," Sana remarked.

"Yeah, but coffee actually tastes good," Adeena said as she stared at the red liquid in her glass and wrinkled her nose. Unlike her older brother Amir, she wasn't strictly observant in her Muslim faith. She enjoyed an alcoholic beverage now and then, but she was a cocktail drinker. Wine and beer held little appeal to her raging sweet tooth.

Elena was the beer connoisseur of our group. If she had more time, she'd probably be brewing her own for the shop, but her hands were already full with the cafe, tending to her family's greenhouse, and occasionally helping her mom out at El Gato Negro, their family restaurant.

I was somewhere in between. I liked most alcohol but didn't really love any of them. I was more of a mood or social drinker, though my good friend Jae was doing his best to teach me about the wide world of ciders. "What do you think, Yuki?" As Yuki was a fellow casual drinker and restaurant owner, I wanted to get a sense if this was a good business decision. I was all for supporting family (even if that family was Ronnie), but I had my own business and partners to think of.

Yuki echoed Sana's seal of approval. "I don't have Sana's good taste, but I really like it. Do you know if he makes white wine, too? Akito would consider it heresy, but white wine pairs just as nicely with Japanese food as sake does, and I'd love to offer a few varieties at the restaurant."

"I'm visiting the winery tomorrow, so I'll make sure to ask. See if I can get more samples, too." Tita Rosie had taken me aside earlier and gently nudged me into agreeing to go with her, so might as well use the visit to help my friend.

Yuki grinned. "I know the PTA squad have been resistant to making your shop their new hangout, but I guarantee that will change once you add this to your menu. Few things basic moms love more than wine and gossip."

We all laughed and toasted one another before I poured out shots of lambanog. Even though Ronnie and I called it coconut wine, it was really a liquor similar to vodka or soju. My favorite ones still retained enough coconut flavor to cut through the bite, but not so much it tasted artificial. I hated to give Ronnie any credit, but his was the best version I'd tried (not that I'd had many), and as I sipped the strong liquor, I was hit with inspiration for winter bash menu items. I grabbed my notebook and scribbled down the ideas before getting up to check if we already had the ingredients. One glance at our fully stocked pantry and I knew we were in business. On the way back, I grabbed the plates of cookies I'd baked that morning.

"I promised you all that you'd be the official winter bash cookie testers, so here you go. I made four different flavors and need to narrow it down to two." I set the cookies in front of everyone and kept my descriptions brief to not influence them in any way. "Pinipig shortbread, salabat snickerdoodles, pandan crinkles, and calamansi sugar cookies."

Greedy hands snatched at the cookies, and everyone was silent as they munched on the sweets, sipping wine or coffee to cleanse their palate before moving on to a different flavor.

Adeena was the first to speak up. "Do we really need to choose only two? I think all of these would be popular with our customers. A little something for everyone, you know?"

Yuki nodded as she reached for another salabat snickerdoodle. "I agree. These are all so good and different, plus they all have a holiday feel to them, if that makes sense. I honestly can't choose."

"I just got a great idea for a mason jar trifle using Ronnie's lambanog, and I think it'll be too much to assemble those as well as four different cookies for the party on top of the regular cafe baking," I explained. I felt the same as they did, which was why I'd asked for their help, but didn't want to take on too much and end up with subpar offerings.

"I think packaging these as a holiday cookie sampler box would be a great idea. If you make the dough, I could help with the baking and boxing them up. I'm sure Katie would help, too," Elena said.

Katie Pang was the teenager in charge of our social media—we'd taken her on as an apprentice (not many Shady Palms students went on to a traditional university, so our local high school had recently started an apprenticeship program where students could elect to get on-the-job training along with technical education classes) a couple of months ago—and she was already an important member of our team. She came to the shop every day after school to learn how to track orders, supplies, and accounts from me, and she recently started working the register with Adeena every other weekend so she could get experience in all areas of the business. Elena was particularly grateful about the situation since she still helped out at her mom's restaurant and had been stretching herself thin before we had Katie's assistance.

"That's a great idea," Sana said. "You should work with her and Terrence on building your brand and developing an aesthetic for your Instagram."

Terrence Howell was the cafe's graphic designer and one of my oldest and closest friends. We'd drifted apart after I'd left town to go to university in Chicago, but now that I was back, we picked up where we left off. I guess some friendships were just like that. Knowing him, not only would he come up with a gorgeous design for the cookie boxes, he'd also know the best and cheapest place to have them printed out, then come over and help us pack the cookies on top of that. I should probably pick him up a bottle of lambanog tomorrow if I'm going to have him working so hard during the holidays.

"If our coach decrees it, I guess I'm making all four cookies for the winter bash and calling in Katie and Terrence for reinforcements." Luckily, the cookies were all simple to make; the dough improved after being in the fridge for a while, plus they froze well. I could make big batches of dough ahead of time and leave the actual baking to the others if necessary. "The trifle will probably need to be assembled the day of the big bash, so I should start testing that recipe tonight."

"Where's Bernadette? Still at the hospital?" Sana asked, refilling her wineglass.

"She's avoiding Ronnie. Haven't seen her since he arrived." I sighed. "I think she's hoping him being around is a temporary thing and is trying to hide out till he's gone, but I don't see that working considering how small this town is. Plus, you know how our families are."

As if she could sense me talking about family, my phone lit up with a call from Tita Rosie. "Anak? Are you busy later?"

The question was innocent enough, but her apologetic tone put me on my guard. "I'm going to be testing out the final recipes for the winter bash. Why?"

"I want you to come with me to check out Ronnie's business and meet his colleagues. You're smart and observant, and you know more about how businesses work than I do. I need to know if Ronnie or his partners are doing something wrong."

That . . . sounded very unlike Tita Rosie. Everyone else in my life was nosy AF (myself included) but she was good about minding her business and letting people live their lives. Plus, it wasn't like her to be suspicious of her son—she was the only person who bothered giving him the benefit of the doubt when it came to his schemes. The rest of us had been burned too many times.

"If you need me, I'll come with you. But why do we have to go tonight? We were already planning on visiting for lunch tomorrow."

My aunt paused, the drawn-out silence confirming that something was very wrong. "Tita Rosie? Did something happen?"

"I got an email. I think Ronnie's in trouble."

That was nothing new. "What did it say?"

"'Ronnie Flores and Co. have blood on their hands. Pay $50,000 or the world will know what they did in Florida.'"

Chapter Four

"Hey everyone, I'd like to introduce you to my mom and cousin."
After Tita Rosie's rather dramatic announcement, the two of us came up with a plan to make our sudden appearance less suspicious. Which was how, a few hours later, my aunt and I ended up at the winery to surprise Ronnie and his colleagues with dinner and dessert.

Ronnie had given us a brief tour of the winery then led us toward his massive office, promising a more thorough walk-through during operating hours. At his introduction, a petite Filipino woman wearing blue jeans, killer high-heeled booties, and the most hideous holiday sweater I'd ever seen hopped up from her desk and moved toward us. The white guy next to her also got up to welcome us, though at a much more sedate pace. He was also wearing a holiday sweater, but it was a simple snowflake pattern, tasteful and expensive-looking, instead of the explosion of colors and patterns the woman's sweater had. Oh my gulay, did her shirt actually have tinsel and lights *and* bells on it?

The woman took in my startled stare and laughed, holding out her hand. "I'm Isabel Ramos-Garcia, but feel free to call me Izzy. And this is Pete Miller," she said, gesturing to the blandly handsome man at her side. As I introduced myself and shook her hand, she explained, "Xander bet me I wouldn't wear all the atrocious sweaters he bought 'cause he thought I'd want to make a good impression on the townspeople. What he failed to take into account is that I have zero shame and love to win. Besides, who doesn't appreciate a good conversation starter?"

Izzy's handshake was as warm and strong as her smile. I already liked her, which surprised me. If she willingly went into business with Ronnie, king of get-rich-quick schemes, there had to be something shady about her. Especially considering that note Tita Rosie got earlier. Still, as I watched her wrap my aunt in a gentle hug and chat with her in Tagalog, I figured Ronnie was due to make at least one good decision in his life. Izzy was likely it.

I tried to start a conversation with Pete, who seemed nice enough but had none of Izzy's warmth. He returned my greeting and handshake but ignored my attempts at small talk and returned silently to his desk. Izzy and Ronnie had the charm covered, so my guess was he was the numbers guy who didn't have to bother schmoozing.

Ronnie must've noticed mine and Pete's awkward exchange because he left Tita Rosie and Izzy to come join me. "Hey Cuz, can you hand me the sweater that's on my desk? I need to put it on before Xander gets back."

I tossed him the hideous holiday sweater, which he quickly pulled on. "Who's Xander?"

"Ah, how does one even begin to describe a man like Xander Cruz?" The question came from a tall man wearing dark jeans, a fitted green Henley, and a bright red blazer covered with a Christmas light pattern who'd just entered the room and was now approaching us. The lower half of his face was covered with a thick, meticulous beard, and made it hard to tell his exact age (late thirties, maybe early forties?) but it couldn't hide his wide grin. On his arm was a woman I could only describe as expensively beautiful. Not that she wore her wealth in an obvious way, but everything from her caramel-and-honey-highlighted chin-length hair down to her red-soled heels told me this was a woman used to the finer things in life. Her one concession to the rather festive attire the others wore was a sparkly snowflake-patterned scarf that she wore over her cable-knit sweater dress and sparkly snowflake earrings that glittered with what I was sure were real diamonds.

She surprised me by offering her beautifully manicured hand and a smile even warmer than Izzy's. "I'm Denise Sutton, and this big head here is my fiancé, Xander. We're the main investors for Shady Palms Winery. You must be Ronnie's family. He's spoken so glowingly about all of you, it's nice to finally meet you."

Her perfume wafted toward me; Roja Haute Luxe, if I wasn't mistaken. Sam's mother had worn it and loved to brag how it was "très exclusive" (apparently the perfumer only produced five hundred bottles a year) and cost $3,500 each. So glad I hadn't married into that family.

"I'm Lila Macapagal, Ronnie's cousin. His mom is over there talking to Izzy." I gestured over at Tita Rosie and Izzy, who were so deep in conversation they didn't notice us talking about them. "She runs Tita Rosie's Kitchen and I own the Brew-ha Cafe right next to it. If you two are in town long, you should stop by. We brought dinner and dessert for you all, and I guarantee you haven't had Filipino food as good as what Tita Rosie makes."

Xander lit up. "I love Filipino food! Gotta appreciate any culture that loves lechon as much as us Puerto Ricans."

"I've never had it, but I do love trying new things. Xander has definitely expanded my palate," Denise said, smiling affectionately at her fiancé.

"I'm glad you're here, but I wish you'd let me know you were coming," Ronnie said, looking regretfully at the feast Tita Rosie was laying out. "We all just had dinner."

Tita Rosie froze in the middle of lifting the foil off the tray of green jackfruit adobo. "I'm sorry, you're right. I just thought it would be a nice surprise for you." She chewed her lip for a moment, then started packing everything up. "Well, now you don't have to worry about your baon for tomorrow! Do you have a fridge I can store these in?"

"Thanks, Tita, and don't worry about packing up now. We have a huge fridge in the staff lounge, so we can do it all later. I'm glad we won't have to worry about lunch for the rest of the week," Izzy said, peeking under the foil at all the delicacies my aunt and grandmother had prepared.

"Do any of you have room for dessert, or should I put these in the fridge, too?" I pulled one of my individual buko pandan trifles out of the refrigerated tote bag I was carrying. Considering how little time I had to come up with the recipe, I was proud of how they'd turned out: bright green pandan chiffon cake brushed with a lambanog-spiked pandan sugar syrup, coconut custard, thin slices of juicy red strawberries, all topped off with coconut whipped cream, strawberries, and glittery nonpareils. The whole thing begged you to dig a spoon through the contrasting layers, but not before taking a picture to post on social media, of course.

Izzy clearly knew what was up because she did exactly that: She scooped up one of the mason jars and took an artful photo before grabbing a spoon and diving in. "Mmm, the pandan and coconut go so well with the tart strawberries! Ronnie said you were good, but he definitely undersold you."

OK, I really liked this girl. I made a mental note to introduce her to my crew—Sana would be thrilled to add another WOC entrepreneur to our group. They'd also helped me with cases in the past, so they could help me figure out if Izzy was sus or not. At Izzy's enthusiasm, the rest of the group helped themselves to the trifles I set out on the table. Despite her carefully put-together appearance, Denise had no problem shoveling in large spoonfuls of cake and custard.

"This is so good!" she exclaimed. "I've been sneaking tastes of Ronnie's coconut wine all day; love it by the way, but this takes it to a whole new level. I wonder if we should include recipes as part of the marketing plan. Put them up on the website."

Ronnie grinned. "You've gotta try it with the Brew-ha Cafe's coffee and a shot of lambanog. It's the perfect way to cut the sweetness."

Denise nodded, but Xander said, "Just coffee for me." He looked pointedly at Denise. "You said you had a headache, and you've already had quite enough of that wine. You sure you don't want just a coffee?"

He stressed those last words very carefully, but Denise laughed it off. "Oh, stop fussing, dear. I also said I had a tummy ache, but I was probably just craving sweets. Lila's cake is doing a wonderful job of reviving me."

Ronnie went to the table to pour coffee from the large to-go box I'd brought. "I had a couple special bottles of lambanog set aside for the two of you. Sure I can't tempt you, Xander?"

"Have the twins pack the rest to go and I'll try it later. I'm driving," he explained. "Where are the twins anyway? They're supposed to be helping you."

A snide voice near the door cut in. "'The twins' were walking the floor and taking notes on the general operation like you asked them to."

We all turned toward the speaker to see a tall man who'd just entered the room clutching an iPad. He looked to be around Ronnie's age and wore his disdain and tailored clothing with the confidence of someone several tax brackets higher than me. And though his tan skin and blond hair were not God-given, they were certainly not out of a drugstore bottle. The woman standing next to him was a carbon copy, right down to her matching iPad cover.

She at least took the time to introduce herself. "Despite how Xander and Denise refer to us, we actually have names. I'm Olivia March and this is my brother, Quentin. We're part of Sutton & Cruz Hospitality Services."

"They're our assistants," Denise said, scraping out the last of the trifle from the jar.

"Oh, thank goodness, you all brought dinner," Quentin said, eyeing the trays on the table. He smiled at Tita Rosie and me, his demeanor and tone doing a total 180 from how he'd responded to Xander. "We haven't had a chance to eat yet and figured everyone had forgotten about us again."

Xander choked on the coffee he'd been drinking. "Oh yeah, sorry about that, man. But uh, Ronnie's family brought us a feast, so dig in!"

Olivia hovered behind her brother as he peeled back the foil, inspecting each dish. "Do you have any vegetarian dishes?"

Her brother gave her a look and made a fake throat-clearing kind of noise, and she sighed. "Mostly vegetarian, but maybe seafood is OK?"

Tita Rosie hurried to reassure her. "Oh, we're used to accommodating various dietary restrictions, so we have vegetarian as well as gluten-free options here. Anak, could you point them out for her?"

"So you're a vegetarian?" I asked as I pointed out dishes like green jackfruit adobo, steamed fish, kinilaw, and shrimp pancit.

"Vegan, actually, but I had to change my diet recently due to health issues. That's why my brother is fussing. I'm not even allowed to eat strictly vegetarian anymore," she said, rolling her eyes. She took a big bite of the pancit and hummed her appreciation. "Though I guess it's not so bad if I get to eat stuff like this."

"Yes, heaven forbid I look out for my little sister," Quentin said. With a gleam in his eye, he added, "Since you care so much about your diet, I guess you won't mind me taking the last dessert," and swiped the final mason jar trifle off the table.

"Hey, don't eat it all! I want to try some, too." Olivia pouted as her brother made a big show of closing his eyes in rapture as he sampled the dessert. They came off as caring but rather childish, considering they were several years older than me. But maybe that's what it was like having a twin—someone always by your side to both spar and scheme with. I didn't have siblings, but I had Bernadette and that was pretty much what our relationship was like.

"You can have mine. I don't really like sweets." Pete handed his unopened jar to Olivia, who fluttered her eyelashes at him and thanked him profusely.

Izzy finally tore herself away from my aunt and moved toward Pete's side, placing her hand on his arm. "That's so sweet of you, honey."

Ah, so those two were together? I wondered if it was awkward for my cousin to be the third wheel in a business partnership. It hadn't been a problem for me, but Adeena and Elena were special.

"So, tell us about your company. We've heard a little about it from Ronnie, of course, but I'd love to know what you all do, too. And thanks so much for taking care of my son," Tita Rosie said.

"He is a handful, isn't he?" Izzy said, grinning at him. "But he's also an idea machine. When it comes to Shady Palms Winery, Ronnie's the heart and Pete's the brains."

"What about you?" I asked.

"She's the one with vision. She takes my ideas and Pete's calculations and makes things happen," Ronnie said. The fondness in his eyes and voice made my aunt and me exchange glances. Well, well, well.

"That she does. She's the one who convinced me to invest, after all," Xander said. "Denise admires passion and creativity and was ready to go all in after Ronnie's pitch, but I wasn't so sure. It was Izzy who broke it all down and let me know I wasn't dealing with a bunch of pie-in-the-sky first-timers."

Denise shrugged. "What's the point of having money if you're not using it to help people achieve their dreams? Plus, I had a good feeling about them."

"Yet you won't back *our* business," Quentin said. Although it was Denise he was speaking to, he glared at Xander over his wineglass.

"I'm sorry, darling, but we've talked about this. I trust my gut and Mercedes, and both told me it was a bad idea. Now then," Denise scraped the last bit of trifle from the jar. "I'm ready for another drink."

"Who's Mercedes?" Tita Rosie asked, holding out the tray of cookies I'd brought.

"Her astrologer," Xander said, hand hovering over the selection. He finally settled on a salabat snickerdoodle. "She gives wonderful advice. Denise relies on her whenever she's unsure about something."

"How convenient that you not only introduced the two, but that Mercedes gave your relationship the thumbs-up when Denise wasn't sure if she should accept your proposal." Quentin drained his glass and refilled it. He looked like he wanted to say more, but Olivia put a hand on his arm, and he took a deep breath to calm himself. "Sorry, Denise. I shouldn't have said that."

For an assistant, this Quentin guy sure had a mouth on him. Not that an assistant needed to be constantly bowing down and kissing butt or whatever, but you'd think he wouldn't be so outright rude in front of anyone. Not if he valued his job, anyway. Then again, the way he was dressed, maybe job security wasn't a priority for him?

He drained his glass again and reached for another refill, but the bottle was empty. "I think I've had too much to drink, so I'm going to stay quiet now. Sorry for this less-than-shining first impression, everyone."

Denise and Xander shook their heads, watching their assistant move to the table to uncork yet another bottle of wine. Olivia walked over to her brother and put her hand on his shoulder, speaking to him in low, soothing tones.

Ronnie stepped in to smooth things over before it got too awkward. "Anyway, I've got something just for you two," he said to Xander and Denise as he pulled out a bottle of lambanog from the office's mini fridge. "Wait, why is this the only one here? I set aside two bottles."

"Oh, that was me. I stopped by earlier to see how things were going, and the twins told me you'd set aside bottles for me. Um, for us. So I opened one and poured myself a glass." Denise glanced at the bottle Ronnie was uncorking. "Well, a couple of glasses. The coffee I got from the diner was absolutely awful, so I needed to wash the taste out of my mouth. I told them they could have the rest."

Ah, so the flush on her pale cheeks wasn't just her makeup, and the warmth of her handshake wasn't entirely due to her personality. Considering how much she'd already consumed, I couldn't believe I hadn't smelled the alcohol on her. Then again, her perfume was rather strong. I wondered if that was on purpose.

As I studied her appearance, Denise chugged the lambanog-laced coffee Ronnie had handed to her. As she leaned forward to put the cup on the table, her demeanor swung from elegantly put together to falling down drunk in what seemed like seconds. All those shots she'd had earlier must've finally caught up to her, I thought, watching her sway dangerously on her four-inch heels.

"I think you've had enough. Ronnie, get some water, would you?" Xander commanded as he grabbed his teetering fiancée.

"You know what, dear? I do believe you're right," Denise said, right before vomiting all over him and passing out in his arms.

Chapter Five

"What an absolute disaster," Ronnie said, his head resting on his arms on his desk, while Tita Rosie stroked his hair.

After Denise vomited and passed out, Xander and the twins cleaned her up and packed her into the car with a swiftness and ease that suggested they'd done this before. Xander had insisted it wasn't Ronnie's fault, but Ronnie was still beating himself up over the possible loss of his investors. Izzy and Pete were off whispering in the corner, but I couldn't hear what they were saying unless I got conspicuously close, so I tried to comfort my family.

"It's not ideal, but I'm sure they won't pull their funding just because one of them chose to drink too much. It's not like you were forcing drinks in her hand. And that guy Xander acted like this was a common occurrence. I'm sure it'll be fine."

"We're already on thin ice, and this sure as hell doesn't help." Pete, showing more emotion in that one sentence than he had all night, crossed the distance across their large office to glare down at Ronnie.

"If this is Florida all over again, I'm out. I'm not getting caught up in your mess again."

Florida. Tita Rosie and I exchanged glances, both of us likely thinking of that threatening email. It couldn't be a coincidence.

"Now hold on," Izzy said, rushing over and standing between Pete and Ronnie. "That was not his fault. It was none of our faults and has nothing to do with our business here, so I suggest not bringing it up again."

She stressed that last sentence, casting a subtle glance toward Tita Rosie and me. If I hadn't been watching them so closely, I would've missed it, but it told me maybe there was something to that blackmail note after all. The question was, did I press the issue now in front of everyone or try to talk to them individually and see if their stories tracked? Before I could formulate a plan of attack, Ronnie's phone rang, making the decision irrelevant.

"Xander! How is De—" Ronnie paused, his face draining of color as he listened to the speaker. "We'll be right there. I'm so sorry, I—"

Xander must've hung up, because Ronnie stopped speaking and got unsteadily to his feet. "Denise is in the hospital and it doesn't look good."

Nobody else moved; I think we were all in shock. I definitely was. Tita Rosie recovered first. "Let's go. They need our support." She crossed herself and guided her son toward the door, followed by Izzy and Pete.

Even though I wasn't religious anymore, I took a moment to do the sign of the cross as well. Something told me we'd need it.

We'd all rushed to the hospital immediately after receiving the call, but we still weren't fast enough.

"You're too late. She's gone," Quentin said. He sat with his arm around his sister, who had her head in her hands and didn't bother looking up at us. A box of tissues sat on Olivia's lap, and Quentin's red eyes as well as the tissues clutched in his hand let me know they'd gotten the news shortly before we arrived.

Izzy gasped. "I'm so sorry. Oh no, I'm so sorry. Where's Xander? What happened?"

"We still need to run a few tests, but it was likely alcohol poisoning. My condolences."

We all turned around at that. Xander stood with a doctor, who had just spoken, and my cousin Bernadette. I'd texted her on the way to the hospital, and she said she'd try to get assigned to Denise's room since she was working the night shift. Guess that didn't matter now.

My aunt stepped toward Xander, wringing her hands. "I'm so sorry for your loss. Please let me know if there's anything we can do."

Xander just nodded, his eyes trained toward her but not exactly at her, as if he were looking at something far in the distance. Tita Rosie looked at her son and tilted her head toward Xander, probably signaling him to say something, too. Ronnie just looked at Izzy and Pete, the look on his face begging them to handle it.

Izzy stepped forward and took Xander's hands in hers. "Xander, we're here for you. Just let us know what you need. I'm sure you've got a million things on your mind right now, so if we can lift the burden in any way, please let us know."

That seemed to bring Xander back into the moment. "Yeah. Thanks, Izzy. I just . . . have a lot to process right now. I can't even start planning her funeral yet, since I want the doctors to run some tests and I have no idea how long it'll take. I just don't know."

"You mean, like, an autopsy?" Olivia's face blanched in horror. "They're going to . . . going to cut her up?"

I knew how necessary autopsies were for a death like this, but I privately agreed with Olivia. I'd watched enough crime shows and listened to enough true crime podcasts to know how invasive the procedures were and couldn't imagine how horrible it must be for the friends and family of the deceased to think about.

Her brother pulled her closer, tightening his hold around her shoulders. "I'm sorry, is that necessary? I thought you said it was alcohol poisoning? An autopsy just seems so . . . so undignified."

The doctor had moved a respectful distance away after she'd delivered the news, but she came a little closer to join the conversation. "There were some irregularities that I mentioned to Mr. Cruz, and he wants me to follow up on them. I'm sorry, but I can't speak to more than that." She turned back to Xander. "Again, my condolences for your loss. I'll contact you if I have any questions."

The doctor gestured at Bernadette, who followed her, but not before a quick glance at Ronnie. He made a move as if to talk to her, but she scurried away after the doctor.

"Let's go home, anak," Tita Rosie said. "We shouldn't intrude any longer."

"Do you need a ride home?" I asked Xander and the twins. "Or I mean, to wherever it is you're staying?"

Xander managed a sad smile. "Thanks, but we'll be fine. I appreciate you coming to the hospital. I'm sure I'll see you around."

We all went our separate ways, and once I was back at home, tucked in bed and cuddling my dog, Longganisa, for comfort, I reflected on the day and how we'd gotten to this point. I knew Ronnie would bring trouble, but I thought that threatening email would be the worst of it. Now we had a tragic death on our hands, and part of me (the part that had grown warier and more suspicious over this past year) couldn't help but wonder:

What was the doctor going to find in those tests?

Chapter Six

"What is it about your family that just brings the most drama ever? Did your ancestors break a promise to a wise woman and get cursed? Because it's really starting to feel like it."

I'd just finished telling Adeena and Elena what had happened last night and was too tired to question Adeena's line of thinking.

"Ignore her. We just watched that old movie *Holes* last night and she's being weird." Elena handed me a steaming mug. "Drink this. Mate has almost as much caffeine as coffee, but it's gentler. You seem like you need a boost."

I cupped my hands around the mug, letting the warmth comfort me before taking a sip. "Thanks. And if there's a family curse, its name is Ronnie. I knew his showing up after all these years would lead to trouble."

"Do you think this is gonna cause problems for his business? I know he was really nervous about making a good impression." Adeena poured herself a cup of her signature lavender chai latte and joined us.

I sipped at the mate, enjoying the strong, earthy flavor and herbal, almost eucalyptus-like aroma. "No clue. I hope not. I don't particularly care what happens to him, but I know Tita Rosie would be devastated if the business folded and he had to leave again. Plus, the winery is supposed to bring more jobs to Shady Palms. Marcus just started there as a security guard and Joseph took them on as a client."

Marcus and Joseph were my Ninang Mae's sons and my unofficial cousins as well. Joseph was an accountant, so I was sure he'd be fine if the business folded, but Marcus had been unemployed since he'd quit the Shady Palms police force earlier this year.

Elena sighed, picking at the banana bread on her plate. "My cousins were hoping to get jobs there as well. They're tired of working in the family restaurants but figured they could use that experience to get hired as restaurant suppliers or something. I might tell them to hold off until the winery becomes more stable."

"That's a good idea. Besides, according to Ronnie, in the wintertime, the winery focuses on filtering and fermentation, so they don't need a full staff just yet. Spring is the beginning of their hiring season, so tell them to try then. If the winery's still around, that is," I added.

The bell above the door rang, signaling our first customer of the day, so the three of us split up and headed to our respective areas. While Adeena and Elena handled the storefront, my domain was the kitchen in back. I drained the last of my mate to get my head back in the game—Denise's death was tragic, but I didn't know her, and there was nothing I could do to help her now.

I pulled the cookie dough I'd prepared yesterday out of the fridge, and as I started rolling the snickerdoodle dough in my salabat sugar mix, I thought about making something nice for Xander and his assistants. Despite how Quentin and Olivia had acted toward Denise at the winery, they were clearly shaken by her sudden death. I glanced at the clock—the morning tsismis put me behind schedule, and I needed to speed it up if I wanted to have these baked goods ready for our customers. The cafe came first, I reminded myself. At lunchtime, I'd pop next door and see what Tita Rosie and Lola Flor had planned. There was no way they wouldn't be preparing meals and scheduling condolence packages for Xander and his team.

Decision made, I lost myself in my baking, not realizing how much time had passed till I heard someone at the kitchen doorway. I looked up and a smile shot to my face when I saw my visitor. "Jae! What are you doing here?"

I washed my hands and rushed over to hug him.

Dr. Jae Park, my friend who I was kinda sorta dating, squeezed me extra hard, nearly lifting me off my feet. "Weren't we meeting for lunch today?" He glanced at the racks and racks of cookies I'd churned out, and the bowl of cookie dough I still hadn't finished prepping. "If you're busy, I can pick something up for you."

"Oh shoot, it's that late already?" I glanced at the clock, which said it was somehow afternoon already. "Is it OK if we eat next door? I need to talk to Tita Rosie."

"You know I'd never say no to your aunt's cooking. Is everything OK, though?" He studied me, his eyebrows scrunching together in concern.

I took off my apron and hung it on the hook by the door. "Looong story. I'll tell you over a plate of lechon."

We made small talk as we walked over to Tita Rosie's Kitchen, the easy banter and laughter between us unfurling the knot in my stomach that'd been there since last night.

"So then I—whoa!" Jae was mid-sentence when I jerked to a stop in front of him as I entered the restaurant, making him and the couple behind us almost crash into me. I heard Jae apologize behind me, but I was already on my way to an occupied table.

"Xander? How, uh, how are you?"

Xander was sitting with my aunt and cousin, an absolute feast laid out in front of them: lechon, mixed adobo, bistec, nilaga, some veggie side dishes, and a giant bowl of rice.

Xander waved his hand at the empty chairs in front of him. "Please join us. Your aunt made enough food to feed an army and it's all amazing."

The poor guy was looking rough—he was as perfectly turned out as yesterday and had the same warm smile from before, but the deep circles under his red-rimmed eyes and his ashy pallor let me know he wasn't doing as well as his image projected.

I introduced Jae to Xander and Ronnie. Ronnie wiped his hands on his napkin and stood up to shake Jae's hand, saying, "Hey, Cuz, you didn't tell me you had a boyfriend! Welcome to the family, man." Ronnie looked Jae up and down quickly before tilting his head to look Jae in the eye. Jae was almost half a foot taller than him, and on the slim but solid side, his broad shoulders straining his dental scrubs. "Whoa, and he's a handsome doctor, too? Way to go, Lila!"

I groaned inwardly. I had been putting off this moment since this thing with Jae was too new and my feelings were too fragile to add my problematic cousin to the mix.

Jae was excellent at gauging the temperature in the room and seemed to understand that the situation we'd just entered was rather fraught, based on the look he gave me. He rolled with it, though, shaking both men's hands and giving Tita Rosie's fingers a brief squeeze.

"Nice to meet you both. I own Dr. Jae's Dental Clinic, just a few doors down, so if you have any dental issues, make sure to give us a visit. And thanks so much for inviting us to join you. I haven't tried Auntie Rosie's lechon before, but Lila's been hyping it up. Glad to finally try it." Jae eyed the plate of roast pig with a grin. "Any suggestions on which part to try?"

"The pork belly is my fave," I said as I snagged a few of the crispy, fatty pieces for myself.

"As a Korean, I am never going to say no to pork belly." Jae filled his plate with a little of everything on the table and took his very first bite of lechon. "Oh man. This pork is, like, a spiritual experience."

Xander laughed, the sudden burst of amusement lighting up his entire face. "Now, this guy gets it! Let's dig in, everyone. Don't be shy."

The whole table ate quietly for a while, each refilling our plates several times, enjoying Tita Rosie's food too much to continue the strained conversation.

Joy, our server, stopped by to drop off several dessert platters. "Lola Flor told me to bring these for you. Bibingka, Food for the Gods, champorado, and puto bumbong. All traditional treats for the Christmas season."

We all smiled and thanked Joy before digging in.

"I can't believe how well you're feeding me! This is too much," Xander said.

"It's the least we could do. You shouldn't have to worry about feeding yourself at a time like this. I made extra for your assistants as well," Tita Rosie said.

Xander smiled at Tita Rosie's opening statement, but I couldn't help noticing the tension in his face. My natural curiosity (some would call it nosiness) reared up at that, but I tamped it down and piled a plate with various treats for Jae and me to share. I held out the plate to him and he raised his eyebrows at me—he knew what "a time like this" meant in Shady Palms speak, and he didn't miss Xander's change of expression, either. I gestured that I'd explain later, and he nodded to show that he understood before snagging a piece of Food for the Gods.

"Whoa, what is this?" he said, after taking a huge bite.

"It's like our version of fruitcake," Tita Rosie explained. "We only make it at Christmastime."

Food for the Gods was a rich, buttery date and walnut bar, which doesn't sound all that special, but there was something absolutely addictive about it. Bernadette claimed to hate dates, yet she could eat an entire tray of these bars all by herself, they were that good.

Between the five of us, we demolished Lola Flor's desserts, despite how full we were before they arrived. There truly was a separate stomach for sweets. We all sat around in a sugar haze, making pleasant small talk as Tita Rosie packed up the lunch leftovers for Xander to take home.

"Thank you so much, Rosie. I can't tell you how much this means to me. I—" Xander's ringing cell phone cut him off, and he glanced at the screen. "Sorry, it's the doctor. I'll be right back."

There was a brief pause while we all waited for Xander to step outside, and then Jae leaned in. "OK, so what's the deal?"

"His fiancée died of alcohol poisoning last night. The doctor was supposed to run some extra tests, and I guess she's calling to report the results. That was fast, though," I said.

Ronnie grimaced. "He's got money. Knowing him, he probably greased the wheels a bit to make this a priority. Don't know why he bothered though. It was an open secret that Denise was an alcoholic."

"Anak! Don't speak poorly of the dead," Tita Rosie said, crossing herself.

"I wasn't speaking poorly, I was . . ." He trailed off as the restaurant door chimes announced not just Xander's appearance, but that of the man beside him.

"Hyung?" Jae asked, at the same time Tita Rosie said, "Jonathan? What are you doing here?"

Detective Park, Jae's older brother and Tita Rosie's close friend, walked with Xander to our table. I didn't even have to look at him to know that he had bad news for us.

But it was Xander who spoke first. "The doctor said she called the police with the test results before contacting me. It looks like Denise was poisoned."

Chapter Seven

"What was that?"

Ronnie stared first at Xander and then at Detective Park. His confused glance changed into a hard glare after a quick assessment of the new party—Detective Park didn't need to introduce himself or flash his badge for Ronnie to correctly guess he was law enforcement. "And who is this?"

Tita Rosie shot up from the table and hurried over. "Anak, this is Detective Park. He's a good friend of the family." She looked over at the detective. "Jonathan, what's going on? Are you here for lunch, or . . . ?"

Her voice trailed off as she also looked between Xander and Detective Park. Xander refused to meet her eyes, but Detective Park knew better than to prolong the moment.

"As Mr. Cruz said, the hospital called the police department before informing him of the test results. There's a possibility Ms. Sutton's death was due to outside circumstances."

"You think she was murdered?" I asked, somehow shocked despite my suspicious musings last night. I mean, sure, Shady Palms had been the scene of more than one murder in the past year, but those were people who'd lived in Shady Palms most, if not all, of their lives. They had history here, which meant they also had enemies here. But Denise was new to town. From what I remembered, they'd arrived shortly after Ronnie did and Ronnie had only been here for a week or so. Who would want to kill her?

I came to the same realization the moment Ronnie spoke up. "And you're here because you think I had something to do with it. Aren't you?"

Tita Rosie gasped. "No!" At Detective Park's look, she said, "Jonathan? How could you?"

"I'm not singling you out. I went to Shady Palms Winery first and told your business partners the same thing. They're currently at the station answering questions. I came to the restaurant because they said both you and Mr. Cruz were having lunch here. That's all."

Ronnie looked at me, the expression on his face basically asking, *Is this dude legit?*

I tamped down the sick feeling in my stomach—I needed to focus on the situation at hand, not for Ronnie, but for Tita Rosie's sake. "Detective Park has been horribly, *horribly* wrong in the past, but I think he's learned from his mistakes and knows not to just go after someone because they happen to be the most convenient suspect. Isn't that right, Detective?" Just because he'd become part of the family didn't mean I'd ever let him forget how he'd hounded me over my ex-boyfriend's murder when I'd first moved back to Shady Palms.

"That is correct, Lila. I haven't forgotten my poor behavior toward you. But unfortunately, my job also dictates that I question everyone involved in a case, regardless of previous cases or personal connections. So, Mr. Flores, you're needed down at the station. You too, Mr. Cruz."

Xander started. "Me? What for? I'm busy getting all of Denise's affairs in order."

"The tests you rush ordered only gave us a basic picture, sir. We're ordering more tests and would like a little more background info to narrow down what we're looking for. Hopefully this is all a tragic accident."

"And if it's not?"

"Let's just take this one step at a time."

Tita Rosie reached out to him. "Jonathan . . ."

"I'm so sorry, Rosie. I'm just—"

"Just doing your job. I know. Just like last time." Tita Rosie shook her head. "You're not the only one who learned from their mistakes after Lila's case."

The tone in Tita Rosie's voice made Ronnie and me exchange glances again, and those curious glances changed to shock when she moved behind Ronnie's seat and put her hands on the back of his chair, symbolizing her support. "You can talk to him once our lawyer gets here."

Amir Awan, Adeena's older brother and our family lawyer (not to mention my childhood crush, but that ship had sailed, sadly), arrived with his usual speed and style. Just a touch taller than Jae, Amir was always perfectly coiffed, his suit tailored to hug his gym-sculpted body. He gave Tita Rosie and me each a quick kiss on the cheek and shook the hands of all the men present.

"Good afternoon, Detective. Doctor. And nice to finally meet you, Ronnie. I'm Amir Awan, your family's lawyer. You are not to speak to anyone in law enforcement without me present. Got it?"

"Absolutely." Ronnie crossed his arms and grinned. "So, are we having this conversation here or down at the station?"

"I need time to talk to you in private, get all the facts first. Then we can go to the station together. After all, we wouldn't want to do anything that would impede the investigation, right, Detective?" Amir looked at Detective Park, who sighed.

"Let me assure you that you're not under arrest or even a person of interest. We're not entirely sure what happened to Ms. Sutton. But I also can't stop you from seeking counsel, so I hope to see you down at the station. Soon." He turned to Xander. "Do you need a ride to the station, Mr. Cruz?"

Xander shook his head. "I should probably tell my assistants about this. I'll give them a call and we'll head over together."

Jae waited until Detective Park and Xander left before saying, "Thanks so much for the great lunch, Auntie. And it was nice to meet you, Ronnie. Just sorry it was under these circumstances."

"You called him 'Hyung' when he came in. That was your brother?" Ronnie asked. The look on his face let Jae know what he thought about that.

"Yes, but what he does is not my business. I am here for moral support for Lila and her family, and that's it." Jae stood up and gave my aunt a quick hug. "I'll stop by again soon. Tell Grandma Flor to have a tray of those date and walnut bars ready for me, OK?"

After a quick goodbye, he left, the bell above the door chiming behind him. But before Amir could get started, the door chimed again, and I bit back a groan as I saw who the newcomers were: the Calendar Crew, aka my godmothers, Ninang April, Ninang Mae, and Ninang June. They hurried over to us.

"We just heard!"

"I can't believe it, another murder in our quiet little town? What is this world coming to?"

"I knew you'd bring nothing but trouble."

This last statement was directed at Ronnie. Ninang June stared daggers at the man who'd broken her daughter's heart, and Tita Rosie was quick to jump to her son's defense.

"He didn't do anything! Besides, what are you all doing here? We just learned about this ourselves!"

In response, my godmothers gestured around at the full restaurant, all our customers suddenly turning around and pretending they hadn't been watching us the whole time. My aunt groaned. The town grapevine at work.

"Maybe we should move to the back room at the cafe? Tita Rosie's office is too small for all of us," I offered.

Amir studied Ronnie and then the rest of the group. "You know, I think I should talk to my client in private. Lila and Auntie, you've both got businesses to run. I'd rather not take up any more of your time."

I started to protest, but Amir's eyes begged me to go along with this. As I glanced over at my godmothers, I understood—he knew Ronnie would likely be less than truthful in front of an audience. Particularly a hostile one and one that included his mother.

I stood up. "You're right, Adeena and Elena are probably wondering where I am. Good luck, Ronnie. Amir's the best, so don't make this hard for him, OK?"

Tita Rosie smiled in understanding. "Just give me a minute so I can fix you a plate to go."

I headed next door, eager to let Adeena and Elena know what was going on, and also to get away from my gossipy aunties and the whispering going on at the restaurant. I just knew the Calendar Crew would come over once they were done pumping my aunt for information, and I needed to prepare my partners for the whirlwind that was about to ensue.

Chapter Eight

"Did you hear anything I just told you?"

I'd filled Adeena and Elena in on what had just happened and the two of them sat there staring at me in a worrying silence. The Calendar Crew were coming over any second and I needed the two of them ready to run interference with the customers in case the aunties decided to be their less than inconspicuous selves. I didn't need the news of Denise's death and the doctor's suspicions to spread any more than it already had.

"Yeah, we heard you. This is called processing, Lila, you should try it sometime," Adeena said. "You might have become eerily well-adjusted to this, but news of a possible murder is still shocking to us lesser mortals."

"There's more." I paused to take a fortifying sip of my signature drink, the Brew-ha #1. "Remember that call I got back when we did the cookie and wine tasting? I didn't want to say anything till Tita

Rosie and I had a chance to talk about it, but someone sent my aunt a blackmail letter about Ronnie."

Adeena whistled as I told her the contents of the email. "You telling the aunties about the note?" she asked, refilling my mug.

I shook my head. "I doubt Tita Rosie wants it getting out. There might come a time we need their help looking into it, but for now, it should stay a secret."

"And nothing stays secret with your godmothers. Got it," Adeena said. "So you need to distract them by giving them just enough info to satisfy them, but not enough to make matters worse."

"When the aunties come in, Adeena and I will make a big fuss over them and offer them whatever we've been experimenting with. Make them feel special that they get early tastes, before any of the other customers," Elena said. "Then I can lead them to the back, where you'll have snacks ready, and you can talk to them there while Adeena and I handle the customers. That should put them in the right mind frame."

"What would we do without you, Elena?" I asked, and Adeena echoed my question.

She grinned. "Probably nothing since you two would be too busy bickering to get anything done." The bells above our door chimed, announcing the arrival of the aunties. "They're here. I handle the greeting, Adeena you take care of their drink orders, and then I'll bring them to Lila in the back."

She moved toward my godmothers and Adeena and I took up our positions. While I waited for my godmothers to come to the cafe kitchen, I set out a plate of cookies and checked on the buko pandan chia puddings I'd set in the fridge this morning. The trifles were awesome and definitely something I'd like to explore for the winter bash, but they were also time-consuming. I was hoping these puddings would be a faster and easier alternative. They looked almost as pretty as the trifles, with their layer of salted coconut on top, though I needed to think of easy toppings. If this Ronnie mess became a thing, I knew I wouldn't have the time to dedicate to cutesy individual desserts.

"Lila! Are you hiding back there? What's going on?"

Ninang April, Ninang Mae, and Ninang June all crowded into my kitchen, their hands loaded down with drinks from Adeena and various beauty samples from Elena. A pudding sat at each station I'd prepared for them, and they quickly sat down and dug in.

"Not bad!" Ninang April said, which was high praise coming from her. "I like the texture. This isn't sago, is it?"

"No, those are chia seeds. They're really good for you and set into a nice pudding without needing egg yolks or gelatin or anything like that. Super easy, and they're vegan, too," I said. Not that there were tons of vegans in Shady Palms, but I was always happy to experiment with delicious alternatives for my increasingly diverse clientele. Plus, knowing they could get something not readily available where they were drew in people from nearby towns as well.

I slid the cookie platter in front of them, which contained the four holiday cookies I'd come up with as well as peach-mango crumble cookies, my special of the day. The buttery, sweet base was topped with a dollop of my homemade peach mango jam, shortbread crumbles, and a generous dusting of powdered sugar.

"What do you think of the cookies? Should I add them to the regular menu, or are they better as a seasonal offering?"

"You already have ube crinkles on your permanent menu, so make the pandan crinkles seasonal with an option to special order them. Too many similar items can be boring." Ninang April was the harshest of the trio, but she was also the most practical and offered good (if blunt) advice. "The salabat snickerdoodles would fit in well with your everyday offerings. They could maybe use more ginger, but otherwise they're excellent. That peach mango shortbread is even better, so keep it off the main menu and bring it back for a limited time throughout the year. Makes them special, and people will feel like they have to buy them if they're only available for a short time."

I nodded, scribbling this all down. "Anything else?"

"Yeah," Ninang June said, setting aside her mug. "What mess did Ronnie get into this time? We heard something about a murder. I tried to get Rosie and Bernie to tell me more, but they refuse."

I sighed as all three women leaned forward expectantly. "We don't know that it's murder. One of Ronnie's investors passed away recently, and the doctor said it looked like alcohol poisoning. But there was something not quite right about it, so they ran more tests. I guess they found something suspicious, so they're talking to everyone who knew the dead woman."

"What's her name? She's not from Shady Palms, is she?" Ninang Mae asked.

"I don't know where she's from, but I'm pretty sure she's not from here. Her name's Denise Sutton. She and her fiancé, Xander Cruz, are the main investors in Shady Palms Winery. That's really all I know about her."

My godmothers all reached for their phones, their fingers flying across the screen. "Is this her?" Ninang Mae asked, holding out her phone to show me a picture of Denise. I nodded, and she said, "She's originally from Connecticut, but nothing online mentions where exactly. Her fiancé is from Chicago and they met in grad school. University of Chicago," she added.

"Does she come from money?" I asked.

"Not exactly. Her family seems to have done OK, but nothing special. Comfortable middle class, I suspect. But listen to this," Ninang June said, her eyes lit up. "She's a widow. Her previous husband was a very wealthy older man who left everything to her when he passed away last year."

"Last year? And she's already engaged to someone else?" Ninang April let out a harsh breath from her nose. "She killed him for his money, didn't she?"

"Not unless she somehow gave him cancer. Seems the old man knew he was dying and wanted a bit of fun and happiness before he passed. This article says her husband had been friends with her father and wanted to make sure she was taken care of," Ninang Mae said, showing us the online article on her phone.

"Looks like there was a bit of scandal regarding his will," Ninang June said, checking out the article Ninang Mae showed us. "He had two kids from a previous marriage and they got next to nothing. They contested the will, but the old guy's lawyer said he left explicit instructions about their inheritance because he wanted them to 'work for a change.'"

My godmothers continued digging up dirt on Denise while I baked fresh batches of cookies for the cafe. As annoying as it was to have them cluttering up my kitchen, it was nice to have them do all the preliminary research in case this thing with Ronnie and his partners turned serious.

"I need to bring these cookies out for the customers. Do you all need anything or are you done here?" I added that last part, hoping they'd get the hint. Instead, they all held up their empty mugs in response.

I sighed and placed their mugs on a separate tray from the cookies. "I'll tell Adeena you all need refills. Be back in a bit. Let me know if you find anything good."

I made my way toward the front, stopping to chat with a few of my regulars and hype up my cookie selection before filling the snack racks that had held slices of salabat banana bread, calamansi chia seed loaf, halo-halo chia pudding parfait, and our other more "breakfast-y" options from this morning. Considering how quickly the baked goods had been selling out, I made a note to order more shelving so I could offer a bigger selection. Good problems to have.

"How's it going back there?" Adeena asked, as she steamed milk and poured it in the shape of a kitty on top of a lavender chai latte before handing it over to a waiting customer. The fact that she could do something that required such precision while carrying on a casual conversation always amazed me. My lack of accuracy in the kitchen ensured that there would likely never be macarons or other fiddly treats on the menu at the Brew-ha Cafe.

"The aunties are all busy digging into the details of Denise's life and could use a refill. What were they drinking?"

She shrugged. "Just my latest attempt at an ube latte. It's fine, but not quite right yet. See if you can get any useful feedback from them. I don't want to put it on the menu till I've nailed it."

She pointed to the last of the batch behind the counter and turned to help the next customer, so I refilled their mugs and made my way back to the kitchen.

"You all find out anything that connects Denise to Shady Palms, or would be cause for murder? Oh, and Adeena wants your opinion on the ube lattes. She thinks they're not quite right yet and could use some suggestions." I set the mugs in front of my godmothers and helped myself to a peach mango crumble cookie. Dang, they were good. As much as I hated it when the Calendar Crew were right, Ninang April was spot-on about these. I wondered how a mango cala-mansi version would turn out. More experimenting was in the future . . .

"Not really. Mostly just articles about her company and their var-ious investments. In addition to the Shady Palms Winery, she's in-volved with a couple of other food-related businesses and hotel chains, all Midwestern companies. Her fiancé seems to be a bit of a character, though. And so handsome," Ninang Mae added, as she scrolled through her phone.

"Joseph is the accountant for the winery and Marcus works security there, right?" I asked, naming her two sons. "Can you ask them if they've noticed anything suspicious? Money issues, people lurking who don't work there, strange calls, anything that might give us a motive."

"Of course! I'll talk to them tonight and make them tell me everything." She started to text her sons and then stopped to look at me. "You know, Lila, if you and Dr. Jae aren't exclusive, you should really give Marcus another shot. Times are changing; it's good for you to have a younger boyfriend."

I fought the urge to roll my eyes and turned to Ninang April and Ninang June, who were both sipping at their lattes and jotting notes in the spiral pads they both carried around with them. I was about to ask what they were writing when the two women started arguing over the correct way to structure a suspect list.

"A mind map flows better and allows you to make connections you might not make with a straightforward list!"

"Yes, but a list allows you to stay organized, which means you're less likely to miss important clues!"

This went back and forth for a while (I was on Team List, though Team Mind Map was making some good points), and what started as funny quickly turned tiresome as my godmothers started getting weirdly personal with their rebuttals ("Oh, you think you're so smart? All that thinking is why you're going bald!").

My cell phone rang and I grabbed it from my tote bag, eager to get away from my ninangs' bickering. "Hey, Amir! Are you guys all done with the questioning?"

"I'm sorry, Lila, but I'm going to need you and Auntie to get down to the police station immediately." Amir paused, likely sensing I needed a moment to process that statement.

I clutched my phone. "Is . . . What should I tell her? Why do we need to be there?"

"The final test results are in. Denise Sutton died of methanol poisoning. The detective has no choice but to hold Ronnie and his partners for questioning."

Chapter Nine

B efore you start in on me, I recused myself from the investigation. I didn't want anyone accusing me of favoritism or anything like that."

Detective Park met us in the lobby of the Shady Palms Police Department, hands out as if to ward off the verbal beatdown he was expecting from my grandmother and me. Surprisingly, it was my aunt who came at him.

"Susmaryosep! You thought having the best and most experienced member of the SPPD off the case was going to help me?" Tita Rosie clutched her worn purse, both hands shaking as if she were fighting the urge to hit him with it. "Who's on the case?"

Detective Park just stared at her, his mouth hanging open, and didn't answer.

"Jonathan! Who is investigating my son's case?" Tita Rosie asked slowly, every word punctuated by her heavy, deliberate steps toward him.

"Oh, um, it's Feliks Nowak. He's a good kid. He transferred over from Chicago recently, and I've been training him since the sheriff finally realized we need more detectives on the force."

"So he's your protégé?" Lola Flor asked.

"You could say that."

She grunted her approval. "Good enough. Now where is my grandson? We'd like to speak with him."

"He's still being questioned, but Mr. Awan is with him, so you have nothing to worry about. Well, I . . . He's being looked after, is what I meant," Detective Park said, after the three of us glared at him. "They should be done soon, so why don't you all take a seat and I'll go check on them?"

Lola Flor took a tissue out of her purse and wiped down three seats before gesturing for Tita Rosie and me to sit down next to her. The three of us sat in silence, glaring at Detective Park until he left to see how Ronnie and Amir were doing.

We sat there waiting for what felt like hours (but according to my phone was only twenty minutes) before Ronnie and Amir came out, followed by Izzy, Pete, and a fresh-faced detective who didn't look much older than me.

"Anak!" Tita Rosie flew out of her seat, cradling Ronnie's face in her hands. "Are you OK?"

"I'm fine, Mommy," Ronnie said, turning red as his mom fussed over him in front of everyone.

"We are not fine, Ronnie. We are in deep fu—" Pete started, but Izzy cut him off.

"How about we talk about this later? In private?" She lifted an eyebrow, glaring at her business partners in warning.

Detective Park cleared his throat, and we all turned to look at him. "I wanted to introduce you all to Shady Palms's new detective. Detective Feliks Nowak, this is Ronnie Flores's family: Flor, Rosie, and Lila Macapagal."

Tita Rosie moved forward to greet him. "Welcome to Shady Palms, Detective Nowak. It's nice to meet you."

Detective Nowak shook her hand, not quite smiling but a pleasant expression on his face nonetheless. "You too. Detective Park has told me all about your wonderful restaurant. I'll have to stop by sometime." He glanced around at the group. "I'm sure we'll all be in touch again soon, but right now I've got a mountain of paperwork to tackle."

With a quick nod, he excused himself and strode toward the back of the station. Tita Rosie waited until he'd disappeared into an office before breaking the silence. "How about we all head back to the restaurant? You must be so hungry."

Izzy groaned, but her expression softened as she turned to my aunt. "I'm sorry, Tita, that wasn't for you, that was for him and this whole situation." She ran her hands down her face and sighed. "We're a little tired right now. Could we maybe—"

"Oh, of course, you must rest. Why don't you come to the house, and I'll make you something to eat there instead?" Tita Rosie said, smiling at the group.

"Uh . . . I don't know if . . ." Izzy trailed off, glancing first at Pete and Ronnie then at my aunt's beaming face.

"Ronnie. Give them our address. We need to get home and start cooking," Lola Flor said, her tone and expression letting him know it was not a request. He tried to reason with her anyway.

"Don't you need to get back to the restaurant?" he asked.

"We closed it for the day to be here. We expect to see you soon," Lola Flor said, ending any discussion on the topic.

"Make sure to invite Xander and his assistants too, OK? They need to eat," Tita Rosie said to an increasingly grumpy-looking Ronnie.

"Yeah, yeah," he responded.

"What was that?" Lola Flor asked, her voice sharp and ready to cut into him.

"Uh, I mean, opo," Ronnie said, switching to formal Tagalog to say "yes" to his mom.

"Lila," Tita Rosie said, interrupting my snickering at Ronnie. "Can you bring some drinks and sweets? Your lola has the traditional dishes covered, but I'm sure our guests will appreciate the variety."

"Of course, Tita. I'll prep them now and should be home in half an hour or so. I just need to fill Adeena and Elena in since I had to leave so suddenly."

Tita Rosie nodded. "They're your business partners and part of the family, so they deserve to know. Tell them they can come too, though I'm not sure they want to close the cafe so early."

"I'll pass along the message."

"Oh, and Lila?" Something in my aunt's voice made me hesitate at the door and study her more carefully.

"Whatever you do, don't tell your ninangs."

I'm sorry Pete couldn't make it. He had to go handle a bunch of paperwork at the office due to the, uh, problems we learned about earlier today. He made me promise to bring home a plate, though," Izzy said, grinning at my aunt and grandmother. She sat on the couch with Longganisa, my adorable dachshund, on her lap. Longganisa was wearing the newest outfit that Naoko Sato, my friend Yuki's daughter, had designed for her—a reindeer costume, complete with an antlered hood. You'd think Longganisa would hate it, but she was all about cute head coverings. Anytime the hood slipped off, she'd butt her little head against your hand until you pulled the hood back up, and then she'd bask in her maximum cuteness. I loved my vain little girl.

Izzy rubbed Longganisa's belly, cooing at her like she was a baby. "You are just the cutest puppy in the world, aren't you? How does it feel to be the cutest ever?"

It was really quite adorable. Ronnie must've agreed because he took a picture of the two of them with his phone, a soft smile on his face. When he saw me watching him, he forced a laugh.

"You are so ridiculous. Weren't you just telling Xander that Poe was the cutest dog in the world? You two-timing Poe now?"

"Every dog is the cutest dog in the world, Ronnie," Izzy said, all matter-of-fact. "How have you not learned that by now?"

"Xander has a dog? What kind?" I asked, handing Izzy a glass of water.

"The sweetest pittie mix named Poe. I asked if he was named after Edgar Allan Poe or the Star Wars character or something else, and all he said was 'Yes,'" Izzy said, accepting the drink with a smile before pulling out her phone with her other hand. She swiped through a bunch of photos before holding up her phone to show Xander with a black-and-white pit bull mix. The dog's tongue was hanging out, smiling big for the camera, and Xander's grin was equally big and endearing.

"Aww, so cute! Did Xander bring Poe with him? We should set up a playdate for him and Nisa." Longganisa loved people way more than other dogs, but I was trying to socialize her more. She'd had regular doggy daycare playtime back when I was in Chicago, but now that I was back in Shady Palms, her social life had taken a hit. And I know how that sounds, but I said what I said. Animals needed friends sometimes, too. (And no, she wasn't getting a sibling. Lola Flor was very clear on her one-pet-maximum rule.)

"Yeah, he was able to find a place that allowed pets. The twins are in charge of taking care of him when Xander has to be out at meetings, but I know he takes Poe on runs along the river a couple times a day," Izzy said. I filed that information away for later—if Longganisa and I ran into him during one of our runs, maybe that would be a natural and totally not awkward way to set up a playdate.

"That reminds me, he sends his regards, but said he needs some time to himself. He also has plenty of leftovers from lunch earlier," Ronnie said, likely to stop his mom from worrying that poor Xander was going to starve to death alone in his hotel room.

"Small group for dinner tonight," Tita Rosie said, looking disappointed.

"Amir said he'd try to make it, but he has another case he's working on that might result in a late night. Adeena and Elena should be here soon. The cafe closes at six today, and they said they'd head over once they were done."

No sooner had I said that than the doorbell rang, announcing their arrival. I hurried to let them in.

"We brought the drinks and treats you asked for!" Adeena announced before enveloping Tita Rosie in a big hug and doing mano to Lola Flor. Elena followed suit, and then the two of them made their way to me, Izzy, and Ronnie, plopping down on the loveseat across from us.

"This is Adeena Awan and Elena Torres, my best friends and partners at the Brew-ha Cafe. You two have met Ronnie already, and this is Isabel Ramos-Garcia, one of his partners at the Shady Palms Winery."

"Great to meet you two! You can call me Izzy, by the way. Ronnie told me all about your new cafe, and I'd love to check it out soon. He said the food and drinks are great and there's 'a lot of plants and stuff,' so I know I'll love it." She grinned at him as she did the air quotes, her tone a perfect imitation of my cousin.

Elena smiled at Izzy. "Yes, all the 'plants and stuff' are from my family's greenhouse. Whether you're looking for tea, bath salts, lotion, or just a nice plant for your office, I've got what you need."

Elena was such a natural seller that even when she was doing a sales pitch during a casual conversation, it never felt pushy or out of place. It must've worked on Izzy, in any case, because she said, "I was just telling Ronnie and Pete that our office was depressing and needed some major redecorating! All my plant babies are at home, but I'd love to add to the collection."

Elena handed her a business card. "Come by tomorrow if you can. I'm bringing in some potted yucca plants tomorrow morning and they always sell out immediately. I could set one aside for you, if you want."

"That would be great! I—" Izzy paused mid-sentence to glare at Ronnie, who tried to hide the fact that he was yawning and failed.

He tried to shrug it off. "I'm sorry, Iz, but plants are boring."

She raised an eyebrow. "To you. Plants are boring to *you*, but not to me. I have to listen to you and Pete talk about basketball and your fantasy leagues all the time. The least you could do is not insult my interests."

To his credit, Ronnie flushed and apologized immediately. "You're right, I'm sorry. I never thought of it like that. That was really shi—uh, really rude of me. I'm glad you found someone you can geek out with."

He smiled at Elena, who was looking him over coolly, likely wondering if he was worth acknowledging. Apparently he wasn't, since she turned to Izzy without saying anything to him. "If you're really interested, you can stop by the greenhouse sometime. My mom started a community garden section recently, and you're welcome to claim a plot."

As the two of them swapped phone numbers, Ronnie looked on proudly, prompting a laugh from me. "Aww, are you happy that she's making friends? That's surprisingly sweet of you, Ronnie."

He shushed me, glancing over to make sure Izzy hadn't heard me. She continued chattering happily with Elena and Adeena, paying him no mind. "I was worried that she wouldn't meet anyone she clicked with here. She's a major extrovert and craves company and stimulation. She has, like, fifty million hobbies and likes trying new things. It

wasn't a problem in college or in Florida, but here in Shady Palms ..."
He shrugged. "I never had many friends here, and there's, like, no social scene. I felt bad having her hang out with just Pete and me night
after night."

"I'll introduce her to the rest of my crew. If she likes working out,
my friend runs a fitness studio and she can join us for classes."

"I think she'd really like that. Thanks, Lila."

The fondness in his eyes was killing me. I just had to know what
their deal was. I cleared my throat and asked, "So, how long have she
and Pete been dating?"

"Since college."

"Oh wow, that's a long time. Are they engaged?"

"For the past five years, yeah."

"Oh." I looked over at Izzy and spotted the shiny rock she was
sporting on her left ring finger. "So ..."

"None of my business." Ronnie's tone was matter-of-fact, but the
expression on his face let me know he wanted to make it his business.
Interesting. Then again, Izzy was adorable, and Ronnie had always
been a messy bench. Count on him to not only fall in love with his
best friend, who happened to be his other best friend's fiancée, but
also go into business with both of them. The potential for drama here
was absolutely delicious, and I couldn't wait to fill the Brew-has in on
this. Hopefully, they were gathering juicy tidbits from Izzy as well.

"Hoy, wash your hands. It's time for dinner," Lola Flor called from
the dining room.

Hands washed, I left Longganisa in the kitchen with her bowl of
organic kibble (she preferred to eat while lying on her plush doggie
bed, like the pampered princess she was) and joined everyone around
the dining room table. My aunt said a quick grace, then everyone
helped themselves to the myriad dishes on the table: chicken afritada,

bangus a la pobre, adobong pusit, beef nilaga, lumpiang togue, kang-kong in oyster sauce, and a vegan sisig dish she was experimenting with, as well as mounds of steamed white rice.

"This is a feast! Does your family always eat like this?" Izzy asked as she squeezed calamansi over the vegan sisig.

"Not for an everyday meal, but I knew we were having company and that means I can spend time on more dishes," Tita Rosie said, watching everyone fill their plates before she served herself.

"So, Izzy, how did you and Ronnie meet? And what made you decide to go into business together?" Adeena asked, helping herself to the seafood and vegetarian dishes on the table. I knew I could count on her to get the conversation going. As much as I liked Izzy, the blackmail email Tita Rosie told me about stayed in the back of my mind, something I couldn't quite dismiss as a prank. Especially after what happened to Denise.

"We met in college! Freshman orientation at the University of Wisconsin-Madison; we all happened to be sitting by each other. My family wouldn't let me go away for school, so it was local for me, but Pete's from a Miami suburb and wasn't prepared for Midwestern weather. It was only, like, sixty degrees and you'd swear it was below freezing. He was so miserable that first day at orientation that Ronnie lent him his hoodie and I gave him my beanie. We were all friends after that."

"Aww, that's so sweet! I remember Ronnie saying something about spending time in Florida with you two. Were you in Miami?" I asked. I studied the two of them to see if their expressions would give away anything suspicious about their time there.

"We were in Key West, actually," Ronnie said, piling more chicken afritada on his plate. I'd forgotten it was his favorite when we were kids, but of course Tita Rosie would remember.

"Why Key West?" Elena asked, going for a third helping of both the bangus and the squid adobo. "Isn't it really expensive out there? Even more expensive than Miami, I mean?"

"Yeah, but we were working for this real ritzy resort that provided housing and meals, so it was totally worth it," Izzy said, as she scraped her plate clean.

"The hours were killer though. I'd never seen any place with such a high turnover rate. We were all there for three years and by the time we left, none of the original staff were there."

"It was worth it for the conch fritters. They were famous for them," Izzy explained to the table. "And also—"

"The Jet Skis!" Izzy and Ronnie said this at the same time and cracked up, probably some inside joke between them.

Lola Flor seemed affronted by these high spirits, because she stood up and said, "Rosie, it's time for dessert. Come help me."

I cleared the dinner dishes off the table, and by the time I got back, Lola Flor had laid out the same desserts she'd served us at lunch and Tita Rosie was setting down a tray of mugs. Adeena jumped up to grab the tea, coffee, and sweets she'd brought from the cafe. I hadn't had time to roll each individual salabat snickerdoodle, so I'd made cookie bars instead. They were so much faster and even more delicious somehow that I decided salabat snickerdoodle squares were going on the permanent menu.

"What made you all decide to take over the old winery?" I asked as I reached for one.

The Shady Palms Winery had been around for decades, but it had never been all that notable or profitable. None of the Illinois wine trails tours included it as a stop, and as far as I knew, their only customers were local businesses who were loyal to the town's economy (and/or couldn't afford anything better).

"During off-season, we'd pick up some extra hours at this winery near the resort. Learned all about the process and Ronnie and I both became a little obsessed with the tropical fruit wines." Izzy laughed. "But it wasn't until we met this Filipino guy trying to perfect his coconut wine that we got the idea."

Ronnie refilled both his and Izzy's glasses of water. "Manong Larry! He taught us everything he knew, even introduced us to suppliers who could help get us the coconut flowers we needed. But Key West was way too expensive. Pete started looking around for something cheaper, and when he found out the Shady Palms Winery was for sale, and so cheap, well . . . it felt like fate."

Tita Rosie's eyes filled with unshed tears. "However it happened, I'm so happy you're back. Your business is going to be great for the town, too. I'm sure in your hands, you'll help make Shady Palms a new tourist destination."

He laughed. "Thanks, Mommy. But it's going to take some time. We need a total rebrand and an actual staff before we start thinking that far ahead."

"Ooh, you should hire Terrence to help design your wine labels and website! He did both the restaurant and the cafe, and he's helping us come up with a range of swag to sell." I pointed to one of the Brew-ha Cafe mugs, which Lola Flor was drinking tea out of. Our mugs and tumblers bearing the Brew-ha Cafe logo were already popular, but we wanted to expand our offerings. Even Tita Rosie was turning a decent profit selling Tita Rosie's Kitchen glasses and aprons.

Izzy pulled out her phone to check out the Brew-ha Cafe website. After taking in our clean yet engaging design, fun logo, and all the other design elements that went over my head but Terrence insisted were important, she nodded. "Do you have his card? I'd love to meet with him."

"He's actually coming by the shop tomorrow to design our holiday cookie boxes, so why don't you drop in so I can introduce you? You wanted to see the cafe, and this would be a good opportunity for you both." I checked my messages to make sure I got the time right. "He's usually a morning person, but since we need Katie there too, we're meeting at three thirty. Does that work for you?"

"Oh, that's perfect, actually. I've got a meeting at two tomorrow, so I'll just head over when I'm done. Are you OK with me leading the design meeting, Ronnie?" Izzy asked.

"Of course. You've got a better eye for that stuff than I do, so I'll leave it up to you. Just make sure you let Pete know the proposed costs before signing off on anything. You know how he gets." Ronnie grabbed another cookie before turning his attention to me. "Who's Katie, by the way?"

"Our apprentice and social media whiz. She's only in high school, which is why we have to wait till she's out of class to have our meeting."

"Oh wow, you just opened your shop and you've already got an apprentice? Maybe we should—"

Lola Flor sighed and set her mug down with a thud. "Enough! I'm so tired of all this small talk. Are you not going to tell us what you talked about with the police?"

Ronnie was so stunned by Lola Flor's sudden outburst he didn't realize he was holding his coffee mug all tilted until hot coffee poured into his lap. He swore loudly, then bit his lip and apologized after catching his mother's disapproving look. "There's not much to tell. The doctor said it looked like Denise died of methanol poisoning, but they have no idea how it got into her system. So the police need to do some investigating. Wanted to know if we'd seen anything out of the ordinary or had any theories about it. That's all."

"That's all? Then what really happened in Florida?" I asked.

Izzy and Ronnie both whipped around to stare at me and then at each other. Ronnie recovered first. "What do you mean? We already told you about our time in Florida. There's not much else worth talking about. We worked hard, found a new passion, and wanted to strike out on our own. That's it."

Anyone who didn't know my cousin would buy the sincerity in his voice, but I *knew* him. There was so much more he wasn't letting on, and I wouldn't let him keep doing that to Tita Rosie.

"So then why is somebody blackmailing your mom?"

His face blanched. "What are you talking about?"

"Lila!" my aunt warned, but it was too late. Lola Flor's head snapped up at that, and her stare drilled a hole into her grandson.

"What did you do this time?"

"Nothing! I—"

"Then why is someone emailing your mom saying that she needs to pay up or they'll tell everyone how you've got blood on your hands?"

Izzy choked on a piece of bibingka and had a coughing fit. Ronnie thrust his glass of water at her, but she waved him off. "I'm fine, I'm fine. That just . . . surprised me." She took a sip from her own glass before taking a deep breath and facing my aunt. "Tita, I'm sorry, but for legal reasons, we really can't talk about that. But I can assure you, Ronnie didn't kill anyone, or harm anyone in any way, for that matter. None of us did. Whoever sent you that message is just trying to stir up trouble and scare you, and I will not let that happen. Please forward it to me. It'll take some time, but I'll find out who sent it."

I raised an eyebrow at her. Was she really going to try and fix this, or was this her way of getting us to drop it? I liked this girl, but that didn't mean I had to trust her. Her being besties with Ronnie was the first red flag, but this . . . I reminded myself to keep my guard up. Few people were who they seemed when you first met them.

"She's got some serious computer skills, and if she can't crack it, she knows people who can," Ronnie said, before addressing Tita Rosie. "Mommy, I swear whoever sent that email is lying. Just give it time. The cops will figure out what happened to Denise and Izzy will find out who's trying to blackmail us, and it'll all be fine. We'll be fine."

Tita Rosie nodded and forced a smile. "OK, anak. I believe you." And knowing her, she did.

But Lola Flor caught my eye across the table and shook her head. We both knew better.

Chapter Ten

"Dang, Lila, you are really doing the most with these holiday cookie boxes. You sure you can handle all that assembly?"

Terrence Howell set down the prototype boxes he'd brought and looked at the various seasonal cookies I'd set out, a gentle smile tugging at the left corner of his mouth. "What do you think, Katie?"

I bit back my laughter as I watched Katie Pang, my teenage apprentice, try not to swoon as she formulated a coherent answer. I always forgot how handsome Terrence was. He'd been a football player back in high school and had also worked construction for years, so he was still strong and powerfully built, unlike most of the other former athletes in this town. He'd been my ex-boyfriend's best friend (after the breakup, he'd sided with me, something I'll always love him for) and was only a few years older than me, but his dark skin had the beginning of lines around his eyes, forehead, and mouth, and his tightly coiled hair, currently in twists, was shot through with gray. I wasn't the only one who'd been having a tough and life-changing year. These physical signs of the stressful life he'd been leading did nothing to take away from his attractiveness (in fact, his crow's feet highlighted his gorgeous, kind eyes) and the young Katie was harboring a (thankfully) innocent crush on him.

Katie started to slump in her seat, then quickly straightened up when I caught her eye. "Um, I know it's a lot of work, but aesthetically, it's a really good choice. Especially if she makes sure each cookie has a different shape or design or something so people are drawn to the variety boxes. The photos would just be more interesting. Visually, I mean."

I nodded. "I think Katie's right. Besides, I've tweaked the cookies so that the only time-consuming ones are the pandan crinkles, since I have to roll them individually. Everything else uses pans or molds."

"Sorry I'm late! It smells amazing back here," a familiar voice said behind me.

I turned around and smiled. "Izzy! Did you just get here?"

I made sure to keep my voice and expression friendly—I didn't want to tip her off about my suspicions, and who knows, maybe she really was as cool as she seemed.

She entered the cafe kitchen rocking another loud holiday sweater (this one was red leopard print and had a picture of a llama wearing glasses, a Santa hat, and a puffball-lined collar with snowflakes all over it), a half-empty Brew-ha Cafe mug in hand. "I got here a while ago, actually, but was chatting up front with Adeena and Elena and lost track of time. I'd fully planned on being here at three thirty. Sorry if I kept you waiting."

"Not at all! We were going over the prototype boxes that Terrence brought and discussing design ideas. Pull up a chair and I'll make the introductions." I quickly introduced Terrence and Katie, who both shook her hand, and said, "And this is Isabel Ramos-Garcia. She's part owner of the Shady Palms Winery and was hoping to talk to Terrence about branding."

Izzy picked up one of Terrence's sketches for the holiday cookie boxes. "I like your work. It's very clean, but still has a touch of whimsy. It suits the cafe perfectly, and I think you'd be a good match for us as well."

He smiled and thanked her. "Could you tell me a little more about your business after I finish this final sketch? I want to incorporate Lila and Katie's feedback before I forget."

While he sketched, I got the dough for the calamansi sugar cookies out of the fridge. "Katie, could you bring us all another round of drinks? I want to get started on this next batch while these two chat. Help yourself to anything from the pastry case as well."

"Will do, boss!" Katie saluted me and took Izzy's and Terrence's orders before heading out to the front.

Izzy smiled as she watched Katie bounce away. "She seems like a good kid. And I caught the tail end of her spiel about visuals, so she seems smart, too. How did you find her?"

Terrence and I exchanged glances. He hadn't been around for most of the drama that'd happened in the summer, but he was well aware of the circumstances that brought Katie into our lives. "Um, her best friend, Joy, is a server at Tita Rosie's Kitchen. She's the one who introduced us."

Which was totally true and yet nowhere near the full story.

Katie arrived as I was loading the sugar cookie dough in the cookie press. With a slight push, perfectly star-shaped cookies scented with delicious calamansi citrus juice and zest popped out, and I quickly lined two baking sheets with them.

Izzy watched me with interest. "How do you decorate them? I don't see any bowls of icing or sprinkles or anything."

"I don't decorate them. I think they taste better as is," I said. "Plus, the decorations take forever and we don't have time for that."

"Aww, but decorating the cookies is the best part! I mean, nobody actually likes sugar cookies, do they? It's just 'cause they're pretty and making them together is fun. At least it was in my family. Though we didn't have to churn out a ton as a business," Izzy said as she took her mug from Katie and thanked her. "Makes sense that you wouldn't have the time on top of everything you're doing for the shop and party. And I'm guessing your family's doing something for Simbang Gabi?"

Simbang Gabi was a Filipino Catholic tradition consisting of nine masses in the nine days leading up to Christmas. It was usually accompanied by traditional snacks like bibingka and puto bumbong after each service and a huge feast on Christmas Eve—my aunt and grandmother went all out every year to plan festivities with our friend and parish priest, Father Santiago. Shady Palms had a decent-size Filipino population and an even larger Catholic one, so this celebration had spread to become a large community event. In fact, the town's winter bash always took place the weekend before Simbang Gabi so there was no worry of overlap, particularly because the town council made it a point to emphasize that the winter bash was a strictly secular celebration.

"Yeah, Tita Rosie and Lola Flor will be working on something, but I'm usually not involved in the planning. I'd rather figure out something we can do here as a special wintertime promo to get people excited about our winter bash booth."

"Why don't we have an event here at the cafe? Like, sugar cookie decorating for the family or something?" Katie asked, helping herself to a fresh cookie from the tray. "Or even classes where people can make the cookies together from start to finish, based on your recipes and instructions."

"Oh wow, that's brilliant, Katie. Now that the cafe is more established, community engagement is key to bringing in more people and keeping them as customers," Terrence said.

"That is brilliant," I agreed. "Let me talk it over with Adeena and Elena and I'll let you know. We'd need your help if we actually do this."

Katie happily agreed, the grin on her face and slight blush on her cheeks letting us know how pleased she was with the compliments.

Terrence flipped to a clean page in his notebook. "All right, Isabel, let's begin our consultation. What can you tell me about your business? And what exactly would you need from me?"

"First of all, call me Izzy, please. Second, we're hoping to make Shady Palms Winery notable not only for our delicious local varieties, but for our specialty wines based off popular Filipino fruits."

"Oh wow, that's really cool. What gave you the idea for the specialty wines?" Terrence asked, jotting down notes.

"We met a Filipino vintner when we were down in Florida and really loved the tropical fruit wine he was making and wanted to produce our own. But we needed a place that wasn't as expensive or competitive as Key West, and thought Shady Palms was the perfect place to build our niche."

Katie laughed. "You couldn't have chosen a better spot. Not only is there zero competition here, our town's name matches your brand perfectly."

At our blank looks, she said, "Shady Palms? Palm trees? Tropical fruit? Am I the only one who made that connection?"

Izzy thunked her forehead with the heel of her hand. "How have I not seen that till now? You really are quite brilliant. 'Enjoy a taste of the tropics right here in the Midwest.' Terrence, I don't know if this is asking too much, but I think the vision here is Midwestern sensibility with island vibes. Does that make sense?"

Terrence nodded, his gaze fixed on his sketchbook as he scribbled furiously. "I'll pull together some preliminary sketches and send you my estimated quote as well."

"That'd be great. Once you have everything drawn up, would you be able to meet my partners and me at the winery? We'd need their OK on this as well. Plus it would be good for you to see the space since we'll probably need signage and things like that."

He stood up and pulled out his business card. "Sure. Just let me know when. I gotta head out for another project, but I'll be in touch soon."

Terrence gathered his things and I handed him a bag of goodies I'd already packed for him. "Thanks, Terrence. Make sure to say bye to Adeena and Elena as you head out. I think Elena has something for you. And if you have time, pop next door to say hi to my aunt. She was asking about you a few days ago."

"I'll walk you out," Katie said, gathering the empty mugs on the table. "I'm supposed to take over the register soon anyway. Do you need me to do anything else back here, Lila?"

I hid a smile. "I should be fine. Thanks, Katie."

The two of them headed out, Izzy's eyes dancing as she watched them leave. Once they were out of earshot, she said, "She has the biggest crush on him, doesn't she?"

I laughed. "She's not exactly subtle about it. Don't worry, I've already talked to her and she knows that nothing will happen between them. He'd never go for it since he's too old for her, plus he's already engaged. She just likes being around him, which I understand."

"He's engaged?" She shook her head and sighed. "Of course a man that good-looking and talented wouldn't be single. When's the wedding?"

"Ah, that's a bit . . . complicated." And a story that I didn't want to get into right now, so time to turn the conversations toward her.

"How about you? Any idea when you and Pete are going to have your big day?"

Izzy smiled tightly and fiddled with the ring on her left hand. "Not really. We wanted to make sure we were on stable financial ground before moving forward. I mean, do you have any idea how much a decent wedding costs?"

My lips pulled in a lopsided line as I attempted a nonchalant smile. "Well, yes, actually. I was engaged last year."

Izzy stilled. "Oh. I'm so sorry."

I shrugged. "Don't be. Walking in on Sam cheating on me was horrible, but to be honest . . . I don't know if anything less than that would've opened my eyes to what a mistake marrying him would have been. There were so many red flags, and I ignored them because I wanted things to work. I *needed* them to work."

She turned her mug around and around in her hands. "That's good then. So, you're happy now?"

I smiled at her, a real smile. "Absolutely. I'm working my dream job with my two best friends, I'm dating someone who treats me better than I could've imagined, and I get to be close to my family. It's not all sunshine and roses, but I don't regret a thing."

"Sometimes I wonder what we're waiting for, but I don't believe in half-assing things. If I'm doing something I care about, I need to go all in. I can't really commit to two major life events at the same time, though, you know? Not equally, anyway. So we're prioritizing the winery to secure our future." She sighed and took a sip of her drink, looking so down that I held out a freshly baked calamansi sugar cookie.

Izzy smiled her thanks and took a bite, her eyes widening at the crisp, buttery tang. She quickly gobbled down the rest of the cookie, and I could see that my baking had worked its magic. Contentment radiated out from her, and her tense expression melted into a dreamy smile.

"But you know what? Once the winery's a success, and I can finally focus on wedding planning?" She grinned at me. "It's going to be an event to remember."

"That makes sense," I said, turning back to my baking so she'd feel more comfortable talking. "You at least know where you'd want it to be? Since you're from different cities, there's probably a lot of talk from both families on where to hold the ceremony."

She'd mentioned last night that her parents hadn't wanted her to go away for college, so I imagined she came from a strict and/or close family. I bet they'd want to be part of the wedding planning.

Her loud groan let me know I was right. "We haven't been able to come up with a good compromise, so it might be a destination wedding where everyone has to travel. I wish we could just elope, but I couldn't do that to my parents and his parents would never forgive us, either."

"You both have strict parents?"

"His are strict. Very old-fashioned, very conservative. I don't even want to think about the fight that's sure to happen when they find out I'm not changing my last name." She shook her head and sighed. "Mine are just . . . We're really tight, but I'm the oldest, so you know how it is."

"I'm an only child and my parents died when I was young, so not really. But I can guess. Oldest daughter of immigrant parents?" I asked, remembering how so many of my friends in college bonded over the fact that they were the eldest daughter born in an immigrant family, and all the responsibilities and pressure that entailed.

She winced. "Right, I knew that. Sorry. And yeah, that's exactly it. So it's fine. I'm not in a rush and neither is Pete. We've got plenty of time. Besides, I'm kind of enjoying the freedom."

At my questioning look, she explained, "My parents would never have let me move out of the house before marriage, particularly with two guys across the country, if Pete and I weren't engaged. Florida was my first real taste of freedom away from my family, and I loved it."

"So then why did you leave?"

"I told you, because of the winery. There was no way we'd be able to aff—"

"Yeah, but that's not the only reason. Right?" I didn't want to push too hard, but there was a reason some rando was trying to blackmail Tita Rosie, even if Izzy wanted to pretend it was nothing.

"Look, Lila, we've all got stuff in the past. But I'm handling that email problem, OK? I know we just met, but you've got to trust me on this."

I continued rolling balls of pandan cookie dough in powdered sugar, heavily coating each dough ball so they'd get their customary crinkle look after baking. This wasn't the time to push since I had no bargaining chips yet, so I just let her sweat it out in silence for a bit before changing the subject.

"How does Ronnie feel about yours and Pete's relationship? He ever complain about being the third wheel or anything like that? I mean, you all live together, don't you?"

"As far as I know, he doesn't care. The only thing he's asked about our engagement is why we're bothering. According to him, the only point of marriage is for a tax break or insurance, and since that isn't happening for either of us, we should just keep everything the way it is." She frowned and reached out for a piece of shortbread to dunk in her coffee. "I think he's just afraid it'll change things between us, which is ridiculous. Pete and I have been together almost the entire time the three of us have been friends. Why would a wedding change that?"

I was still reeling from Ronnie's feelings about matrimony and wondered how much of that was shaped by his parents' marriage before I thought to ask, "Has Ronnie been in a serious relationship since you've known him?"

She burst out laughing but forced herself to stop when she saw I was serious. "Um, not exactly. There was one girl we thought would finally be the one to get him to settle down, but, well, I'm sure he's told you all about it. At least they're still on good terms, all things considered."

"He's still friends with his ex?" That was surprising, considering the string of broken hearts he'd left here. "And what do you mean, 'all things considered'?"

She studied me carefully, as if she thought I was joking again. "He never told you about her?"

"Was she his college girlfriend? Or someone from your time at the resort?"

"I really don't think I should be the one to tell you about her. It's not my place. But I'll tell him to be more open with you. If he hasn't told you about her, I wonder what he has told you about his life." She said the last part quietly, almost as an afterthought.

"Izzy, Ronnie hasn't contacted us in fifteen years. I don't know a thing about him after he walked out on us. I didn't even know he went to college. Like, how could he have even afforded it? Especially being from out of state?"

Izzy reared back, staring at me in disbelief. "Fifteen years? That can't be right. I mean, he said that it'd been a while, but we thought . . . well, never mind what we thought." Her brows knit together, likely wondering how much she could say without betraying her best friend's privacy. "Anyway, he was a scholarship student. Worked odd jobs around campus for money. Spent every break with my family to save money on food and housing. He told us his family was broke and he didn't want to be a burden, so we assumed that was why he never visited you all or talked about you much. I always got the sense that he'd gotten in trouble here and wanted a fresh start."

I laughed, but there was no amusement or joy in the sound. "Yeah, you could say that."

It was hard to remember a time that Ronnie wasn't in trouble. Vandalization, drugs, fights; you name it, he'd been hauled into the Shady Palms Police Department for it. And while my cousin was no saint, the fact that he acted out made him an easy target whenever something went wrong in our town. As angry as I was at him for abandoning Tita Rosie, I knew why he did it. Could even understand it. I sure as heck was still pissed about it all.

He was maybe seventeen when a party he was at got raided. Our previous mayor's son got caught with a large amount of, shall we say, illegal substances, and convinced the arresting officers that it belonged to Ronnie. Sheriff Lamb and the rest of the police department were only too happy to pin it on the town troublemaker, despite several witnesses saying Ronnie didn't do it. The only thing that kept him out of juvie was the help of Adeena and Amir's dad, who was still a practicing lawyer back then. Instead, Ronnie had to pay a huge fine (meaning Tita Rosie had to pay a huge fine) and got sentenced to 120 hours of community service, the maximum possible in Illinois. The day after he'd worked his last community service hour, he was gone.

I sighed, the memories of those tense, sad days flooding my head. "Izzy, has he said anything to you about how he feels being back?"

She looked hunted, as if she knew both answering and not answering would confirm what I already knew. "He's nervous. He wouldn't tell me anything specific, but he admitted that much. But he's also happy to see you all again. And he's trying hard, Lila. He really is. Whoever he was as a kid, he's become a good man. I swear it."

I lifted an eyebrow and sipped at my drink to avoid responding. I didn't want my skepticism to push her away; we needed more time to bond so she'd eventually open up to me about what happened in Florida. I didn't believe for a second that Ronnie's shady past wasn't finally coming to bite him in the ass. Luckily, she got a text at that moment, the message making her sigh and stand up.

"Pete said the twins are coming over to the office, so I've got to head back. Thanks for introducing me to Terrence and the food and drinks and the chat and just . . . everything."

I smiled at her. "Of course. If you're free tomorrow, want to hang out with me and my friends? There are other people I'd like to introduce you to."

"I'd like that!" We exchanged numbers and she grinned as she waved goodbye.

Fine, I'll admit it. I liked her. I liked her a lot. I could see her becoming part of the Brew-ha crew, just like Sana and Yuki had.

Just a shame that she kept lying to me. Guess I'd have to dig a little deeper to find out what she was hiding. Here's hoping neither of us regretted it.

Chapter Eleven

I wouldn't consider myself a morning person, but I'd been helping at the restaurant since I was a kid and was now the baker at my own cafe, so mornings and I had reached a grudging truce.

Not this morning though.

Whether it was the stress of preparing for the winter bash, the mess that Ronnie was in, or just the pull of a toasty, warm bed on a freezing Midwestern morning, I could not bring myself to get up. After the third time I hit snooze, Longganisa must've decided she'd had enough because she burrowed under my blankets and stuck her cold wet nose into the bare sliver of skin on my back that was poking out from my sleep shirt.

"Ah! OK, OK, I get it, Nisa."

Rubbing the wetness away, I got out of bed and washed up before letting Longganisa out into our fenced yard. I wasn't scheduled for a shift at the cafe, but I should probably pop in anyway. There was always more work to do there, but at least it came with a decent cup of coffee. I sighed at that dreary thought and got up to feed Longganisa and scarf down some pandesal before I headed to my room to get ready for the day. Longganisa raced up the stairs in front of me, but partway up, she turned around to face me and let out a sharp bark. Her reproachful gaze let me know that I hadn't been spending enough time with her, and I sighed again. "You're right. I know what we both need."

Anytime my brain refused to shake the morning cobwebs on its own meant it was time to go on a run. I hadn't been as diligent as I was during warmer weather since it required a lot of prep for both Nisa and me, but considering there wasn't snow on the ground yet, it shouldn't be too bad. I went back to my room to change into my workout gear, Nisa trotting behind me, and once I was ready, I put her in her matching outfit and booties to protect her paws from the freezing pavement.

Properly outfitted, we made our way down to the Riverwalk, our favorite place to run. It wasn't as crowded as usual due to the early hour and crisp morning air, and Nisa and I were able to quickly get into a comfortable rhythm as we made our way down the path that snaked alongside the river. The air bit at my skin and my breath came out in puffs of steam, but my head was finally clear and Nisa was panting along happily beside me. We slowed our pace when we got near the footbridge that would let us cross the river, not just for safety (though that was important, and the town had finally installed handrails along the sides) but also because it brought up bad memories from the summer. At the head of the bridge was someone I hadn't expected to see but should've.

"Good morning, Xander!" I called out.

Xander had a tight orange knit hat pulled down over his ears and was leaning on the rail, looking out over the water, his dog waiting patiently at his feet, but he didn't even glance my way. Did he not hear me, or was he ignoring me? I was only a few feet away, so he must've heard me. Maybe mornings were his special time to decompress, and he didn't appreciate the intrusion. It was awkward, but probably best to keep it moving and leave him alone.

Just as I'd made that decision, he glanced in my direction and started, then recovered with a quick smile. He reached up and removed wireless earbuds from under his knit hat. "Lila! And who do we have here?"

I tightened my hold on Nisa's leash since Longganisa and his dog, Poe, if I remembered correctly, were barking and circling each other warily. Nisa calmed down after a few good sniffs. Poe still had a low growl going till Xander stooped and rubbed his neck—Poe's eyes half-closed and his tongue flopped out in pleasure. What a good boy.

"This is Longganisa," I said, also stooping down. "And that's Poe, right? Could I pet him?"

"Sure. He's quite friendly; just make sure you don't move too quickly since sudden movements startle him."

I held out my hand for him to sniff, and when he lowered his head to me, I gave him a good scratch behind the ears. "Nisa absolutely loves attention, so feel free to pet her if you want."

Xander obliged, and he soon had Nisa flopped on her back for belly rubs. He squatted beside the dogs, both of them vying for his attention, which he gladly gave. It was super adorable, and nice to see such a genuine smile on his face. He looked up and caught me watching him, a smile on my own face.

"What?"

"Nothing. I was just thinking that you looked really happy playing with the dogs. And I know that you haven't had a lot to be happy about lately. So, I don't know. I hope you're OK."

He studied me for a moment before saying, "I appreciate that. Would you—"

A cyclist trying to walk their bike across the bridge brushed by us, making Xander falter when he caught the stink eye they were throwing him, and I noticed Xander and I were blocking the path. He must've realized this too because he said, "Poe and I need to continue our walk. Would you and Longganisa like to join us?"

"We'd love to! It's been a while since we've had company on our runs."

We rejoined the path and set out at a light jog. Xander and Poe were keeping at the leisurely pace Nisa and I preferred since anything faster was bad for her back, which I appreciated, but as I glanced at Xander, I couldn't help but notice how fit he was. "Are we slowing you down? You seem like you'd prefer a faster pace," I said.

"We're fine. His legs and joints resist anything too fast, so I'm used to it. If I'd wanted a real workout, I would've just gone to the gym, but I'm enjoying the fresh air." He pulled his knit hat farther past his ears. "Do you come here often?"

"Yeah, it's mine and Nisa's favorite spot. We haven't come as often as we'd like since I've been so busy with holiday planning and baking, but I really needed it this morning."

"Any particular reason?"

"Just stressed about getting things done in time, nothing major. How about you? How are things going with the . . . with everything?" I wasn't sure how to end that question—With your fiancée's funeral planning? With the hospital tests? With the police? With your brand new business venture?—so I hoped that leaving it open-ended would get me answers to a few of those things.

He suddenly stopped and bent over, hands to his knees as if he were worn out and needed to catch his breath. And despite our slow pace, that's exactly what he was doing, taking deep, ragged breaths in and out as if he'd been sprinting for the last mile. Nisa and I both came to a stop as well, and she trotted over to him and put a paw on his foot to comfort him.

I bit my lip. "I'm sorry. It's none of my business. If you don't want to talk—"

"No, I'd love to talk. To be honest, there are things I need help with, and I don't know who to turn to."

"What about your assistants?"

He scowled and then shook his head quickly, as if to shake off the ugly expression. "There are some things they're assisting me with, but others could use a more . . . delicate touch."

"Why don't you come over to my aunt's restaurant for breakfast? I only had bread and coffee and could use something a little more substantial. We could talk there."

He finally faced me, and for once didn't force a smile. "You know what? I'd like that. Can you ask your aunt to set up a private table? I just need to drop Poe off—"

"Actually, why don't we drop Poe and Nisa off at the cafe? We're dog-friendly and I have a special space set up for her in my office, though I haven't used it yet. I'm sure these two would appreciate some time to hang out, and Elena can test her organic dog biscuits on them."

"Oh, that sounds great. Sometimes I worry that he gets lonely in the big house without . . . without company," Xander said, pausing partway to swallow a lump in his throat.

"I'll let my aunt know to set up a breakfast table for us in the private party room, and we'll drop the dogs next door. See you soon."

Xander examined the spread, which included our usual DIY silog platters—garlic fried rice with a choice of fried or scrambled eggs and various proteins: longganisa, tocino, tapa, sardines, dried fish—as well as pandesal, cheese, coconut jam, condensed milk, bibingka, and champorado.

"Your aunt is going to spoil me. How can I go back to cafe con leche and pan after all this?"

He watched what I was doing and then copied me: one plate for savory, one plate for sweet, and a bowl for the champorado. I was in a sardines mood this morning (don't knock it till you've tried it) and heaped the fish with its garlicky tomato sauce on top of my rice before adding a fried egg. Xander piled a bit of everything on his plates and dug in with an enthusiasm that made me smile.

"Oh, I'm so glad you're enjoying your food!" Tita Rosie entered the room with a tray containing pitchers of water and calamansi iced tea plus carafes of hot coffee and tsokolate. She set the drinks on the table and sat with us, dishing up a small bowl of champorado and swirling condensed milk on top. She dug into the creamy chocolate porridge with a smile, and after a few spoonfuls she helped herself to a piece of tuyo.

"Did you skip breakfast with Lola earlier?" I asked, dipping a chunk of bibingka into my tsokolate. My aunt and grandmother ate breakfast together every morning before opening up the restaurant, and I wasn't used to her attacking her food with such energy.

Tita Rosie took a sip of coffee and nodded. "We're catering a holiday lunch for a business in Shelbyville, so I needed to get in early to make sure everything was ready. I'd forgotten to pick up the trays and boxes I needed the other day, so I had to run out again. I got back not too long before your call and haven't had a chance to eat yet. I need to leave soon, but I'm so glad I waited so that I could share a meal with you two. I've been meaning to check in on you, Xander. Please let me know if you need anything from us."

Xander speared several pieces of tocino and added them to his plate before responding. "Actually yes, there is. It's not common knowledge, but Denise and I bought a house on the outskirts of town and had been in the process of moving in. It was only meant to be a vacation home, you know, when we needed to get away from the city, so we didn't bring too much with us. But there's still a lot of Denise's things in the house. I was wondering . . . if it's not too much trouble . . . could you find someone to sort through her belongings?"

Tita Rosie and I exchanged a look, and he must've thought we'd assumed he wanted us to do it because he quickly explained, "Like a professional cleaning service or something like that. I don't really know what's available in this town, but I'm happy to pay for it and I trust your recommendation. Obviously, I'll take care of papers and any personal effects like jewelry, but her clothes, shoes, perfumes . . . anything that can be donated, I'd love for them to handle it. Or if there's a charity in town, I don't know, they can resell her things and keep the money."

"Oh Xander . . . are you sure? It may be too painful to go through her things right now, but there may come a time where you'll wish you had," Tita Rosie said, watching him with a soft look in her eyes. "There's no need to do it all right away."

"There are a few things of hers that I'm keeping for sentimental value, of course. But she'd hate for me to hold on to all those things when they're no longer needed. And Denise loved her charities, so I'm sure this is what she'd want. I just can't handle it right now."

"What about your assistants? They knew her personally, so I'm sure they'll know better than us the value of those things."

Xander wiped his mouth with a napkin. "It's fine. They're busy with other, more pressing tasks. And I think it's a better idea to hire people who didn't know her or the true value of her possessions to make these kinds of decisions anyway." My aunt and I exchanged another look. Neither of us missed the tension hidden in Xander's seemingly innocuous words. Denise and her assistants had seemed to get along just fine, but it was hard to miss the strain between Xander and Quentin. I wondered what their beef was. Maybe Ronnie had the details?

Tita Rosie turned her attention back to Xander. "I'm honored that you'd trust us with something as personal as that. Of course we'll help you. However, instead of paying for a service, why don't I ask my church outreach group if they'll help? We could use anything you donate to raise funds for the programs we run," Tita Rosie said.

Ooh, what a great idea. Tita Rosie and Father Santiago were always struggling to fund the community outreach programs they ran, and the Simbang Gabi festivities often included a raffle and fundraising event. Denise's donations would not only net a huge amount, but sorting through her belongings would give me a reason to search for clues to her death. Morbid, I know, but if those tests pointed at anything other than an accidental death, we'd need every opportunity we could get to collect information.

We exchanged numbers and discussed a possible schedule before turning back to demolish the rest of our breakfast. About twenty minutes and a second jar of coco jam later (Xander had started just eating it with a spoon), Xander scraped out the last of the champorado in his bowl and leaned back in his seat, sighing in contentment.

"I needed that. Thanks for inviting me over, Lila. And thanks for this amazing meal, Rosie. Is your mom available? I'd love to thank her as well, maybe buy a few jars of her coconut jam to take home with me."

Tita Rosie lit up. "Sure! Wait just a minute and I'll bring her here."

Xander waited until he saw Tita Rosie disappear into the kitchen and said, "I'll be right back. Need to run to the register and pay real quick before your aunt says it's on the house." He headed to the front of the restaurant, where Joy was ringing up another customer, showing that he understood exactly how Tita Rosie operated. Smart man.

I was in the middle of checking my texts (a quick check-in from Adeena about the dogs: *They love the sweet potato dog biscuits!* and a sweet *Good morning!* message from Jae) when Lola Flor's voice boomed behind me.

"Where did he go?"

I jumped, dropping my phone to the floor. Thank goodness for screen protectors. I stooped to pick it up and tried to think up an excuse. "Um, bathroom?"

Tita Rosie peered out of the room and sighed. "Your ninangs have him cornered at the register."

The three of us stepped into the main area of the restaurant and sure enough, the Calendar Crew formed a semicircle around him, trapping him at the register. "We better go save him," I said. "Lord knows what they're saying to him."

But when we made our way over to them, the group was laughing and chattering excitedly together.

"Oh, you're going to love it, Xander!"

"I mean, it's no Monte Carlo, but they've got a great buffet and some good people watching opportunities."

"If you do well enough on this trip, maybe you can join us on mahjong night. Father Santiago refuses to gamble, so we need a new fourth."

It wasn't hard to guess what was going on, but I decided to ask anyway. "What're you all bugging Xander about?"

The Calendar Crew turned to me, all three of them grinning. "He's meeting us at the casino later! We're going to have so much fun!"

"I have a few errands to run, but I'll meet you at the buffet in a few hours." Xander aimed his key fob at a fancy-looking silver SUV, and the purr of the auto-start kicked in. The Calendar Crew rushed outside to check out his car, and he turned to us. "I just wanted to thank you all again for your hospitality. I really appreciate it. Lila, is it OK if Poe stays with you a bit longer? If I'm running late, I'll have one of the twins swing by."

The casino seemed like an odd place to go considering he was still in mourning, but as I've learned, people grieve in different ways. Maybe he was just trying to get his mind off things and grasped at any opportunity to do so. It's not like he had much of an outlet here in Shady Palms considering the only people he knew were his assistants and the winery crew, all people who might be involved in his fiancée's death.

I assured him we were happy to watch over his dog, and Lola Flor held out a bag with several jars of coco jam as well as some of her pastries and rice cakes. "You need to eat. Keep your strength up, diba? There's plenty more where that came from."

Xander accepted the bag, a sheen of wetness in his eyes that disappeared after a few blinks. "I know you're all busy, but can I tempt any of you to join us? It should be a good time."

Lola Flor's eyes glowed in excitement, but a look from Tita Rosie had her turning around and stomping back to the kitchen. Tita Rosie said, "Thanks for the offer, but I'm afraid we can't. Are you sure you'll be OK with the three of them? They can be . . ."

"A lot. Like, a lot a lot," I said, gnawing on my lower lip as I glanced out the restaurant's large glass window to see the three of them still clamoring to peer in the windows and case the car's interior.

He grinned. "I've dealt with plenty of aunties in my life, Lila. Don't worry about us. We'll play a little poker, eat too much at the buffet, maybe waste some money at the slots. It's not like we're going to Vegas. How much trouble can they possibly get up to?"

The loud blare of his car alarm made us all jump and stare at my godmothers, who had all backed away with their hands in the air as if they'd had nothing to do with it. Xander's forehead creased, and my aunt did a quick sign of the cross.

"I'll pray for you," she said.

Xander turned to me as if asking if she were serious, and I just shook my head.

"Good luck, buddy. You'll need it."

Chapter Twelve

O of, Xander's a braver man than I'll ever be if he willingly went to the casino with the ninangs."

Ronnie shook his head and took a sip of our house blend. I'd gone over to the cafe after breakfast and was greeted by Ronnie, Izzy, and Pete, who were all seated at the counter, chatting with Elena. Well, Ronnie and Izzy greeted me; Pete was too busy picking pieces of candied ginger out of the salabat banana bread to notice me. He was also drinking our house blend, but Izzy had a mug of Adeena's special spiced hot chocolate in front of her, and Elena was sipping on atole. Adeena was busy helping a customer, so I poured myself some atole and joined them at the counter.

"Yeah well, let's hope their chattering will be distracting in a good way. He looked grateful for the company," I said.

"We wanted to give him some space, but maybe we were giving him too much space. He doesn't know anyone else in this town and could probably use help getting Denise's affairs in order," Izzy said, a look of chagrin crossing her face.

"He definitely could. He asked Tita Rosie and me if we could recommend a service to go through Denise's things and help him decide what to donate and whatnot."

Izzie and Ronnie exchanged glances, but it was Pete who finally spoke up. "That's strange. He just met you. Why wouldn't he ask Quentin and Olivia to handle it? They were Denise's . . . I mean, stuff like this is literally their job. Maybe they don't know this town the way you do, but Google exists."

"I wondered the same thing, honestly. Not that I have a problem helping out, but . . ." I paused, trying to figure out how I wanted to word this. It seemed like Pete was friendly with them, so I didn't want to repeat what Xander had said. I went for a half truth.

"It seemed like he wanted someone who didn't have a personal connection to Denise to go through her possessions. He wants everything to be donated, so he figured it'd be easier for people with no attachments."

"I still think it's strange, but whatever. I hope he's at least paying you to do it," Pete said, biting into his now-ginger-free banana bread.

Izzy dropped the cookie she was about to dunk into her cocoa, the chai gingerbread biscuit landing in her mug with a splash. "How could you say that? That man just lost the love of his life, and all you can think about is squeezing him for money?"

"First of all, you're the one always going on about boundaries and knowing your worth and women's labor, blah blah blah," Pete said, rolling his eyes. "It's not like these are dear friends who'd be happy to help. He's imposing on total strangers. You don't think that's weird?"

Izzy frowned, reaching for a napkin to clean up her mess. "Well, I guess—"

"Besides, 'love of his life'?" Pete snorted. "Her money, maybe. But not her."

"That's a terrible thing to say!" Izzy burst out.

Even Ronnie jumped in. "Yeah man, that's way too harsh. We don't know him to be judging him like that. And he's still our investor, you know. So watch what you say. We still need him, and you're the one always harping on about keeping 'the money' happy."

Pete shrugged and turned back to his banana bread. "Whatever, man. Let's hope he doesn't blow it all at the casino then."

Ronnie and Izzy exchanged looks again, as if this were something they'd had to worry about before. Interesting. I'd have to ask the aunties about this later.

"While we're on the subject, well, I know it's not my place, but I couldn't help noticing some tension between Xander and Quentin. What's the story there? Do any of you know?" I asked.

Ronnie shrugged. "It's been like that since we've met them. Quentin was always fine with Denise, but whenever Xander wanted him to do something, it would get done, but not without a heap of attitude. I wonder—"

Izzy cursed loudly, making the rest of us startle at the sudden interruption. She was staring down at her phone but glanced up at the silence. "Oh, sorry. I, um, forgot I had some stuff to do today. I'll see you all later." She shrugged on her jacket and bag and ran out the door, both men staring after her.

"She's been doing that a lot lately," Pete said, almost to himself. Ronnie didn't respond, just continued watching Izzy's departure with a strange look on his face.

There was an awkward pause before Ronnie cleared his throat.

"Anyway, we were just here to drop off samples. We're hoping to clear out a good amount of the old winery stock by spring to make room for our new varietals. Let us know if you like any in particular and we'll give you a great discount."

"Let me put together a to-go bag for you all. I'm sure you've got a lot of work to get through," I said, filling the (super cute, designed by Terrence) paper bag with the last of the morning's pastries and tossing in a few cookies as well. "I need to make some fresh bakes for the case anyway."

Pete mumbled his goodbye and thanks before grabbing the to-go bag and heading out. Ronnie waved at Adeena and me, stopping briefly near the door to flirt with Elena, who'd moved to help a customer, and make her laugh before heading out.

"How's your morning been?" Elena asked, rejoining us to set a vase filled with pine tree clippings and pinecones on the counter.

The scent of the fresh-cut sprigs filled my nose, sharp, sweet, and refreshing, and I leaned forward to better appreciate the invigorating yet calming aroma. "Not bad. A little strange, maybe. How are Nisa and Poe doing?"

Elena let out a squeal and gestured for me to follow her. In the corner of my office that I'd fixed up for Nisa but hadn't used—I was still uncomfortable with the idea of bringing her to work, but dog-friendly cafes were popular and she was well-trained, so I needed to get over it—Nisa and Poe were curled up in her large dog bed together, napping peacefully. Poe's tongue was out in a permanent blep as he slept, and Nisa's head was tucked under Poe's chin, narrowly avoiding his tongue.

"Oh. My. Gulay. This is the cutest thing ever!" I whipped out my phone and started snapping a million pictures.

Elena nodded. "I know. I had no idea I needed small dogs spooning in my life, but this has made my entire week. They are so sweet together."

"Adeena said they liked your sweet potato dog biscuits?"

She lit up. "Yep! I think coming up with a line of healthy, organic pet treats could generate a bunch of revenue, especially now that people know dogs are allowed in the shop."

It was Katie's idea to make the place pet-friendly since it'd make for really cute pictures for social media and marketing, and she was absolutely right. After Adeena came up with a recipe for a healthy pup cup late in the summer, and Katie posted flyers around town of Longganisa in a Brew-ha Cafe onesie slurping up a pup-kin spice latte, our business had become a beloved family hangout spot.

I took one last photo and tucked my phone away. "Sounds good. Do we need to work out a kitchen schedule for your baking, so the human cookies don't get mixed up with the dog ones?"

Elena nodded. "That would be a good idea. I can bake at night since the biscuits need time to cool and crisp, while yours are better fresh-baked. I might look into growing catnip in the greenhouse for cat treats. The recipe I use for Bella uses salmon or tuna, and I don't want to stink up your kitchen."

I laughed. "Much appreciated. And I kinda love the idea of you making kitty edibles for our customers."

Elena grinned. "Glad to see you finally coming around on that."

I'd had a pretty hardened stance against drugs—and a rather unforgiving view of drug users, thanks to Ronnie and his good-for-nothing father—for most of my life, but events earlier this year had taught me how rigid and narrow-minded I was when it came to this. Becoming friends with Elena opened up my mind a lot more and reminded me that people were complex beings who wouldn't always make decisions that I agreed with. It seemed obvious now, but at the time I hadn't realized that my separating people as "good" or "bad" based solely on their substance abuse problems was super ableist and problematic.

Though I had to admit that I was very much a work in progress. Case in point, my sometimes not-so-kind thoughts about Denise and whether or not she was actually poisoned, or if she'd just drunk so much it'd built up over time. Hmm, I should probably do some research on methanol poisoning to see if that was possible.

I shook my head and refocused on the adorable scene in front of me to get those dark thoughts out of my mind. I pulled my phone out again for one more picture. "I should send this to Xander, I'm sure he'd appreciate an update on his pup. A pupdate?"

"Good idea. And then we should both get back to work," Elena reminded me, after a gentle laugh at my pun.

After I sent Xander the picture, we both left my office, with Elena heading back toward the front and me making my way to the kitchen. A thorough handwashing (and quick tucking up of my hair into my baking hat), and I was ready to tackle something new. I flipped through my bujo to look at ideas I'd jotted down. The selection I'd set out this morning—salabat banana bread, calamansi chia seed muffins, chai gingerbread cookies, ube crinkles, and mango peach crumble cookies—had all but sold out in the two hours we'd been open, so I knew I had to whip up more of the same. That would keep the ovens pretty busy, so maybe something no-bake?

I got to work on the banana bread and calamansi muffins since they'd take the longest to bake, and by the time I got the quick breads in the oven, I had it: ube white chocolate fudge! I gathered the ingredients, and in less than fifteen minutes, the mixture was ready and I poured the liquid fudge into the pan I'd prepped. It needed time to chill, so while it cooled, I removed the bowls of cookie dough from the fridge and swapped in the fudge.

As I rolled the chai gingerbread cookies in their turbinado sugar mix, I thought about what Katie said about having a cookie decorating workshop. This gingerbread, combined with the calamansi sugar cookies, would be the perfect traditional-with-a-twist base for a holiday workshop. If I could find festive, yet not-Christmas-specific cookie cutters (or at least not *only* Christmas-related cookie cutters), we were in business. I'd have to ask Katie to do some research for me. I wished that everything we came up with to promote the business wasn't so last-minute—even with the winter bash, I felt like we'd been planning for forever, but had only pinned down what we were doing less than two weeks before the event. Then again, we were a new business, so it made sense that we were just throwing spaghetti at the wall to see what would stick. And to be honest, I couldn't stop myself from coming up with more and more dessert ideas to try out, so my menu for just about any event was constantly changing. In some ways that was good, since the customers loved the variety and finding new things each time they stopped by. But it was terrible for planning, and people were quick to complain when a beloved item happened to not be on the menu that day. Like I said, we were a work in progress.

The quick breads were done, so I moved them to the cooling rack and popped in the cookies. As I sat and waited for them to finish baking, I flipped to an empty page in my journal and jotted down notes about all that had been going on:

•*Blackmail—Izzy said she was handling it. Check in w/ her? Get Terrence to help?*

•*Denise—Methanol poisoning. Do research. Possible accident? Who had access to her?*

•*Xander—Grieving widower? Pete says it was money, not love. Both? Talk to Calendar Crew about him.*

•*Ronnie—What is he up to? Why did he really come back? How did he get the money to do anything? See if I can find any articles about him in Florida.*

•*Pete—So boring.*

That was as far as I'd gotten before the timer went off for my cookies. I removed them from the oven and let them set for a moment before moving the cookies to the cooling racks. The salabat banana bread was still too warm to slice cleanly, so I put the loaves in the fridge for a few minutes while I brought the muffins out to refill the case. By the time I made it back to the kitchen, the loaves were just cool enough to slice into, and I made quick work of them. The cookies were too hot to bring out, so while I waited, I texted Terrence about help tracking the blackmailer.

On top of his graphic design skills, he was a computer whiz and had helped Adeena and me more than once during our high school sleuthing days. Back then, it was mostly combing through people's social media and hacking into people's email to get evidence of cheating partners or get rid of incriminating photos, but now we were in the big leagues, and I could only hope Terrence knew how to find our culprit. He wrote back, *I'll do what I can once I finish this project! Just forward me the email.* With that taken care of, I killed time playing with Nisa and Poe, who'd woken up from their naps. Realizing I hadn't heard from Xander after sending him that photo, I texted him again with an update.

Nisa and Poe are getting along great! When will you pick him up? I can bring him to my place if you're getting back late.

This time he answered right away.

Sorry, just saw this

Can you drop him off at my place?

Twins should be stopping by later tonight to take care of him

After he sent me his address and key code, I responded with a thumbs-up emoji and put my phone away. "Hey, you two, looks like we're going on a road trip! Get ready, because we're leaving soon."

Both dogs just looked at me and went back to snuggling on the dog bed, which they'd dragged under my desk. I suddenly remembered the cookies and rushed back to the kitchen, bringing them out to a fully packed café. Seeing the crowd, I grabbed a Brew-ha Cafe emblazoned dog shirt that looked like it'd fit Poe and a bandana for Longganisa. I dressed up the dogs and led them out to the front for some easy marketing. Sure enough, there were a few groups distributed throughout the cafe, but they all came together to gush over the dogs and take pictures.

Elena made a big show of giving Nisa and Poe her homemade dog biscuits, pointing out how much they loved them (and the dogs *really* loved them—Elena even got Nisa to do a little dance before she earned her treat) and how her recipe was so much healthier than store-bought dog treats. The consummate salesperson, she announced that anyone who posted a picture of Nisa and Poe in their Brew-ha Cafe gear on social media, tagged the Cafe account, and talked up the new dog biscuits in their caption would receive a ten percent discount on anything else they bought that day, fifteen percent off for the dog biscuits. Katie, our social media expert, directed people on which hashtags to use and started taking her own pictures to post on our account.

While Elena watched over the dogs and Katie guided our customers, I went back to my office to grab the dogs' winter wear. There was no real reason to hurry since Xander said his assistants wouldn't be over until nighttime, but I wanted to get Poe back before the usual afternoon rush to get more baking done. I waited till the customers had taken all the dog pics they needed before putting Poe's puppy parka and boots back on, then got Nisa ready as well. Not gonna lie, another reason I wanted to head over right away was because I was excited about getting to check out Xander's house when he wasn't around. I wouldn't do any digging just yet (that could wait till we were given the OK to sort through Denise's belongings), but it wouldn't hurt to take a quick look around, get an idea of who we were dealing with.

At the last minute, I decided to pack a baggie of dog treats for Poe and a separate treat bag for Xander—even though he wouldn't be there, Tita Rosie and Lola Flor raised me to never show up at someone's home empty-handed. Once the dogs and I were finally ready, we made our way to the door, stopping at the counter to let Adeena and Elena know where I was going. Katie was straightening the bags of coffee that Adeena had just hand-roasted, but she abandoned her task when she overheard me.

"Can I come with you? I want to play with the dogs more!"

I handed her the leashes. "Sure, I wanted to talk to you about your cookie decorating workshop idea anyway. Let's roll."

Chapter Thirteen

I'm not sure what I was expecting, but it definitely wasn't this."

Katie stood in front of the renovated farmhouse Denise and Xander had bought as their vacation home, casting a critical eye over the building that was in desperate need of a paint job and the barren landscape surrounding it. I could tell she was expecting something more high-tech and glamorous, and to be honest, so was I, especially after Xander mentioned a key code.

"The general structure seems to be in great shape, and I'm sure the land surrounding it will be gorgeous come spring. I bet they'd planned on using the space as a fun couple's project to renovate together," I said, typing in the code on the keypad in the newly installed door.

"Oh, you're probably right. That's so sad. I hope he—Whoa!" Katie cut herself off mid-sentence as she stepped into the heated front room and took in the lavishly decorated space.

The interior was decorated in a way that read as a rich city person's idea of country living, but in like, eighteenth-century England. That's the only way I could describe it. It toed the line of ostentatious and gaudy but landed just barely on the side of tasteful. Everything looked plush and posh, and what furniture and decorations could be polished had been done so, so that they seemed to emit a soft glow. The stone fireplace took up a third of the wall and had stacks of firewood next to it. The rug in front of it looked so lush, I longed to kick off my boots and socks and sink my bare feet into it. There was an honest to goodness china cabinet and a silver serving tray on a side table next to it. This was a house you invited landed gentry to for a nice glass of sherry or port and fine cigars after a fox hunt, or for having intimate dinner parties where you served excellent boiled potatoes to the local vicar.

Poe and Nisa pulled on their restraints, eager to explore, and I removed their boots, as well as my own, before letting them off their leashes. They both careened toward a room in the back, Nisa following Poe's lead, and Katie and I followed them into a spacious kitchen. Next to the dishwasher sat an empty food bowl, full water bowl, and a dog bed that was at least three times bigger than Poe and definitely hadn't been bought on sale at Costco (like Nisa's). The two dogs lapped at the water, then sat expectantly next to the empty food bowl.

"Sorry, babies, but you already had treats earlier and it's not time for dinner yet. You'll have to wait a bit longer," I said, setting the bag of goodies I'd packed for Xander on the counter along with Poe's clearly marked bag.

They glared at me for a moment before a noise from above sent Poe rocketing up the stairs with Nisa close behind, both of them barking their heads off. Katie and I exchanged glances before running to the stairs ourselves. She was about to climb ahead of me before I came to my senses.

"Wait, we don't know who or what that was. You stay down here and be ready to call 911 if we need help, OK?"

She nodded and pulled out her phone, and I carefully started up the stairs. Was I making the dumbest horror movie 101 decision by going upstairs to investigate a suspicious noise alone? Possibly, but my dog was up there, and I couldn't leave without her.

But maybe you shouldn't go up there unarmed? Bless you, Common Sense, for coming just when I needed you. I went back downstairs and looked around for a weapon to protect myself with and found a fire poker leaning against the fireplace. The sharp point was a bit much, but it was heavy and could do damage if I swung with enough force. I'd been on the softball team in elementary school and hoped muscle memory would serve me well in case I had to fight to save the dogs. In a home invasion (or any mildly dangerous situation, really), my first instinct was to GET OUT, but considering I could no longer hear Nisa or Poe, that wasn't really an option.

"Who's there?" I called up the stairs. No real point in going for stealth considering the dogs would've alerted them to our presence, if they hadn't heard us already.

"Ugh, hurry up and come get your dog!" someone answered. They sounded vaguely familiar, but I couldn't place them. I looked at Katie and motioned for her to stay there. She held up her phone with 911 already dialed but not put through and gave me the thumbs-up.

I started up the stairs, then realized that the intruder could easily rush me and knock me down. I wasn't going to risk a broken neck for whatever this was. I stayed near the bottom of the stairs and called out, "Show yourself or we're calling the cops."

The dogs started barking again, the sound getting louder as they followed the intruder to the stairs. Quentin March stood at the top, hands up.

"Hey, I think there's a misunderstanding here. Will you please call off your tiny attack dogs?"

He smiled at me, probably trying to project innocence and charm, but I wasn't going to let my guard down just yet. I called the dogs, and they came down the stairs to nestle at mine and Katie's feet.

"What're you doing here?" I asked, lowering the poker but not letting it go.

"What are *you* doing here?" he shot back. "I'm Xander's assistant, I'm in and out of here all the time. I just came over to feed the dog."

"A little early, isn't it? Xander said you wouldn't be over till later tonight." It was barely lunchtime.

He cleared his throat but held my gaze. "Yeah, well, you caught me. I have plans for later tonight and wanted to feed him early so I could skive off later."

Hmm, that made sense in theory, but something about it struck me as sus. "Xander didn't tell you I had the dog?"

"That man never tells me anything. I assumed Poe was home, like he usually is."

Ooh, that bitterness I detected the first time we met was back. I just had to find out what their beef was. Then I realized something.

"Wait, if you were supposed to be feeding Poe, why were you upstairs?"

"Oh, uh . . ." His eyes darted back up the stairs. "Now that Denise is gone, Xander wanted me and Olivia to start going through her things. She's out on another errand for him, so I thought I'd get started without her."

"Really? How interesting." I leaned against the banister and eyed him, trying to look cool and in charge. "Why don't you tell me what you were really doing?"

He grinned at me. "Are you trying to play detective? That's so cute."

Katie said, "Hey, Lila is a great detective! She already, well . . ." She trailed off, wanting to defend me, but not wanting to talk about certain events from the past.

I put a hand on her arm. "It's fine, Katie. Why don't you take Nisa and Poe to the kitchen? You were working on a new trick with Nisa, right?"

Katie eyed Quentin warily but agreed. "Just shout if you need me. I have my phone ready in case, you know." She shot Quentin one last glare before disappearing with the dogs.

Once she was gone, I turned to him and pointed with the poker to emphasize my point. "Cut the BS. Even if you did come here early to skip out on dog duties later, which I totally don't believe, by the way, you definitely weren't here to sort out Denise's affairs. And before you say anything"—I held up a hand to cut him off since he looked ready to argue—"I know this because Xander asked my family to help handle her belongings earlier this morning. And he left very specific instructions on who he did and did *not* want involved."

I gave him a meaningful look. "You going to talk, or do I need to call Xander? Or better yet, the police?"

An ugly look crossed Quentin's face. "I knew it! I knew he was going to try and cut us out. That son of . . ." and here he let out a string of increasingly colorful curse words. He was really quite creative with his language once he got going.

"Sooo . . . are you going to explain yourself, or . . . ?" I held up my phone to make a point.

"Fine. I'm coming down the stairs to talk to you, so don't freak out and hit me with that fire thing you're obviously trying to intimidate me with."

I liked keeping a healthy distance between us, but it did feel rather ridiculous to keep my neck craned up to talk to him since it was such a tall staircase. I backed away from the stairs but kept the poker in hand. "Fine. But don't move too fast or too close. My family knows I'm here, by the way. And so do Xander and my business partners. Just in case you get any funny ideas."

He came slowly, almost elegantly, down the staircase and was close enough that I could hear him sigh. "Honestly, the things you come up with. I know you live in the middle of nowhere and must be bored out of your mind, but must you concoct these ridiculous scenarios?" He stopped roughly five or six feet away, just out of swinging reach. "So, what do you want to know, Nancy Drew?"

I rolled my eyes. Like that never gets old. "What were you doing upstairs?"

"If you *must* know, Denise was my stepmother. She married my father for his money, but before her was my mom, who actually loved him. After she died, my father had the nerve to use *her* ring to propose to Denise. That ring has been in the family for generations, and I was not going to let Xander pawn it to cover his gambling debts."

"Xander has a gambling problem?" I asked, my heart sinking at the thought of him at the casino with the aunties. Pete had hinted as much back at the cafe, but I was hoping it was just idle gossip. I filed away the fact that Denise was his stepmom to examine later—it explained why Xander and Denise employed the twins together, despite Quentin's rudeness to Xander. I also remembered the Calendar Crew mentioning something about the stepkids in that article they found.

He snorted. "Are you kidding? The only reason he can keep his investments afloat is because of Denise's money. Addicts seek comfort in each other, I guess."

Addicts? "Did Denise have an alcohol problem?"

He tilted his head, an amused smile twisting his lips. "You saw her that night. What do you think?"

I grimaced. Yeah, that wasn't too hard to figure out. The question was whether or not that contributed to her death, making it accidental rather than straight-up murder. I thought about having the aunties research or asking Ninang June, since she used to be a nurse, but since they seemed to be friendly with Xander, I wanted them to focus their attention on him. They were better placed to drag information out of him than I was. But maybe I could talk to Bernadette. She wouldn't be thrilled about getting involved in Ronnie's mess, considering their history, but I couldn't see her outright refusing. As long as I provided the proper enticement, that is.

Quentin must've gotten annoyed as I stood there in silence thinking through all that, because he finally said, "Are we done here?"

"Not yet. Not if you want me to keep quiet about this."

He grumbled, but said, "What else do you want to know?"

"Why are you here trying to steal the ring? You don't think Denise left it to you and your sister in her will?"

This time he erupted in full-out belly laughter, bending over and clutching his stomach. "Wow, you're actually pretty funny, did you know that? Look, Denise may not have been my favorite person, but I still cared about her. After my mother died, my dad didn't know what to do with us, so he married Denise and we became her problem. She was . . . kind to us. Which is more than I could say about my dad." Quentin took a deep breath, his expression now sober. "I'm gutted about what happened to her, especially since that means Xander's the one running the show now. But if my own father wouldn't leave us anything in his will, you think she would?"

"Your father didn't leave you anything? Why would he do that?" The words flew out of my mouth before I could figure out a more roundabout, sensitive way to ask. Nothing like poking at an old wound to get answers, Lila. Though that did solve the niggling bit of information I couldn't remember earlier regarding that article about Denise—it had mentioned their father leaving them nothing because he wanted them to "work for a change."

"Because Olivia and I were good-for-nothings who 'didn't deserve a handout' and had to prove ourselves before we were allowed anywhere near his money." He grinned as he said this, but I couldn't help but feel there was a deep pain hidden behind his nonchalant tone.

"Prove it how?"

"That's none of your—"

"Hey, Lila? Adeena just called and wanted to know what was taking so long. Are we OK?" Katie came out from the kitchen and stood in the living room area with us, her phone pressed to her ear.

"Put her on speaker," I said. When she did, I said, "Hey Adeena, we're just handling something that suddenly came up. If we're not back at the cafe within the hour, call Detective Park and let him know we were at Xander's with—"

"I'm done here!" Quentin said, brushing past me on his way to the door. Katie and I followed him out and saw him go around the house, where there must have been a garage or more parking spaces since he soon pulled out in a large bright blue SUV.

"Who was that?" Adeena's voice asked from Katie's phone.

"One of Xander's assistants," Katie said.

"Ooh, he did not sound happy. Let me guess, you cornered him about the case and forced him to spill?" Adeena asked.

I went back in the house to collect Longganisa and our things. "Girl, make sure you've got something good prepared, maybe one of Bernadette's favorites. I need to message her real quick, but we'll be back soon. I've got so much to tell you!"

Chapter Fourteen

S o, the only reason you invited me over is because you wanted to
see how much I know about methanol poisoning? Are you serious?"

Bernadette leaned back in her chair and crossed her arms, the
mother of all scowls across her face. I may not have been entirely
truthful when I'd messaged her, but considering her feelings about
Ronnie, I knew she wouldn't have come if I'd been direct about why
we needed to talk. Time for a half truth.

"Of course that's not the only reason I invited you over! Like I
said, we missed you here. You haven't been over in forever and we
were getting worried you weren't coming back. That you were going
to let Ronnie keep you away from us."

I infused my voice with all the sincerity I actually felt—I mean,
yes, there was an ulterior motive to me having her over, but nothing
I'd just said was a lie.

"It's true," Adeena said. "In fact, Sana and Yuki were here a couple of days ago asking about you. And I know Elena's upset she couldn't be here, but she had to leave early to help her mom."

Bernadette's frown eased ever so slightly, but her arms remained tightly crossed and I knew she wasn't ready to drop her guard. What more could I say to show how much we needed her? A lightbulb went off.

"Besides, I need your help brainstorming more Christmas-themed bakes for Simbang Gabi and Tita Rosie's Noche Buena party. Adeena and Elena are great for more general ideas, but they don't know traditional Filipino Christmas dishes the way you do."

The Brew-ha Cafe's involvement in my aunt's party was a recent development. As in, I'd been forced into it just a few hours ago. I hadn't thought my aunt would want me to contribute to the festivities since her parties were known for providing delicious, traditional Filipino food to people longing for a taste of home, so I figured my fusion desserts wouldn't fit in.

But Bernadette hadn't been able to stop by until after her shift, close to the cafe's closing time, so I'd left Nisa in my office and taken Katie out for lunch at the restaurant. After serving us, Tita Rosie had asked me what drinks and desserts the Brew-ha Cafe would be providing for the festivities culminating at the end of Simbang Gabi and was shocked when I told her I'd assumed she and Lola Flor didn't want me involved. She spent, like, ten minutes wringing her hands and talking about how important it was for our family to work together, and how much Father Santiago missed me, and really, Lola Flor wouldn't mind *that* much about having to share a table with my nontraditional sweets, no really, she'd only grumbled about it a few times . . . and so I'd been roped in to helping my aunt and grandmother with their Simbang Gabi festivities and big Christmas Eve party.

"If it's Christmas, you know you've got to make puto bumbong," Bernadette said, taking a sip of Adeena's latest attempt at an ube latte.

Puto bumbong was a purple rice cake made from a special variety of heirloom rice in the Philippines. It was steamed in a bamboo tube and served topped with butter (well, margarine, usually, but I'd finally convinced Lola Flor to start using butter), sugar, and coconut. It was traditionally served during Christmastime and a huge pain to make—even Lola Flor said she was happy she only had to make it during Simbang Gabi because she couldn't be bothered with it the rest of the year.

"There's no way I could get the rice on such short notice, and Lola Flor needs her whole stock to prepare the traditional version. I'm not sure how I'd make a modern version of puto bumbong anyway, so let's table that till next year."

Bernadette surveyed the array of cookies, quick breads, and the ube fudge I'd made earlier that day. "What about a cupcake? Your halo-halo cupcakes were a hit this summer, but you haven't come up with a new cupcake recipe in a while."

I shook my head. "Cupcakes are a great idea, but like I said, I wouldn't be able to get the purple rice in time, and there's no substitute for it. I guess I could make ube cupcakes, but those aren't particularly Christmas-y."

"Then how about a bibingka cupcake? Lola Flor's bibingka is always delicious, but I think a cupcake would be a fun way to tempt people too scared to try the traditional version because of the salted duck eggs." She drained her mug. "Adeena, this was great, but I think it needs more ube halaya and less ube extract. And maybe a touch of vanilla for balance?"

"OMG, I love you!" "Oh my gulay, you're a genius!" Adeena and I burst out, our praises overlapping each other. We looked at each other and burst out laughing.

Bernadette gave us both a smug smile. "Does that mean I finally get to have a drink named after me?"

"Absolutely. Do you want this ube latte named after you, or did you have something else in mind?" Adeena asked.

"I want you to make a spiced version, similar to a pumpkin spice latte. Once you figure out a spiced ube latte good enough to name after me, let me know so I can try it out."

Adeena made a note of that on her phone, and I pulled out my journal to jot down my ideas for the bibingka cupcake. "We owe you big time for this, Ate Bernie. And, um, not to ruin the moment, but I was hoping we could talk about . . . you know."

Bernadette sighed and gestured to Adeena for a refill. Adeena got to work on the revised version of the ube latte while Bernadette told me all she knew about methanol poisoning.

"Sorry, but your theory of the methanol building up over time doesn't hold water. It's not like arsenic. However, the timing is interesting. I'm pretty sure symptoms don't usually show up till about twelve hours after ingestion. Though I suppose it depends on how much methanol she ingested and how quickly her body metabolized it. There are a bunch of other factors to take into account as well, but still, if she displayed symptoms immediately after drinking the coffee Ronnie gave her, either he added a ton of methanol to her drink, which is unlikely since you probably would've noticed that, or she'd ingested it much earlier in the day and all the extra alcohol made her nauseous."

I raised an eyebrow. "You realize you just said Ronnie was the one who added the methanol to her coffee, right?"

Bernadette hesitated, glancing back and forth between Adeena and me as if unsure whether to share the next bit. "You, uh, might want to talk to Detective Park. And to your brother, Adeena. I'm not saying Ronnie did it. But there's been talk around the hospital. I can't say too much, but there might be some evidence you don't know about. Some pretty damning evidence."

And that's all she'd say about that, insisting that she'd told us too much already and she didn't want to get in trouble with the hospital.

Still, she'd given us plenty of food for thought. And I knew what my next move would be.

Chapter Fifteen

"What's this evidence you've been hiding from us, ah? You think you're so smart we wouldn't find out?"

Lola Flor heaped food on Amir's plate first, then Ronnie's, each spoonful punctuated by the harsh tone of her questions. Usually our meals were more casual, family-style affairs where everyone helped themselves, so for Lola Flor to take it upon herself to serve them breakfast meant she was piling guilt and judgment on their plates along with garlic fried rice and eggs.

Ronnie and Amir glanced at each other, the latter giving Ronnie a look as if to say, *It's your family and your case, you handle this.*

Ronnie picked up his spoon and fork. "We weren't hiding anything. We were just waiting for the results of their investigation. They wanted to test the bottle of lambanog and Denise's coffee cup before moving forward. There's nothing to tell until they get those results."

"And even if they find traces of methanol in those pieces of evidence, there's still a chance to prove it wasn't put there on purpose,"

Amir said, picking up his silverware as well and spearing a piece of beef tapa. "I did some research, and lambanog is rather infamous for causing methanol poisoning if poorly made. Not that I'm saying your product is poorly made," Amir rushed to reassure Ronnie. "It's more of a last-ditch defense if they find something. Accidental death is a serious offense, but still better than murder."

Amir kept his voice carefully neutral, not judging, not placating, just stating the facts of the case, but Ronnie erupted. "So even you think I had something to do with it!"

"I do not. I just want to prepare you for the possibility that—"

"That what? That I'm such a screw-up I killed a woman, even accidentally? That's what you all think, isn't it?"

"Anak, why are you so angry? We don't think that. And Amir is just doing his job. It's smart to look at all the possibilities, don't you think?" Tita Rosie said, reaching out to put her hand on her son's. Ronnie snatched his hand away.

Tita Rosie's face fell, and a sheen of tears glittered in her eyes. She cleared her throat and excused herself, grabbing the nearly full plate of beef tapa and saying it needed a refill. We all watched her disappear into the kitchen before rounding on Ronnie.

"What the hell is your problem? You do realize we're trying to help you, right? And that your mom is the one person who's been by your side and fought for you through everything? If you want to complain and throw a tantrum, whatever, Lola Flor and I are used to it. But you do *not* treat Tita Rosie like that. Do you hear me?" I thought my voice would rise higher and higher until I was screaming at him, but it turned out when I was furious, my voice got lower. Harder. Meaner. And as I delivered that speech, I leaned closer to him until he nearly fell off his chair trying to back away from me. "I said, do you understand me?"

His eyes darted around the table, from Amir to Lola Flor, then to Adeena and Elena, who'd both been silently eating and pretending to mind their business. I'd wanted them there because Adeena knew all Amir's tics and I knew Ronnie's, and I figured together we'd be able to see through those two if they tried to lie to us. Elena was a good judge of character and great peacemaker, but even she refused to break the tension that was simmering around the table. It was Lola Flor who finally ended it.

"When your mother comes back out here, you are going to apologize to her. Sincerely. I don't care if you have to get on your knees; you are going to show her how sorry you are and how much you appreciate her. You are then going to tell us everything you know about this case, and why you reacted so strongly when Amir mentioned poorly made lambanog. You tell us the truth, or you are banned from our home and restaurant, and you can take care of your own legal fees."

Tita Rosie arrived at that moment and set the platter back down on the table without meeting anyone's eyes.

"Thanks for the refill, Auntie. You know this is one of my favorites," Amir said, reaching over to help himself to more beef tapa.

Tita Rosie chanced a small smile and thanked him, but her eyes kept straying toward her son, who refused to look up from his plate.

We all continued eating, except for Lola Flor, but no one was willing to break the strained silence. Lola Flor glared at Ronnie, unblinking, unmoving, her hands folded in front of her next to her untouched breakfast plate. Adeena was serving herself a third bowl of champorado when Ronnie suddenly burst out, "This isn't the first time someone's gotten sick from my lambanog."

Adeena dropped the ladle on the table, mid-serving, and the rest of us whipped our heads around to look at Ronnie. Did this fool just say what I thought he said?

"What happened?" Amir asked, leaning back to study Ronnie appraisingly. "I'm sorry, but this might have bearing on your case, especially if it's on your record."

Ronnie sighed and rubbed his hands up and down his face, and I could hear the slight rasp as his hands moved over his unshaved stubble. "We weren't directly involved. Me and Izzy and Pete, I mean. I mentioned Manong Larry before, right? The vintner who taught us about wine-making and lambanog?"

I nodded and motioned for him to continue.

"He was a great guy, and he was teaching us everything he knew since he wanted to retire. He knew we wanted to buy the business and he loved the idea of passing on his methods. 'The new generation carrying on his work,' he said, so he made us all comanagers of the company. But his floor manager was a real jerk, always cutting corners and harassing the workers. He was Manong Larry's nephew, so he felt he had to keep him on, but he wanted me to keep an eye on him. I thought I was doing a good job, but I was juggling so many things: learning how to prepare the wine, how to run a company, handling paperwork, and now I had to watch this guy? I guess . . . I messed up."

"How so?" Amir asked.

"Lambanog isn't hard to make, but you have to be careful since the drink has high levels of methanol if not properly distilled. You were right about that. Not a problem if you take the time to do it well, but we didn't know that the manager had been trying to speed up production to meet growing demand in the area. He had workers coming in after hours when we weren't around to supervise him." He shook his head, slowly, sadly, and his shoulders sagged with the weight of what he was about to say. "A lot of people got sick. One of Manong Larry's friends died. It didn't take the authorities long to make the connection between the alcohol we produced and the affected people. One of the factory workers confessed what the floor manager had been making them do, so Manong Larry and the rest of us were off the hook, but his business was ruined. He shut everything down and moved back to the Philippines, and we moved here to try and start over."

"But why continue with the lambanog production after such a scandal?" Lola Flor asked. "Didn't you learn your lesson?"

Ronnie bit his lip. "Manong Larry took care of me. Treated me like a son. It's thanks to him I finally have a passion in life, and I want to carry on his tradition of introducing Americans to Filipino-inspired wine and liquor."

Treated him like a son. Those words stuck with me, and I could see the effect they had on Tita Rosie, too. A complete stranger had treated Ronnie like a son, cared for him as if he were a member of the family. Unlike his own father, who was emotionally abusive at his worst, and absent at best. No wonder Ronnie acted the way he did.

"So, this tragedy in Florida . . . is that what the blackmail email is about?" I asked.

"It has to be. There's nothing else I've done in Florida that's worthy of blackmail. Unless . . . No, that's gotta be it. Maybe someone related to the guy that died?"

"Or connected to them in some way, otherwise how would they know about it?" Adeena poured herself another cup of tsokolate, her curiosity finally overruling her earlier attempts to mind her business. "Actually, how would the blackmailer know how to contact Auntie Rosie? Or even that you were here in Shady Palms?"

Ronnie frowned. "I've been wondering that myself. There were a few articles released about us buying the winery in business and wine-related publications, but nothing big. And most people don't know that we were involved with Manong Larry since our names weren't on any of the paperwork yet. Though I'm sure if you looked us up, there'd be pictures of us together since we did work for him and attended local events together."

"It's also really weird that only Tita Rosie got the messages. Have you gotten one yet? Or Izzy or Pete?" I asked.

Ronnie shook his head.

"So it's just your mom who got one." I paused, wondering about the implications of that. Why only our family? Were we just first in line and Izzy and Pete would get one next? What would it mean if they didn't? "Have you received any more threatening emails, Tita Rosie?" I asked.

"I don't know," she said. We waited for her to elaborate, but she just tore off a chunk of bibingka and popped it into her mouth.

"When you say you don't know . . . do you mean you haven't checked your email recently?" Ronnie asked.

She nodded. "Your Isabel said she would handle it, so I didn't think I needed to. The only people who email me are old classmates and people in the Philippines, but they could send me a Facebook message if they really needed to speak to me."

Ronnie opened his mouth to speak, but Lola Flor and I glared at him so hard, I was surprised his overly gelled hair didn't catch on fire from the intensity of our stares. He cleared his throat and started again. "Mommy, I think letting Izzy know about any more emails you get will be really helpful. The more information she has to work with, the easier it will be for her."

Tita Rosie put down her bibingka. "I'm sorry, anak, I didn't think of that. It's just that the first email frightened me, and I didn't want to risk seeing more."

Ronnie's face fell and he reached out to take his mom's hand. "No, I'm the one that should apologize. You were just trying to help. You've always been the one trying to help me. And I'm sorry somebody used me to scare you. Why don't you give me your email and password so we can monitor the situation without you worrying?"

My aunt's face brightened at her son's attention, and my stomach twisted in discomfort. Ugh, what was this feeling? Did I eat too much? I poured myself some salabat to settle my stomach. At least I now had Tita Rosie's email info to pass on to Terrence—after Ronnie's latest admission, I definitely wasn't comfortable leaving it all up to Izzy.

Our breakfast party broke up soon after that, and I headed next door with Adeena and Elena to open the cafe. The lengthy meal put me behind schedule, so I didn't have time to make my usual quick breads (despite the name, they took quite a while to bake) before customers arrived. I checked the freezer and found ube scones, as well as the layered chai scones I'd experimented with during the fall. Perfect. I whacked those in the oven and pulled the bowls of cookie dough out of the fridge. Once everything was prepped, I grabbed a Brew-ha #1 and settled in to concoct a bibingka cupcake.

Bibingka was made from rice flour, so this cupcake would be as well. Hmm, that would make this cupcake gluten-free. Maybe I should have my friend Valerie over to taste test my first batch. She was my gluten-free guinea pig, and only too happy to help out with my experiments. I made a note to text her, then got to work figuring out how to make the final product more cupcake-like and less dense bibingka–like. Of course, the answer would be to do a mix of white flour and rice flour, but I liked the idea of keeping it gluten-free. Maybe if I messed with the proportions of leavener and liquid ingredients? I lost myself in the magical alchemy of baking, pausing only to bring out the fresh scones and cookies for customers and to refill my coffee cup.

I finally came up with a cake base that seemed right and debated whether the coconut should go in the cake or be sprinkled on top. Hmm, probably better to test both and see. Cupcake trays filled and in the oven, it was now time to come up with the right frosting. I decided to go with cream cheese, both to mimic the cheese slices that usually top the bibingka and because cream cheese frosting was the best frosting. Don't @ me.

It was delicious but tasted like a regular cream cheese frosting. It needed some *oomph*, something that let people know it was a bibingka cupcake. As I analyzed my grandmother's bibingka, layer by layer, I realized what was missing: the salted duck eggs. I was a huge fan of the sweet and salty combination and knew if I used the salted duck eggs sparingly, I'd have a winning combination on my hands.

I ran over to the restaurant to see if Lola Flor had any spare duck eggs and stopped short when I saw Detective Park in our kitchen, comforting a distraught-looking Tita Rosie.

"What happened?" Remembering what Ronnie said this morning about the investigation, I asked, "Did the test results come in?"

Detective Park nodded. "I'm here in an unofficial capacity since Detective Nowak is busy talking to Mr. Cruz and the other Shady Palms Winery owners. There were extremely high levels of methanol in Ms. Sutton's coffee mug, as well as the bottle that your cousin used to serve her. We have no choice but to shut down the winery and inspect their inventory to see if this was an accident, or if someone purposely used a tainted bottle."

"But . . . what does this mean for my son?" Tita Rosie asked, her eyes begging Detective Park to give her good news.

"Nothing good, I'm afraid. If the evidence points to them, there's a chance he and his partners will be charged with involuntary manslaughter due to criminal negligence." He shook his head. "Again, I'm just here as a friend, but Rosie . . . you have to know."

Tita Rosie shook her head and held out her hand as if to stop his words, but he continued. "There could be some other explanation, and rest assured that the team is investigating all avenues. But I think you have to prepare for the possibility of your son facing serious jail time. I wish there was more I could do."

My aunt broke down, and as Detective Park wrapped her in his arms, I started to ponder our next steps. What now?

Chapter Sixteen

Was there anything better than a karaoke party after a really, really bad day? (I mean, was there anything better than a karaoke party, period? But that's not the point right now.)

After receiving the news that her son's livelihood, as well as his freedom, were in danger, Tita Rosie wisely reached out to Isabel to make sure Ronnie didn't turn to one of his more destructive coping habits to deal with this blow. Ronnie's dad used to drown his sorrows in alcohol and gambling back when he lived with us, and there was a time we worried Ronnie was following his father's path. Isabel reassured her that Ronnie had tamed his wild streak, but I wasn't so sure—even more than me, Ronnie had felt trapped growing up in Shady Palms, and this situation was bad enough to get him to revert. Whatever my feelings were toward him, I didn't want Tita Rosie to relive those troubling times.

My aunt, being who she was, was also very concerned about Isabel and Pete's well-being and asked if there was anything she could do to help. She'd remembered Ronnie mentioning how his partners had really wanted to attend one of our karaoke parties, and well . . . a bit of back and forth later—with me taking over partway through the discussion since my aunt had to deal with the restaurant and Lola Flor's grumbling—and we'd come to the decision to shut the restaurant down early, prepare a feast, and invite our friends and family over for karaoke. Izzy was absolutely craving a night out, Ronnie needed to be surrounded by people who cared about him and could watch out for him, and Pete . . . well, who knew what Pete actually wanted, but this party would be a good way to find out.

A karaoke party might seem like a silly solution to a very serious problem, but I sensed that Tita Rosie suffered from the same helplessness I felt—until those lab results came in, there wasn't much either of us could do about the case. But she still needed to feel like she was doing something, anything, to help her son and his friends. So, if nothing else, we could provide the morale boost everyone needed, a night to cut loose, eat well, and have some fun.

Well, I say "we" but really the morale boost aspect was 100 percent Tita Rosie—she was a saint who always thought the best of people and helped out in any way she could. I, on the other hand, knew that there was a possibility my family would be playing host to a blackmailer, maybe even a murderer. Tita Rosie may refuse to entertain that thought, but I'd be a fool not to. However, since she insisted on proceeding this way, I planned on using this as an excuse to gather the suspects together in a safe space. I needed to get to know the people around Ronnie and the winery a bit better, and maybe see if I could glean any new info to pass on to Detective Park. Just because he wasn't officially on the case didn't mean he couldn't nudge the investigation in the right direction. It might not be much, but it sure wasn't nothing.

Tita Rosie had been kind enough to host a couple of karaoke

nights at the restaurant so I could have fun with Adeena, Elena, and Jae, but we hadn't had a party for our more extensive circle of family and friends in forever. There was absolutely nothing like belting out a song that perfectly encapsulated how you felt and getting a 100 from the karaoke machine, or getting the crowd to clap and cheer and sing along for the chorus (some people hated when others butted in while they were singing, but for me, audience participation was all part of the performance).

My mom had me sing for the restaurant when I was a kid, putting on nightly performances for our customers, and as much as I hated having all those people stare at me, I completely forgot about it once I had the mic in my hand. I'd dreamed about maybe going pro someday, and my mom encouraged it (Lola Flor absolutely did not encourage it, and it was the subject of quite a few fights between her and my mom), but in the end, I decided not to take something that I loved so much and that brought me so much comfort and turn it into work. I had similarly worried that turning baking from a hobby into my day job would ruin the magic, but since I was so used to working in food service, it had been a surprisingly smooth and natural transition.

I finished setting up my table just as Ronnie and his partners came in with a dolly loaded with wine cases. "Whoa! I know a little liquor makes us all better singers, but this is a bit much, don't you think?"

Tita Rosie didn't approve of drinking, but if Ronnie insisted on doing it, at least he was doing it where she could monitor him. I loved that my aunt was operating on "cool high school mom" logic for her thirty-plus-year-old son. Though I had to say it was a good call on her part, considering how much alcohol they'd brought with them.

"All the lambanog has been confiscated, but they left the other varieties since they claimed this was an issue specifically regarding the coconut wine," Izzy explained, as she hefted one last case on top of the pile in the corner, shooing Pete and Ronnie away when they tried to help her with the heavy load. "We wanted to clear out the old stock anyway, so might as well put this all to good use, since who knows how long it'll be before they let us operate again."

Not wanting to linger on that last statement too much, I said, "Let me introduce you to my friend Sana. She loves your cabernet sauvignon, and also runs the best fitness center in town."

I went around doing the introductions—Amir was here with Sana, and Yuki was sitting with Adeena, Elena, and Bernadette (yes, I'd finally convinced her to come hang out). Terrence couldn't make it, but I'd passed along my aunt's login information and he promised to get back to me within a day or two. After taking the winery crew around the room to meet everyone, I left Izzy and Pete to cuddle in the corner, my main hostess duty now done. I went to join Detective Park and Jae, who were helping Tita Rosie, Lola Flor, and me with the food and refreshments (Jae also knew what I was up to and promised to schmooze with the winery people and report back to me). Longganisa was wandering the restaurant, waiting for people to drop food so she could pounce. And Ronnie was fiddling with the karaoke machine, throwing an occasional glare at Detective Park. Detective Park, for his part, either didn't notice or didn't care since his attention was focused solely on Tita Rosie, and I loved to see it. Despite our issues earlier this year, he was a good man and he adored my aunt. She deserved more than her fair share of love and adoration.

"Stop glaring or your face will get stuck like that," I said, handing Ronnie a cup of tsokolate.

He accepted the cup, but not before making another face. "That doesn't make any sense."

"I know, but I really need you to stop trying to set our good friend on fire with your mind. Don't want to draw too much attention to our family with all that's going on, and it's probably not good for the restaurant."

He snorted and opened his mouth to respond, but Xander and the Calendar Crew chose that moment to make their dramatic entrance.

"We're here! Let the singing begin!" Ninang Mae announced.

Xander strolled in with my godmothers, the usual grin on his face, but I couldn't miss the concerned looks the Calendar Crew were sneaking at him. What were they doing together? Did they go to a casino again? After all that'd happened, I'd forgotten to warn them about his gambling addiction, but seeing them together reminded me that I'd have to talk to them about it soon.

This motley crew arriving together made a strange sort of sense, but what was surprising was that they were followed by Xander's assistants, Olivia and Quentin March. Surprising but advantageous (for me, at least). They were the ones I'd talked to the least, so seeing how they interacted with everyone should prove illuminating. I couldn't get a good grasp on them—Olivia seemed nice enough, but I wasn't sure how I felt about Quentin, especially after that episode at Xander's place. He'd seemed sincere over his sadness at Denise's death, but I'd been fooled before.

One thing that quickly became obvious about the siblings was that they were used to finer things and grander parties. I watched the two of them as they eyed the restaurant's décor and all the people in attendance, not bothering to hide the fact that they were analyzing everyone and everything—and finding them wanting. However, I noticed both twins' eyes light up when they saw Jae, which filled me with smug pleasure. Even they weren't immune to his hotness.

"I'm so glad you all could make it!" my aunt said. She waved Xander and the twins over to the tables on the side, which were set up buffet-style: no fewer than ten dishes covered the savory table, a wide range of foods to meet the varying dietary needs of our friends and family. The table next to it was dedicated to sweets, with Lola Flor and me battling it out for space and dessert dominancy. And next to that was a table with a wide array of drinks, both alcoholic and nonalcoholic, courtesy of the Brew-ha Cafe and the Shady Palms Winery.

The various groups converged on the food, and the room was soon full of laughter and conversation mingling with the clinking of silverware. As usual, my aunt, grandmother, and I waited till everyone served themselves before filling our plates. I looked around the room, wondering which group to join first, when I noticed Xander sitting at a table by himself, toying with a glass of water. He'd pick it up and take a sip while scanning the room, lower it back to the table, pause for a beat, then rinse and repeat. He might've even been just pretending to drink, because the glass looked full each time he lowered it. Was he using this gathering as an excuse to study all the suspects together, like I was? Or was he here to find out what we knew about the case and how much of it pointed to him?

I couldn't help but observe, like I had when he was alone on the bridge, that when he wasn't surrounded by people, he didn't seem to feel the need to put on a happy face. Even though the room was packed, he looked so . . . lonely. I wondered why the twins weren't with him since they didn't know anyone else, but they were off with Pete and Izzy, chatting animatedly. Well, Pete and the twins were, anyway. In a strange reversal, Pete seemed to be having fun and Izzy looked bored out of her mind. I made a mental note to have Sana and Yuki welcome her more completely into the circle once everyone had finished their first plates.

I'd almost made it to Xander's table when Bernadette surprised me and set her plate down there first. "Mind if I join you?" she asked him.

Xander jerked his head up to look at her and stared for a moment before shaking his head, not in a negative way, but as if to clear it. "No yeah, of course. Please join me. Sorry, I was spacing out a bit. I'm Xander Cruz."

"Bernadette Arroyo," she said, shaking his outstretched hand. "It was getting a bit crowded over there," she gestured toward the table with Adeena and our friends, all cracking up at whatever Adeena was saying (probably one of her ridiculous stories about our customers, based on her wild gestures). "Besides, I haven't had a chance to introduce myself yet."

He smiled gratefully at her, but then his forehead creased as he studied her more closely. "I appreciate it. Though . . . forgive me, but have we met before?"

She pressed her lips together firmly, as if not wanting to bring down the mood with what she was about to say. "I'm a nurse at the Shady Palms Hospital."

His eyes widened in remembrance. "Oh! You were the one . . . the night that . . ."

Xander kept starting and stopping his sentences, either not knowing how to finish them or finding them too painful to continue. I finally jumped in.

"Hey, you two! Mind if I join you? I'll be making the rounds soon but wanted to relax a bit before then."

Xander waved his hand at an empty seat. "There's plenty of room. And anyone who's a friend of Poe's is a friend of mine. He loved those dog biscuits you left us. Poe is my dog," he explained to Bernadette. "A four-year-old pit bull mix."

"Oh, I love dogs," she said, smiling sweetly. "Do you have any pictures of him?"

"Since when do you love dogs?" I asked as Longganisa waddled over to us. She must've recognized Xander from our run because she got all excited and started sniffing and jumping up to push at his legs for pets, which he obliged with a chuckle.

"What? I've always loved dogs. Isn't that right, Nisa?" Bernadette cooed at my dog. Nisa, dressed as a gingerbread person cookie, just stared at her, her dark brown eyes asking, *Girl, why you lying?*

As if she could hear Nisa's thoughts, Bernadette backtracked. "I mean, I haven't always loved dogs. But Nisa grew on me over time and now I really like them. As long as they're not too slobbery, that is."

Xander chuckled. "It's fine, not everyone is a dog person. To be honest, I first got Poe because I thought a puppy would be a good way to meet women, but I had no idea how much work a puppy would be! Still, I wouldn't trade him for anything. He's saved me more times than I can count by just being there. Plus, Denise didn't even like dogs when we met, but Poe won her over."

The smile that'd come over his face as he shared this faded, and he cleared his throat. "Excuse me, I need a refill." He grabbed his empty plate and headed back to the buffet.

I waited till he was out of earshot before saying, "Are you serious? Ate Bernie, his fiancée just died. In a suspicious manner, I might add. Please don't tell me you're trying to make a move."

I wasn't sure what upset me more: the idea of Bernadette moving in on a grieving widower (well, would-be widower) or the idea of Bernadette hitting on a potential murderer. Both very different reasons, but no less icky.

Bernadette's eyes widened like a child who didn't realize the word they'd just repeated was profanity until they saw their parents' reactions. "I—that's not what I was trying to do, I swear! It's just, he looked so lonely, and I felt bad for him, but I had no idea what to say so, I don't know, I tried to be relatable . . ." She bit her lip and shook her head. "Ugh, he probably thinks I'm some opportunistic gold-digger, trying to flirt with him while he's feeling low. Don't let me drink anything tonight. I don't need to make a fool of myself any more than I already have. Especially in front of him," she added darkly. I thought she meant Xander until I saw her gaze focused on Ronnie. They'd been doing an admirable job of pretending the other one didn't exist, but on a night like tonight, who knew how long they'd be able to keep it up. *Please let them just both be cool for once*, I begged silently.

Xander returned, his refilled plate in one hand and a glass of red wine in the other. So much for him sobering up. "Could I get either of you a drink? It's mostly leftover stock from the previous owners, but they do have some of the new varietals they were testing out."

"Oh, no thanks. I'm, um, I'm on call tonight," Bernadette said.

"Oh, that's a shame," Izzy said, sidling up to our table with an open bottle of red. "How about you, Lila? Care for a glass? We might as well drink up before the cops seize it all."

She was careful to keep her voice light and a smile on her face as she said it, but I felt rather than heard the tension in her voice.

"Sure, why not? A drink or two will loosen us all up come karaoke time," I said. She set down the empty wineglass she'd been carrying and filled it up. I thanked her and took a sip of the excellent (to my untrained palate) wine. "So, what's your go-to karaoke song? You are singing, right?" I looked back and forth between Izzy and Xander, curious to see what their song choices would tell me about them.

Izzy swirled the liquid in her glass, giving her answer some thought. "Taylor Swift is my go-to, but which song I choose depends on my mood and the general vibe. Do I want cute, poppy TayTay? Murder Angst Taylor? Heartbroken Tay? There are so many possibilities, but I'm not sure which one is right just yet."

"You really need to hang out with us more. Adeena has this whole theory that Taylor Swift is actually noir AF and deserves her own crime anthology and podcast. It's become a whole thing." Adeena was nothing if not passionate about her interests, and by passionate, I meant relentless and obsessive (as an example, see our earlier argument about Christmas music).

"Noir, huh? I can see that." Izzy nodded to herself, mulling that over. "I think I know what song to choose. How about you, Xander? Are you singing?"

Xander watched her top off his wineglass and took a big swig before answering. "Probably not. No offense, Lila, but I'm not exactly in a singing mood. I just needed to get out for a bit, you know?"

I assured him that no one would be offended if he chose not to sing, and that we were happy to be there for him. Bernadette and Izzy quickly agreed, and Nisa barked up at him, as if she, too, wanted to let him know she had his back.

"I appreciate that. It still doesn't feel right, being in that house without her. Poe is doing his best, but—"

The twins chose that moment to swoop in on the conversation. Quentin stood over Xander, clutching a half-empty glass of wine. "Yes, I'm sure you must be absolutely devastated, Xander. Is that why we had to drag you away from the casino earlier? Gambling away your grief, I'm sure." Xander winced, and Quentin took a self-satisfied sip of his drink before delivering his line with a blasé air that fooled no one. "And you're doing it with Denise's money, as usual."

Xander shot up out of his seat so quickly Quentin staggered back a few steps, the smug look on his face slipping away as Xander towered over him for a few tense seconds. There was noise and chatter and laughter all over the restaurant, but in the little pocket of space the six of us were standing in, it was dead silent. Then Nisa started growling, the sound starting low in her chest until it seemed to emanate from her entire body, her stance fiercely protective as she stared Quentin down.

Quentin inched behind his sister (who rolled her eyes at him) to hide from my tiny attack dog, and Bernadette let out a harsh laugh. The sound seemed to bring Xander back from whatever dark place he'd been in, and he smiled down at Nisa. "At ease, girl. I'm going to check out the desserts, maybe get a refill. Excuse me."

We watched him head straight to the beverage table, where he popped open a fresh bottle of wine, refilled and then knocked back the entire glass in one quick, smooth movement, and filled it again before heading toward the Calendar Crew with the wine bottle in one hand and his glass in the other.

"Quentin, can't you lay off for just one night? We're trying to have fun, remember?" his sister said.

Quentin smoothed his hair back, watching Xander's capering with narrowed eyes. "I'll try, but he just makes me so mad. Look at him, acting all wounded when we know he's been sneaking around with his astrologer friend. He just wants an excuse to keep blowing Denise's money without looking like the bad guy."

Olivia shushed him, looking around to make sure no one but us heard him. Pete joined us during the lull in the conversation.

"That looks like trouble," Pete said, coming up to us and sliding a casual arm around Izzy. He nodded hello at Quentin and Olivia, before gesturing to Xander, who was laughing and drinking with my ninangs and grandmother.

Izzy snuggled closer to her fiancé. "I hope not. Tita Rosie has been good enough to put this all together for us, and I'd hate for anyone to take advantage of her hospitality."

"When is the singing going to start, anyway? We were promised karaoke," Olivia said, looking around the room. "I thought there'd be private rooms, or at least a bar, but this is just a restaurant, isn't it?"

I counted to ten in my head the way Elena taught me before responding. "This is not *just* a restaurant, but you're right, we should get the party started. Ronnie!" I called to my cousin across the room, who'd been hovering around his mom and Detective Park all night. He turned to look at me and nodded his head as if to say, *What?*

"You know what time it is!" I walked over to the karaoke machine and put in a Powerline song from *A Goofy Movie*, a blast from our past.

Back when we were really young, we'd actually hung out together and wore out the tape watching this film.

"Aww yeah!" He rushed to the makeshift karaoke stage we'd set up and grabbed the mic. He was way more of a showman than I was—I may have liked to perform, but he was a true entertainer, combining his near-perfect vocals with his smooth dance moves (Bernadette was a dancer and long ago admitted that it was his dancing that had seduced her way back when). Even when performing silly moves like The Perfect Cast, he still looked good. At the end of the song, he took a bow to loud applause, with both Bernadette and her mom, Ninang June, reluctantly clapping along.

Probably figuring she'd been nice enough, Ninang June stepped onto the stage and elbowed him off. "Yes yes, galing naman," she said dismissively. "But let's show you how it's done."

She pointed at the rest of the Calendar Crew, who cheered when the Tagalog version of "My Heart Will Go On" started playing. Once she was done, Ninang Mae and then Ninang April performed their songs, all three of them going with their usual Celine Dion choices.

Over the next couple of hours, most of the partygoers had their turn up at the mic and the Calendar Crew went multiple times. They had everyone singing and clapping along (well, those of us who knew the song) to their group rendition of "You Don't Own Me." My aunt loved Bette Midler, and *The First Wives Club* was a movie on constant repeat at my house.

Once they were done, they took a bow and called Xander up, who'd managed to avoid singing the whole time. He tried to fend them off, but those three were stronger than you'd think.

"Don't worry, buddy, I know the perfect song for you. I've heard you sing it enough to know you know the lyrics," Quentin said, a wicked grin spreading across his face. "Let Me Love You" by Mario started blasting, and Adeena cheered.

"Ooh, what a throwback! I love this song," she said. "Hey Sana, make sure to ask Amir about his R & B phase! I know so many age-inappropriate songs because of him."

Sana laughed and wrapped her arms around one of Amir's. "Oh, I definitely need to hear about this."

Amir looked like he wanted to melt into the floor. "Uh, maybe later. I don't want to miss Xander's song."

Xander opened his mouth as if he were going to start singing, but nothing came out. He just stood there silently, clutching the mic so hard his hand was shaking. Ninang June, taking the hint, turned off the song, and Xander dropped the mic on the stage then headed straight to the drinks area. He poured and gulped down a full glass of wine, then poured another, keeping his eyes down on the table and refusing to look at any of us.

"Hmm, maybe I pushed a little too hard this time," Quentin said, coming up beside me to watch Xander guzzling wine like it was Gatorade at the end of a football game.

"What . . . why is he reacting like this?" I asked. "Is singing in public traumatic for him or something?"

"No, Xander loves attention. This isn't our first karaoke rodeo. The reason he's mainlining bottles of wine is because my dear brother chose Xander and Denise's song. Xander played it while proposing to her," Olivia said as she joined us. "It was really quite romantic. Room decked out with her favorite flowers, song playing over the speakers, big heartfelt speech, Poe with a pillow tied to his back holding the ring, the whole shebang. Mind you, her husband, who was, you know, *my father*, had just died, so maybe not in the best taste."

She paused to sip at her glass of wine and let us stew in the discomfort her words brought. "I don't approve of my brother's antagonism to our employer, but I do understand where he's coming from."

She swirled her glass of wine, watching Xander with a mixture of distaste and something else (maybe pity?) on her face. "Quentin, you better handle this. You were the one who set him off and you know what he's like when he drinks this much. There's nothing I hate more than a weepy man, and I don't want ... Ah, too late."

I turned back toward Xander just in time to see him burst into tears and stumble into the table of drinks, his arms swinging out to knock everything over. Jae grabbed the table before it fell, but several bottles and glasses rolled off and smashed on the floor.

"Stop that," Xander said, knocking over another bottle. "They're supposed to break!"

He lunged toward Jae but slipped in the wine that had dribbled out from a fallen bottle. Detective Park managed to catch Xander before he landed on the broken glass. "Whoa there, big guy. I think you've had enough."

"I want to go home," Xander slurred. "I want to go home, please."

"I'm sure you do, but you can't drive in this condition and I'm not a taxi service." Detective Park looked around at the group to see if anyone would volunteer.

Nobody did for a moment, but then Quentin sighed and stepped forward. "This was my fault, so I'll take him home. And to think, this party was just getting fun."

Pete put his hand on Quentin's shoulder. "If you're having fun, you can stay. I was getting tired anyway, so I can take him home."

Quentin looked Pete up and down. "You? Since when have you wanted to help Xander?"

"I mean, if you want to do it, don't let me stop you. Just figured Xander's a big guy, and you ..." Here Pete mimicked Quentin by looking him up and down, taking in his slim build and carefully put-together appearance, so at odds with Pete's gym-toned obviousness and "rich boy bro" image he had going. "You don't really look like you're up for it, know what I mean?"

Quentin looked ready to claw Pete's eyes out, but Izzy stepped up. "Don't let him get to you, Quentin. He's just using this as an excuse to get out of karaoke since he's been complaining about it all night. Isn't that right, dear?"

Pete winced at the ice in Izzy's voice, and Olivia, who might as well be named Marie Kondo, since she seemed to love mess, joined in. "Now, Pete, is that true? Don't be so boring, we want to hear you sing. Let my brother take care of him. He's the one who got him going, after all."

Now both Quentin and Izzy were pissed, Pete looked panicked, and Olivia had a weird smug expression on her face. And of course, Detective Park and Jae were still struggling with a drunk Xander, who kept trying to run away but didn't have the coordination, so Amir and Ronnie had to join the fray. I was standing around watching them all with Adeena and Elena, wishing I had popcorn for us to share.

Pete finally broke the tension. "Sorry babe, but I'll make it up to you next time. Quentin, if you want to be useful, you can help clean up Xander's mess. Don't just leave it for Ronnie's family to handle."

We all looked over to my aunt and grandmother, who'd put on gloves and found a broom and dustpan to clean up the spilled wine and broken glass. To my surprise, both twins walked over to help them.

Ronnie and Izzy helped Pete get Xander to his car, and they all went to wash their hands before rejoining the group. Xander's display had killed the party vibe, though, and Yuki (who made it a point to avoid drama due to her own drama-filled past) announced that it was late and she had to get back to her husband and daughter. She gave me a quick hug and left. I wondered if everyone else would follow suit.

Adeena leaned close. "Should we just help clean up and leave?"

Olivia, who was pouring herself a fresh glass of wine from a bottle

Jae had managed to save, said, "No, it's still so early and we haven't had a chance to sing yet! Don't let Xander ruin the only fun thing that's happened since we got here."

Ronnie and I glanced at each other. It was his party; I wasn't going to make the call. I may not have gotten any concrete evidence, but I'd learned enough about the people involved to fill several notebooks and was ready to call it a night if he was. He looked at the people gathered around, everyone looking like they were having a good time, except for Lola Flor (but she never looked like she was having a good time unless she was at the casino or mahjong table). "You helped clean up and we've still got so much food. It'd be a shame to make my family put together this feast and have nobody enjoy it. All right, Olivia, let's see what you've got!"

She grabbed her brother and dragged him to the front of the room. "You ready, Ryan?" Olivia said with a wink.

Wait, Ryan? Who was she talking to? She held a pose while Quentin fiddled with the karaoke machine. Suddenly, "I Want It All" from *High School Musical* started playing, and I laughed. Classic. And extremely fitting.

"*High School Musical* fans? Yes! I think we're going to get along just fine," Adeena said, as she and Elena clapped and cheered.

Jae was alone at a small table, so I went over to join him. "Eventful night, huh?"

He laughed. "You can say that again. Let no one say the Macapagals don't know how to throw a party."

We laughed and cheered as Olivia and Quentin put on a show. Jae shook his head as they took a bow and stepped off the stage. "I know I just met them, and I have no idea where that song is from, but I feel like it fit them perfectly, don't you?"

"You can tell a lot about someone by what song they choose for karaoke, you know," I said, helping myself to a lumpia from his plate.

He leaned back and put his arm around my seat. "Oh yeah? So, what does the *Titanic* song tell you?"

"Any Celine Dion song means that person thinks they can sing and they want to show off. Choosing the *Titanic* song means they're trying too hard. It also just means that the singer is probably Filipino."

"Amir's choice of 'My Way'?"

"He's only thirty and he chose Frank Sinatra. Shows he's old-fashioned. He might think the lyrics mark him as a trailblazer, but he's just playing it safe, as usual."

As we chatted, the twins queued up another song since the one they chose was just a snippet from a movie. Once they'd finished their super-legit rendition of "What I've Been Looking For," pulling off Broadway-worthy Ryan and Sharpay impressions, Adeena darted forward.

"Yes, it's my turn! This one's for you, babe," she said, pointing dramatically at Elena.

Any other person would be expecting a sweet ballad, or at least a heartfelt rendition from one of the couple's favorite musicals. But Elena knew her girlfriend, and once Adeena started vamping to "I'm Too Sexy" by Right Said Fred, she just laughed and cheered.

"I don't even have to ask what this song choice means. This song is pure Adeena, which means utter chaos." Jae paused and considered. "Well, at least she's chaotic good. Unpredictable, a bit of a pain to rein in, but a great person to have on your team."

I nodded at his geeky and perfect encapsulation of Adeena's personality, and shouted along to mine and Adeena's favorite line, "No way I'm disco dancing!"

"So then what does your go-to song say about you? I mean, almost everyone here is choosing older songs, but 'Ribbon in the Sky' by Stevie Wonder is an interesting choice. This might've been my first time hearing it."

I did a fake pearl clutch. "Well, clearly your parents didn't do right by your musical education because that song is amazing." Adeena's song ended, and I paused to cheer for her as she preened a bit before leaving the stage. "Anyway, it was my dad's favorite song. My mom loved to entertain, but her singing was OK at best. My dad though . . . he had *lungs*."

Jae smiled at me. "So that's where you got your singing voice, huh? Ronnie has a great voice, too. If it runs in the family, I'm guessing your aunt and grandmother can also sing?"

We looked over at Tita Rosie, who was laughing together with Detective Park and Izzy. Ronnie was talking to Amir and Quentin and pretending he wasn't watching his mom being courted, but I knew better. I'd learned his tells as a kid, back when he used to rip us all off at card games (how many thirteen-year-olds had a neighborhood gambling ring?), and despite his cool demeanor, I knew he was sweating on the inside.

"Tita Rosie has a pretty voice, but she doesn't like attention. I've only heard her sing during church and sometimes around the house doing chores. As for Lola Flor . . ." I shrugged. She didn't really approve of mine and my parents' love of entertaining and performing. *So mayabang*, she'd complain. *Always needing attention and out gallivanting at all hours.*

"Yeah, that sounds like her," Jae said, smiling at my aunt fondly. "If I said my karaoke song was 'Adore You' by Harry Styles, what would that say about me?"

I tilted my head. "I'm not familiar with that song, actually."

He grinned. "Great. That means I'm up."

A funky pop song started playing and Jae put his all into portraying a guy who didn't need his lover to say she loved him, he just wanted to show how passionate he was about her. Jae's musical talent mostly extended to playing instruments, but what his voice lacked in smoothness, he made up for with enthusiasm and sincerity and oh my gulay, he was looking me dead in the eyes as he sang as if there was no one else in the room and I was ready to melt under his heated gaze. Ready to do lots of things, honestly, none of which would be appropriate in front of a crowd, particularly one that included my aunt and grandmother.

Adeena screamed when she heard his song choice and was busy shooting knowing looks at me and wolf whistles at Jae, while Elena was jokingly fanning herself. Jae finished the song and handed the mic to Izzy, who'd gone up to the stage to take her turn.

Adeena plopped down next to me. "Dang girl, I'm not even into men and I thought that was supremely hot. Looks like I'm not the only one."

She gestured toward the little group that had gathered around Jae, which included Izzy, Olivia, and Quentin, all of whom were gazing at him adoringly.

Sana and Bernadette came over to join us, the latter with a wicked glint in her eyes. "OK, good, I see you all looking in Jae's direction and wanted to know: One, what was up with that hot-ass song, and two, are you OK with his groupies throwing themselves at him? Because I remember you being jealous AF in the summer."

"I'm not jealous, I'm a Scorpio; it's different." I tried to brush off her questions. "And it's fine. We are both grown, independent adults who are dating, but we've never talked about being exclusive. So he can do whatever and whoever he wants."

Adeena, Elena, Sana, and Bernadette all looked at one another and burst out laughing. Adeena wiped away the tears that were streaming down her face from laughing so hard. "You think you of all people could lie to us? With your loud face? And us knowing everything about you?"

I crossed my arms and cursed my lack of a poker face. "Could you at least let me have some dignity? I am trying to be better and handle my jealousy better than I did during the summer. Personal growth and all that."

"You are trying, I'll give you that," Sana said, pouring me a glass of wine. "Jealousy must run in your family because your cousin does not seem to appreciate all the attention Izzy is giving Jae. Do you think it's because she's engaged to his friend and he's being protective or . . . ?"

I accepted the glass and glanced over at the group to see my cousin trying to inconspicuously slide in next to Izzy. "OK, do you also get weird vibes between those two? Because I'm ninety-nine-point-nine percent sure he's in love with her, and I know she cares about him, but I can't tell if it's romantic or not."

"It's Ronnie, which means drama and trouble and broken hearts, so I'm gonna go out on a limb and say yes. And that her fiancé is aware of it as well. There's no way those three have been friends and business partners for so long without him being aware," Bernadette said, her voice dripping with a disdain she didn't bother to hide.

"I do remember him being a messy bench," Adeena said, observing Ronnie and Izzy with interest. "You don't think they're secretly part of a throuple, do you? I mean, the three of them went to school together, moved to Florida together to work, came to Shady Palms so they could own a business together, and now they all live together, right? That's totally polycule behavior."

"I could see that on Ronnie and Izzy's part, but not that guy Pete. He strikes me as someone who doesn't know how to share, if that makes any sense," Elena said.

While we pondered that, the Calendar Crew sidled up to us and I knew it was time for their "observations" (aka judgments) on the people around us. I was surprised it had taken them so long to do so—the restraint they'd showed all night was admirable, practically a Christmas miracle considering the spectacle Xander had made of himself. But I guess the scene the girls and I had been guilty of gossiping about was too juicy for them to ignore.

"Ay Lila, are you just going to stand there and watch those vultures move in on your man? Shameless!"

"I thought that Isabel had more sense, yet there she is, an engaged woman flirting with someone who's already taken."

"Of course she doesn't have sense. She went into business with Ronnie, didn't she? That alone tells you there's something wrong with her."

I raised an eyebrow at that double standard considering they were now besties with Xander. "Well, Xander went into business with Ronnie and you seem to approve of him just fine. What do you do when you're all out together?"

The aunties shook their heads and clicked their tongues. "Oh, that poor man."

"He's not a bad man, Lila. He just has a problem, that's all."

"We only took him to the casino that one time. Once we learned about his troubles, we made him leave early. Today, he joined us for card games and mahjong with Father Santiago. No money on the line—we bet little things like loser has to bring lunch for everyone, or drive us around for errands. Things like that. We wouldn't encourage his addiction. What kind of people do you take us for?"

I chose not to comment on that.

"So he's spending time with Father Santiago?" The priest was a good friend to my family and me. Despite my lapsed connection to the church, he was one of the people from my past that I clung to. He was kind, understanding, and (unlike me and just about everyone else in my life) completely nonjudgmental. He truly just wanted to listen and help in whatever way he could. If Father Santiago had accepted Xander into the flock, then Xander was in good hands.

"What have you learned about his life before Shady Palms? Does he ever talk about Denise?" I was going to pretend to be all nonchalant about these questions since I didn't want them to get suspicious, but then I remembered who I was talking to. No point in expending the energy when 1) they welcomed any chance to dish the tsismis and didn't care who they were talking to or about, and 2) they could see right through me.

"I don't care how badly he's in debt, there's no way he killed his fiancée for the inheritance. I can tell these things," Ninang Mae said.

"How bad is his debt?" I asked.

"Hoy! Mae!" Ninang June hissed. "Honestly, this is why no one wants to tell us anything."

I looked at her. "Why are you covering for him? You might know something that could help with this case."

Ninang April tsked. "Mae is too sentimental and June thinks Ronnie had something to do with the murder."

"April! Why would you say that?" June asked at the same time that Mae said, "You're probably right."

I held out my hands. "Wait, go back. Why would you think Ronnie had anything to do with this?"

Ninang April rolled her eyes. "She's still nursing a grudge over the way he treated Bernie when they were in high school. As if that's a reason to accuse someone of murder."

"That's not the only reason! It's the fact that Rosie's been getting blackmail letters about him and has been hiding it from us!"

Record scratch moment. "Wait, how do you know about that?"

The three of them looked at me with varying degrees of amusement and disappointment. "Honestly, Lila. All this time and you still underestimate us? You could've come to us from the very beginning and we would've given you the background on everyone involved. You Macapagals are so stubborn, I swear . . ." Ninang April said, waving her hand dismissively.

I glanced across the room at my aunt and grandmother, who were chatting with Detective Park far enough away that they wouldn't overhear us. Still, I leaned forward and lowered my voice. "Tita Rosie doesn't want to draw too much attention to the blackmail letters because she's worried the SPPD would consider it an admission of Ronnie's guilt. If you could maybe talk to her in private sometime? Try to convince her to let Detective Park know what's going on at least? I've asked Terrence for help, but he's been busy and I'm not comfortable leaving it all up to Izzy."

"Leaving what up to me?" Izzy asked, as she joined our circle.

"Susmaryosep! Don't sneak up like that. You want to give us all heart attacks?" Ninang June pressed her hand against her chest.

Izzy tilted her head. "Sorry. I didn't think I was being particularly stealthy. Ronnie and I are getting ready to leave and I was coming over to say good night when I heard my name."

"I hope you had a good time. We had a pretty big crowd, so most people only got to sing one or two songs. Next time we'll have only the girls over so we have more time to ourselves," I promised.

She smiled. "I appreciate that, but are you going to pretend that I didn't overhear you talking about me?"

I looked at my godmothers, who all shrugged. "It wasn't about you, per se. It was about those emails you're looking into for Tita Rosie. We were wondering how your search was going."

She made a face. "Ugh, considering the limited number of people who would've known about the incident, I thought I'd be able to narrow it down easily, but no dice. I have a friend who's trying to track the IP address for me, but it's taking them some time since their day job keeps them pretty busy. Hopefully once we narrow down where the emails originated from, we can figure out who this creep is."

"Let us know if there's anything we can do to help," Ninang Mae said. "You'd be surprised at what we can dig up."

Izzy smiled politely. "I'll keep that in mind. Anyway, thanks so much for arranging this party for us. I had a great time and it was so nice getting to chat with all of you." She looked at Sana. "See you at yoga tomorrow morning?"

Sana grinned. "Bright and early! I have extra mats if you don't have your own."

"I brought mine with me, but I'm trying to convince Pete and Ronnie to join me, so that's good to know about the extra mats. Anyway, I need to thank Tita Rosie and Lola Flor before I leave, so good night, everyone!"

Izzy waved at us, a bright smile on her face as she hurried over to my aunt and grandmother.

"Do you think we can trust her?" Adeena asked, looking at me but posing the question to the group.

I watched Izzy and then Ronnie give Tita Rosie a kiss on the cheek and noted the pleasure that beamed out of my aunt at the attention.

"Absolutely not."

Chapter Seventeen

The next day, Ronnie hung around the house and restaurant all day. Now that his work with the winery was on pause, he had nothing but time and he seemed to want to spend it with his mom. Which would seem sweet if I didn't know him so well—he was down, and Tita Rosie, while not usually physically or verbally affectionate, was still the sweetest, most nurturing person in the world. He wasn't spending time with her to make up for all the years he wasn't around, he was doing it for himself.

"Don't you have better things to do?" I asked, after Tita Rosie went to the kitchen to get him another serving of chicken afritada. It was around lunchtime, and Tita Rosie and I were going to meet Xander soon. He'd called me that morning to apologize for his behavior the previous night and invite my aunt and grandmother and me over for lunch. He wanted to cook for us to thank us for our hospitality, and afterward we would get started on clearing Denise's belongings out of the house.

"I think last night showed me that I'm not coping well. So if you have time after lunch, I'd be grateful if your church group could start clearing her belongings out of the house while I go to Chicago and talk to my therapist. If you need anything from the city, let me know."

Since the Calendar Crew were also part of Tita Rosie's church outreach group, it was easy to get them to agree to help sort through Denise's things and keep an eye out for clues (which Tita Rosie wasn't entirely comfortable with, but hey, this was for her son so she couldn't complain). Lola Flor couldn't join us since someone needed to stay behind and run the restaurant, but she had a two-page grocery list ready for Xander—hope he liked Seafood City as much as we did. Ronnie, of course, wasn't accompanying us, despite being the reason we'd been dragged into this whole mess. Tita Rosie returned with a full platter of chicken afritada and asked if I was ready.

"You sure you can't join us, Ronnie? I thought you wanted to make a good impression on your investor. Don't you think he'd be touched that you came out to help?"

He ladled the tomato-based stew over the heap of white rice on his plate. "Nah, he'd probably find it uncomfortable. Gotta keep your professional and personal life separate, you know? Besides, I'm busy today."

Lola Flor, who'd come out with Tita Rosie, frowned at him. "I thought you were here because you had nothing to do. Isn't that what you said when I asked why you were freeloading off us instead of working?"

"Oh, uh, I got a message from Pete about our accounts. He wanted to teach me some stuff about the software since we have some time on our hands." Ronnie leaned back in his chair, looking satisfied with the excuse he'd clearly just come up with. His phone rang and vibrated on the table, and he speared a potato before glancing at it. "See? That's probably him now . . ."

He trailed off when the name "Penny" flashed across the screen. "Sorry, Lola, Mommy, I've got to go."

And without a glance back, he ran out of the restaurant, leaving his full plate, his confused mother, and his pissed-off grandmother and cousin behind.

I may not be on your level, Rosie, but I have been known to throw down in the kitchen on occasion." Xander grinned and swept his arm out to indicate the arroz con gandules, tostones, and pork chops.

"This all looks wonderful, Xander. Thank you so much." Tita Rosie smiled at him and took the seat he offered. "April, Mae, and June will be here soon to help; they're just running a quick errand at the church."

"No problem. I made plenty, so it should be easy to save them all a plate." Xander turned to the fridge. "I was even able to find Malta in the next town over, but if it's too sweet for you, I also have Topo Chico."

I was too preoccupied swooning over the amazing spread Xander had prepared for us to hear his question. "What was that? Sorry, I was too busy ogling our lunch."

He laughed and held out a bottle of Malta and one of Topo Chico. "Which would you prefer?"

It'd been ages since I had the syrupy sweet malt beverage, so I eagerly grabbed the bottle of Malta. "I'm so excited! It's been forever since I've had Puerto Rican food. I tried it for the first time in college and got addicted. What I wouldn't give for a jibarito joint in Shady Palms," I said, ladling heaps of arroz con gandules on my plate. The rice and beans looked so simple, but one bite was like tasting the rice of the gods.

Xander groaned. "Oh man, jibaritos. I still haven't mastered making them at home. You'd think it wouldn't be too hard since I can make tostones, but somehow smashing and double-deep-frying plantain discs is different than doing that to a whole plantain to make a sandwich."

Jibaritos were a Chicago Puerto Rican specialty, consisting of steak or pork, lettuce, tomato, onions, and garlic sauce sandwiched between smashed, fried plantains. They were both simple and utterly decadent, and when a craving hit, nothing else would do.

"I need your recipes, Xander. It's been way too long since I've been able to satisfy this hunger. Do you think the tostones would work in an air fryer? I'm afraid of deep frying, but Elena has an air fryer at her place."

Xander piled a few of the fried plantains on his plate. "No yeah, definitely. That's how I used to make them back home since Denise wasn't a big fan of fried food. I adapted a bunch of my recipes for her, and they were still pretty good."

His eyes and voice got soft as he said this, and Tita Rosie and I exchanged glances. She was probably thinking of ways to ease his grief, but all I could think about was the twins hinting that Denise wasn't the first woman he'd hooked up with to get to their money. That his charm was just a mask he wore to hide his true intentions. That he'd been cheating on Denise with his astrologer friend, and together they'd been swindling her out of their inheritance. I liked Xander, but I couldn't discount what his assistants said, because who knew a person's true nature better than their assistant? The power imbalance alone revealed quite a bit about them. Though I didn't know anything about the twins, either. Maybe it was time to get Xander's side.

"Hey Xander, before we begin . . . I know the twins are Denise's stepkids. Do you really think it's best to not have them involved in some way?" There was more I wanted to say, but I couldn't word it in a way that didn't sound judgmental, so I shoved a spoonful of rice into my mouth to stop talking.

Xander sighed. "I know what you're thinking. Pretty cold of me to ice out the people who are technically Denise's next of kin. But they always got real weird when it came to her money, and I'm tired of the disrespect. It's not like I'm not letting them be involved in other ways, though. They're out right now coordinating her memorial service and handling things with her family."

I heaped more rice on my plate. "Oh, that's nice. But why keep them as your assistants? With Denise gone, there's no need to stick with them, is there?"

His hand touched his chest lightly. "She felt a sense of obligation to her first husband. He was a great guy, and he thought if his kids worked with Denise, they'd learn to appreciate hard work and build their own legacy. The twins only receive their allowance if they stay employed, so Denise hired them. I know she'd be worried about them, so I keep them on for her, but I'm not going to pretend we're one big happy family."

He cut into his pork chop, the meat almost flying off the plate with the ferocity of his movements. "I have no idea what's in her will, but I hope she provided for them so I don't have to deal with them for much longer."

Wait, but didn't that go against what he just said about wanting to keep them on because Denise would be worried about them? I said as much.

He put his knife and fork down and sighed. "Don't get me wrong, they're not all bad. Olivia's been great and she actually seems like she's interested in learning about the hospitality business. I'm going to have a talk with Quentin about his attitude, though. That's just one more stressor I don't need right now, so if he doesn't shape up, he's gone."

Good thing I hadn't told him about my run-in here with Quentin. I didn't want to be the reason he lost his job when he was just trying to find a souvenir of his mother. Which reminded me . . .

"I hear you. And we respect your wishes. Just . . . Quentin mentioned that Denise's ring from her previous marriage was a family heirloom. It belonged to their mother. Do you think they could have it, no matter what the will says?"

Xander didn't reply and I thought I'd finally pushed too hard, overstepped my boundaries. I looked over at Tita Rosie, who had been quietly enjoying her food.

She met my eyes, then turned her attention to Xander. "I wouldn't dare to presume that I understand, but if that ring belonged to their mother, it should be theirs. No matter how you or Denise felt about them. It feels unkind to do otherwise. For you, it's just a ring. To them, it's a piece of their mother."

At her words, my hand moved to the necklace I always wore, the last present I'd received from my parents before they passed away. I hadn't known why I bothered to bring up the ring until Tita Rosie said that. Then I knew. Then I realized that maybe I sympathized with the twins more than I realized.

Xander watched me, and I knew his warm brown eyes didn't miss my hand moving to my necklace. His mouth twisted, whether in distaste or from his own sad memories, I didn't know, as he mimicked my movements. "You're right. Guess it's a good thing I'm going to see my therapist today. We've got a lot to talk about."

He set his knife and fork down and looked my aunt in the eye. "You've been very kind to me, and I know you're also in an awkward position, so I'm just going to say it. I'm a little uncomfortable that it's you two and April, Mae, and June handling Denise's things. Not that I suspect you all of anything," he quickly added, "but I can't pretend that your son and his partners may or may not be connected to Denise's . . . what happened to Denise. None of you are directly involved in this mess, so I'm not going to turn you away when I was the one presumptuous enough to approach you for help."

He paused, looking at the ceiling like the right words to say were up there. "Just . . . please respect my privacy. Mine and Denise's. I may not know anyone here, but I don't appreciate being a source of gossip. Things are already hard enough right now. I hope you understand that."

Well, dang. It's like he knew I was using this as an opportunity to snoop. That one-two punch of honesty and guilt had me rethinking my plans for a moment, but I couldn't back down now. I wouldn't get a chance like this again. Besides, I told myself, I was doing him a favor. Not just with the cleaning, but my snooping had a purpose more noble than gossip. The more evidence I found, the sooner we could figure out what really happened to Denise. Wasn't the truth behind his fiancée's death more important than a teeny, tiny invasion of his privacy? Let's hope he thought so.

We finished our lunch soon after that, and he was even nice enough to pack leftovers for us to take home to Lola Flor and for ourselves and the Calendar Crew. For a rich dude with a ton of issues, he was a really good host.

He led us upstairs to a room at the end of the hall and unlocked the door.

"Is this door always locked?" I asked, remembering the day we ran into Quentin in this house. If he was looking for his mother's ring, how'd he get into her room? Or had he been wandering from room to room trying to find it?

Xander nodded. "I locked it the day she died and haven't been in there since. If you find the ring, let me know. We'd need to catalog it for the lawyer to show it's accounted for, but I'll make sure the twins get it afterward."

He gestured for Tita Rosie and me to enter the room. The two of us walked into a large airy bedroom that had the lightest trace of Roja Haute Luxe still hanging in the air. It had been converted into a walk-in closet, and every inch of shelf and wall space was packed with clothes, bags, jewelry, and other accessories. Her shoe closet alone was enough to make me sigh with longing. Denise and I had very different styles, but I couldn't deny the beauty and understated luxury radiating from every surface.

Xander must've heard my sigh because he looked at me with understanding. "You know, Denise bought so much to prepare for the move that I bet a lot of these things still have tags on them. If there's anything in particular you want, you can have it as payment for helping me out. Just let me know first, OK?"

He waved away my protestations. "Like I said, you're helping me out. Big time. So please choose something for yourself, or I'll have to choose for you."

Tita Rosie smiled her thanks at him. "Do you want to look around first? See if there's anything you want to keep?"

He lingered in the doorway, hand still on the doorknob. It looked like he was about to cross the threshold, then changed his mind and shook his head. "I can't. It still smells like her in here. Maybe locking it up was a mistake." The doorbell rang at that moment, and he took a deep breath, looking like he was trying to pull himself together. "Excuse me, I have to answer that. It's probably the aunties, so I'll just let them in and get ready to go. It's a long drive to Chicago."

He spun around and hurried away, and even though his face was dry, there was no hiding the tears in his voice. Was he really who he said he was, or the excellent actor the twins claimed him to be? Or someone in-between?

A few moments later, the Calendar Crew bustled in with the bags, boxes, and rubber gloves they'd picked up from the church. Ninang

Mae let out a low whistle as she looked around Denise's giant walk-in closet, and the rest of us just nodded our heads in agreement—no words necessary.

"Before we begin, I found out something that might be important from Joseph. Now, don't get upset, Rosie," Ninang Mae glanced at my aunt, "but he told me that the winery's finances are a mess. They were fine when he signed on, but lately there's been some very suspicious activity. Denise must have noticed too because she asked him some rather pointed questions about the operations shortly before she died. He had to be honest with her, of course, you know how seriously he takes his work. Joseph got the impression that she was thinking of pulling out of her investment after talking to him. Xander wasn't around for any of these conversations, so he's not sure if Xander knows about it."

I swore silently. Which gave Ronnie and his partners a possible motive to get rid of her. That's what she was hinting at.

Still, for my aunt's sake, I said, "Thanks, Ninang Mae. But there's still a lot to learn, so keep your eyes peeled for any evidence for how or why Denise died. The winery is just one part of her life, and we know almost nothing about her. Once we find other motives, maybe the case will make more sense. We might never have this level of access again, so let's make it count."

I could only hope that digging around in Denise's things would tell us a little more about this woman whose life had been cut short.

"All right, Tita, let's get to work."

Chapter Eighteen

Several hours, ten giant donation bags, and one coffee break later, Tita Rosie and I had cleared out everything except Denise's shoes and handbags. The Calendar Crew had emptied out everything in Denise's dresser and found a bunch of notes from Xander scattered on her desk and tucked in with her jewelry, so they took them all to another room to read and categorize more easily. Tita Rosie and I had left the bags and shoes for last since those were our favorites. I may not have much in common with my extended family, but we were united in our love of a really nice handbag. Even Lola Flor, who got all sniffy about wasting money on vanity (or anything, really), enjoyed sporting a beautiful new bag at church.

Tita Rosie and I split up the remaining tasks: handbags for her, shoes for me. Either one would've invoked envy in me, but as I stood in front of Denise's shoe closet, which was roughly the size of my bedroom, I was hit with a deep pang of longing. I had finally gotten to a point in my life where I didn't feel wasteful buying a new pair of shoes before my previous ones had worn out, and was slowly amassing a small but tasteful collection. The array in front of me, however . . . I wouldn't have pinned Denise as a sneakerhead, but one entire wall was dedicated to them. I wasn't big on gym shoes other than for exercise, but Adeena, Jae, and Terrence would kill for this kind of selection. There were even several versions of those funky winged Adidas shoes Adeena had been drooling over years ago.

I walked over and picked up the gold pair to see if they were Adeena's size, and as I angled the shoe to get a better look, I heard something move inside of it. I tilted the shoe carefully and a folded piece of paper fell into my outstretched hand. I started to unfold it but stopped when I saw that it was a letter addressed to "Denise, my love." If it was a love letter from Xander to Denise, he wouldn't appreciate me reading something so intimate and private.

I started to put it in the pile of things for Xander to look over, but paused as a new thought came to me: What if it wasn't from Xander? I mean, who hides love letters from their fiancé inside a shoe? The Calendar Crew had already found all those notes scattered on and in her dresser, so it's not like she felt the need to conceal all her correspondence. A hidden letter often implies that there's something in there to hide. What if Denise had a mystery lover that was somehow tied to all that was going on? Xander put on a show of being a likeable, fun guy, but what if he was secretly the jealous type? If he found out his fiancée was cheating on him, would he fly into a rage? Shout and make threats?

Or was he the kind to quietly, vengefully scheme against those who've wronged him?

I shook my head. No need to create wild scenarios before I even knew what the letter actually said. I glanced over at Tita Rosie, who was way too kind and considerate to ever read someone's private correspondence without their permission (the Calendar Crew clearly had no such qualms), but she was busy sorting Denise's extensive handbag collection.

Denise, mi amor,

Mama told me about your latest venture together. A winery, cariño? After everything you've just been through? After everything WE'VE *been through? How could you go back to him? Didn't Puerto Rico mean anything?*

You know he'll just hurt you again. He may love you, but he'll never change. You can't save him. And he can't help you. You'll just continue to make each other worse, and where does that leave me? I can't bear to watch you destroy yourself for him. I refuse. Xander better appreciate what he has. Because if he doesn't, I'll make sure he learns.

Oh dang. So Denise did cheat on Xander, and it was serious. At least on the letter sender's part. I wondered if Denise felt the same. Who was this guy? It seemed like he knew Xander pretty well. I always wondered why people held on to stuff like this, but considering the drawers full of receipts, notes, and random mail, Denise seemed like the kind of person to never throw anything away. Possibly problematic for her, but useful for me.

Were there more letters after this? There was no date on it, but based on the contents, it must've been shortly after the winery venture was announced. Did the letter sender become obsessed with her and plot to kill her when she wouldn't leave Xander for him, all "if I can't have you, no one can" in a made for TV movie-esque plot twist? That "I'll make sure he learns" line was pretty ominous, after all. Or did Xander find this letter and plot his fiancée's death as revenge?

"Anak, what are you doing?" Tita Rosie's voice behind me made me jump and I hid the note behind my back. I turned around to find her and the Calendar Crew staring at me.

"Oh, uh, nothing. Nothing important, anyway. Are you done with the handbags already?"

She looked at me suspiciously but didn't push. "Your ninangs helped, so we're almost done. But didn't you hear the front door just now? I think Xander's home. We're going to check on him. Do you want to come with?"

"Sure. It's about time for meryenda anyway." I slid the note into my sweater dress pocket (that's right, it had pockets!) and followed them down the stairs. We could hear someone rustling around in the kitchen, so we entered the room and saw Xander setting out a bunch of sweets and street food he must've picked up from Seafood City.

"Hey, I'm glad you're still here! I picked up a bunch of stuff from that awesome supermarket Grandma Flor sent me to and thought you could use a break. I was about to make some coffee. Want some?"

We'd already drunk the box of Brew-ha Cafe house blend I'd brought earlier, so we all said yes and slid onto the tall seats around the marble-topped kitchen island where he'd set the food. It looked like he got some of everything from the street food section (kwek-kwek, isaw, chicken feet, fish balls, chicharon, etc.) and at least half a bakery. While he put away his groceries, Tita Rosie arranged everything and opened up all the little to-go cups of the various sauces.

"Wow, you really went all out, huh?" I said, dipping the chicharon into the little plastic cup of spicy garlic vinegar sauce. Pork skin was the most popular way to make chicharon, but I had a weakness for chicken skin and could've easily eaten the entire bag myself. I may have actually done that a time or five after breaking off my engagement with that cheating jerk, Sam.

Xander helped himself to some chicharon too. "Again, Puerto Rican. You think I wouldn't get chicharon? And everything else looked so interesting, I had to try it. All the dishes I've tried at your restaurant have been delicious, so I figured I couldn't go wrong."

"I'm glad you're open-minded, but I'm still surprised you got those." Ninang Mae pointed with her lips at the isaw, or grilled chicken intestine on a stick. I know, not the most appetizing-sounding thing in the world, but when prepared right, they were excellent.

"I eat mondongo and gandinga, so offal isn't exactly scary to me," Xander said, as he opened up a fresh pack of Café Bustelo and prepared the coffee on the stove using a Moka pot. As it percolated, he set out sugar, milk, and spoons. "Were you able to clear out that room? I know there's a ton of stuff, so don't feel bad if you barely made a dent in it."

My mouth was full of chicharon and the aunties were busy filling their plates, so Tita Rosie answered for us. "All the clothes are either in bags or set aside for you to go through. Lila needs more time to work on the shoes, and the rest of us are almost done sorting through her lovely purses."

Xander must've picked up on Tita Rosie's admiration for the bags because he said, "You find any you like, you can have them for free. Consider them payment for doing this for me," he added as he poured the espresso into cups and set them in front of us. "It sounds like there's still tons of work, and it's not right for me to impose on you like this."

Tita Rosie added a spoonful of sugar to her drink. "It's not—"

"Yes, it is, and you've been nothing but kind to me. I was thinking about it on the way back, and it was rude of me to impose on you like this considering I'm a total stranger. So if you don't take them with you today, I'm dropping them off at the church and letting all the aunties there do what they want with them," Xander said, whipping his espresso with sugar till it was slightly foamy.

Ninang June turned toward my aunt. "Rosie, you better listen to him or the three of us will snatch up all the best ones, and you know Tita Flor will have something to say about that."

My aunt smiled. "Well, if you insist. Thank you so much, Xander. How was your trip back to Chicago?"

He shrugged and helped himself to bibingka. "OK, I guess. Good to see my therapist in person. Virtual visits are convenient, but not the same. I thought I'd meet up with friends for coffee, but I'm still not ready to see them, especially the ones who were close to Denise too. I'm sure most of them know what happened, and a lot of our mutual friends have reached out, but I just . . . I just can't deal with them right now. Makes it too real."

"What about your family?" Ninang Mae asked. "You told us that your parents moved back to Puerto Rico, but I thought you still had some relatives around?"

At that moment, I realized how little I knew about Xander and his life outside the winery. Count on the aunties to have grilled him about his family already, but I wondered how much he'd told them about himself.

"None that I'm particularly close to," he said, dipping a fishball skewer into sweet chili sauce. "Oh wow, these are good."

"What about Denise's family?" Ninang April asked. "She's not from Chicago, right? Are they flying out this way for her memorial?"

He shrugged. "Probably. Her parents don't like me much, but they loved her husband and they're close to the twins. That's why I left them in charge of planning her memorial."

"How could anyone not like you? You're handsome, hard-working, and rich," Ninang Mae said, before blurting out, "Oh no, they're racist, aren't they?"

She was always the least tactful of the bunch. Ninang April was merely blunt, while Ninang Mae had a tendency to say whatever was on her mind as soon as it came to her, no filter in place.

Xander laughed. "Yeah no, I don't think that's it. Denise's husband was her father's best friend, which I found kind of gross, but whatever. She had her reasons and he was a good guy. But anyway, they thought I took advantage of her grief by making my move so soon after his death. I can see where they're coming from, but it wasn't like that."

He leaned back in his chair, head tipped against the high back as he stared at the ceiling. "Anyway, there's usually drama when we're all around each other, but I hope for Denise's sake they cool it for the memorial. But until then, I'm avoiding the city."

"Does that mean you'll be staying in Shady Palms for a while?" I asked, grabbing a piece of bibingka for myself. I took a big bite and chewed it slowly, contemplating the flavor and texture. Not bad, but it had nothing on Lola Flor's version or my cupcakes.

"Maybe. Probably. It depends on how this case goes."

As if in response to Xander's last statement, his doorbell rang. After exchanging a confused look with us, he left to go answer the door and came back with Detective Park and Detective Nowak.

"Rosie, Lila, you've already met Detective Nowak. Detective, these are their friends April, Mae, and June. Ladies, he's the one I've been training, and he's been promoted to head this case," Detective Park said, gesturing the new detective forward.

Detective Nowak stepped forward to shake my ninangs' hands. "Nice to meet you. I wasn't expecting a full house, but maybe it's better this way." He gestured for us all to take a seat. "It's good news and bad news time, and it concerns you to a certain extent." The young detective folded his hands in front of him, his posture solemn and respectful. "The good news is that the rest of the coconut wine bottles were fine, so we've cleared Shady Palms Winery to start operations again."

"Oh, that's wonderful!" Tita Rosie said.

Detective Park put his hand on my aunt's arm. "I'm sorry, but he's not finished, Rosie."

Tita Rosie blanched and looked back at the other detective. "Wait, if the rest of the wine was OK, then that means . . ."

He nodded. "We found a puncture in the cork that was much too slim to have come from a corkscrew. We believe methanol was injected into the closed bottle, and that this is a case of premeditated murder."

Xander made a choked sound, but Tita Rosie, the Calendar Crew, and I stayed silent at this revelation. Considering they said it involved us, we all knew what was coming next.

"Your son, Ronnie Flores, and his associates Isabel Ramos-Garcia and Pete Miller are wanted for questioning in regards to the murder of Denise Sutton."

Chapter Nineteen

Ronnie and the others weren't at their home or the winery and they weren't answering their phones, so I texted my cousin and asked for his whereabouts. Tita Rosie wanted to leave a voicemail telling him to head straight to the police station when he got the message, but the detectives advised her against it. They wouldn't tell her why, but they were probably worried he'd run if given a warning. It was already suspicious enough that all three of the winery copartners couldn't be reached. The most I could do was text him saying to come straight to the restaurant so that he knew something was up.

Not too long after I sent the text, Ronnie, Izzy, Pete, and, surprisingly, the twins walked into the closed restaurant to see my aunt and grandmother, the two detectives, Amir, and me sitting in wait for them. I felt bad for Tita Rosie since I knew this ambush would drive a wedge between her and her son, but there was nothing we could do about it.

"What's going on?" Ronnie asked. He eyed everyone suspiciously—considering all the trouble he'd been in in the past, he knew this wasn't a friendly meeting just to talk. He'd spoken to his mom, but it was Detective Nowak who answered.

"Hello again. I'd like you all to take a seat, please." He gestured to the chairs in front of him.

"I'd prefer to stand, thanks," Pete said, his voice as stiff and hostile as his posture. "Would you mind telling us what this is about?"

"Would you mind telling us where you all were and why none of you answered our calls or messages?" the detective returned.

Izzy put her hand on her fiancé's arm, but it looked more like a gesture of support and solidarity than warning. "A family member was rushed to the hospital and my partners were good enough to accompany me to Madison to visit them. We just got back. Amir, is this something we need to discuss in private first?"

Quentin casually dropped into the seat directly in front of the detective and draped an arm around the seat next to him. "I don't see what this has to do with us, but Olivia and I were in Chicago running errands for Xander. He needed us to coordinate Denise's memorial service, which I'm sure he can corroborate for us."

Olivia sat next to her brother. "Why isn't Xander here, by the way? Considering you were all lying in wait, I'm assuming there's a break in Denise's case?"

Detective Nowak said, "We've already informed him of our findings. And Mr. Awan was good enough to meet us here for an initial questioning. He's free to advise you as he sees fit, though we might have to move to the station for formality's sake."

"I've only been hired to represent Shady Palms Winery for possible liability or class action lawsuits regarding your product. However, if the Shady Palms Police Department wants to move forward with this murder charge, I can't represent all of you. It might become a conflict of interest, depending on the department's findings," Amir explained to the group. "As for the Marches, you might want to talk to your family's attorneys. I can't in good conscience advise you to speak to the police without representation."

Olivia grimaced. "I'd really rather not involve them. Besides, we weren't the ones who poured that poisoned drink. So . . ."

She didn't come right out and accuse Ronnie, who'd poured the drink in front of everyone, but she sure as heck hinted at it.

Izzy interjected. "Now wait a minute, I remember Denise saying you two gave her that first bottle of lambanog earlier in the day. Who's to say you had nothing to do with this?"

Detective Nowak looked at Detective Park, who flipped through his notebook to locate his notes from that night. "She's right. I talked to everyone separately that night and more than one person remembered her saying something about drinking earlier in the day and that she'd appeared inebriated even before consuming the laced drink."

Quentin sputtered. "We just gave her the bottle because Ronnie told us he'd set a couple aside for her and Xander. She's the one who took the entire bottle to drink by herself. Besides, wasn't the poison in her glass?"

Detective Nowak shook his head. "The bottle also contained methanol and—"

"Well, then whoever poisoned her added it to the bottle after they opened it up to pour that drink," Quentin said. Like his sister, he was careful not to name Ronnie as the culprit but had all but pointed his finger at him.

"And we found a puncture wound in the cork of the bottle that is inconsistent with the size of the corkscrew used," the detective continued, as if he hadn't been interrupted. "The methanol was injected into the closed bottle, which means anyone who had access to the wine could've added it. The question is who added it and whether Denise was the intended target or not."

He leveled his gaze at the group arrayed in front of him. "What do you have to say to that?"

All five suspects exchanged shocked glances before looking at Amir, who shook his head. *Don't answer that* was his clear message.

"I think it's time we reconnected with our dear father's lawyers," Quentin said to Olivia, who nodded and added, "Until then, we have nothing to say."

Detective Nowak bowed his head toward her. "Understood. I, of course, can't stop you, but I would strongly suggest not leaving town again until this case has wrapped up. And answer your phones next time."

Quentin started to protest, but Olivia put her hand on his arm. "Whatever. Can we go now?"

The detective gallantly swept his arm toward the restaurant door, and the twins left without another word. He waited a few beats before saying, "Well, that's all for now. But we'd like you all to come into the station sometime within the next few days, so get in touch with your lawyers sooner rather than later. Detective Park, I can find my own way back to the station. Take care, everyone."

After the detective left, Pete sighed and wrapped an arm around Izzy's shoulders. The protective action drew my eyes to the couple, and I realized Izzy was shaking. With nerves? Stress? Or was it fear?

"I'll talk to my dad about this mess. He'll handle everything, OK? I've got this," Pete said, dropping a quick kiss to the top of Izzy's head.

She smiled up at him and snuggled closer. "Thanks, honey. Ronnie, are you . . . ?"

"Amir, are you cool with keeping me as your client?" my cousin asked.

Amir clapped his hands on Ronnie's shoulders and smiled at him. "Absolutely. The Macapagals are like family to me, which makes you family as well. I'll do what I can, but we'll need to talk soon. In private."

Amir stepped back and held out his hand, which Ronnie shook. "Thanks, man. Can it wait till tomorrow? It's been a long day."

"Absolutely. I've got some work I need to wrap up anyway, so I'll call on you early tomorrow. Take care, everyone. Thanks for the food, auntie, grandma," Amir said, dropping kisses on my aunt's and grandmother's cheeks, before grabbing his takeout containers and heading out.

"We should go, too," Izzy said. "I need a hot bath and have a new holiday romance novel waiting for me at home. Let's go, hon."

Pete and Izzy bid their goodbyes, and then it was just Detective Park and my family sitting around the table.

Ronnie glared at the detective, who was sitting next to his mom. Detective Park was part of our family now and had done more for us than Ronnie or his dad ever had, something that Ronnie must've resented. "Why didn't you leave with the other detective? We don't need you around right now."

"Anak! Jonathan is our guest and you are not to talk to him like that. Do you hear me?" Tita Rosie's voice was sharper than I'd ever heard it and Ronnie jerked back as if her words had cut him.

"So it's like that? Never thought I'd see the day you choose a man over your son. He's way too young for you, by the way. And you're still married, so great example you're setting for us. You're just—ow!"

Lola Flor had removed her slipper and chucked it at Ronnie midrant. "Hoy! Give me back my tsinelas," she ordered. "And sit down. You think you can talk to your mother like that? You haven't been around in over ten years, and your father," she let that last word drip with contempt, "hasn't been around for even longer than that. You think you have any right telling us how to live? You think you have a right to your mother's kindness? Good thing you're a big shot now, so you can pay for your food and your lawyer fees from now on. I don't want to see you here again until you grow some sense and a civil tongue in your head. And Lila, don't bother helping with the investigation anymore. I'm not risking my granddaughter for this . . ."

My grandmother pushed away from the table and strode back to the kitchen, muttering in Tagalog under her breath. We all watched her walk away, my cousin and me in shock, my aunt and Detective Park with concern. I tried to catch Ronnie's eye but he refused to look at me. He refused to look at any of us. Tita Rosie reached out a tentative hand, but Ronnie pulled away.

"She's right. I'm sorry, I shouldn't have come back."

Tita Rosie let out a choked sob, and Detective Park wrapped his arm around her as she started to cry. Ronnie stared in horror and rushed out the door.

I followed him to the parking lot and stopped him before he got in his car. "You said you weren't going to hurt her. You swore you wouldn't do this again. But I *knew* you'd do this. I knew it!"

I wasn't very physically intimidating (that was more of a Bernadette thing, despite being the same height as me) but I had a surprising amount of upper body strength due to carrying around heavy restaurant supplies and all the baking I did. I shoved him hard enough to hear a satisfying *thunk* as he slammed against his car. I wanted to shove him again. I wanted to keep hitting him until he hurt as much as Tita Rosie was hurting right now. But somehow, I sensed that he wanted that. That he'd welcome the physical punishment rather than deal with what he'd said and done. So I put enough distance between us that I wouldn't be tempted to play into his hands.

"You better make this right. No running away this time. You're grown now, so start acting like it."

Ronnie straightened his coat and looked me over coolly. "Take care of her, OK?"

He got into his car and I stood watching with my arms crossed, watching him flee like the coward he was. Before he pulled away, he rolled down his window and stuck his head out. "And Lila? Lola Flor's right. Stay out of my business. This doesn't concern you anymore."

Then he finally drove away.

Stay out of his business? I wished I could. But the heartbreak and tears on Tita Rosie's face were seared into my brain and I knew I couldn't stop investigating. I was in too deep. Whatever he may think, this case was never about him, not in my mind anyway. It was always about my aunt and her happiness. And I'd do what it took to make things right for her.

Chapter Twenty

A few days passed without seeing or hearing from Ronnie. I would've been more annoyed if I wasn't so busy getting ready for the winter bash. In fact, not having to deal with his drama made preparing for the party way easier since I didn't have to leave the cafe at all hours to chase down clues. The only bit of sleuthing I'd had to do in that time was when Terrence called me to say he'd tracked the blackmailer's IP address to the Shady Palms Public Library. Unfortunately, after a quick trip there, we learned the library computer users' info was wiped after every session and there was no way to see who'd logged in to send that email. Yay for privacy, but that left us no closer to finding out who was threatening my aunt.

Which was why I was extra upset that the day before the big bash, Tita Rosie received another blackmail letter. This time the black-mailer raised the stakes by mailing a physical letter to the restaurant. Knowing Tita Rosie, she would've hidden this from me if I hadn't been the one to take in the mail that day. I couldn't say what it was about the envelope that struck me as suspicious, other than the fact that it was postmarked but had no return address, but I knew something about it wasn't quite right.

I asked Tita Rosie to open it in front of me, and though she gave me an odd look, she didn't argue. Her eyes widened in dismay as they scanned the sheet of paper she'd pulled out—she tried to shove it back in the envelope before I could see it, but I was too quick for her.

Ronnie has killed before and now he's killed again. If you don't want us to turn in the last piece of evidence against him, wire us $250,000 before the end of the year. This is your final warning.

"Tita Rosie, this is getting serious. They're escalating the situation and we can't just wait around for Izzy to handle it. Besides, as much as you'd like to pretend otherwise, she's a suspect in this case. We can't trust her. Terrence looked into the earlier emails and all he could find was that they were sent from the Shady Palms library. If we want to take this further, we need to talk to Detective Park."

"We can't! Ronnie's already in so much trouble. This will only make things worse and I can't do that to him." Tita Rosie made a grab for the letter, but I danced out of her reach. She was more agile and persistent than I gave her credit for and it took all my effort to dodge her attempts.

"What are you two doing?" Detective Park and Jae had entered the restaurant without us noticing and were now standing next to us, both of them watching me try to stay out of Tita Rosie's reach so she couldn't snatch the letter away.

"Detective Park! Just the man I wanted to see," I said as I darted toward him and thrust the letter into his hand.

"Wow, I'm like, right here, Lila," Jae said.

"Jonathan! That is my personal correspondence, don't look at it!" Tita Rosie said, her voice frantic as she tried to take the letter back from him.

Detective Park looked at me, his eyebrows raised. "If it's her mail, I don't—"

"It's a blackmail letter. She's received several emails, but this is the first physical letter that I know of."

His head whipped to the side to look at my aunt, who was wincing in anticipation of his reaction. "Rosie?"

She didn't respond.

"If it's something criminal, I'm afraid I'm going to have to take a look," he said, opening and scanning the letter, his expression darkening the more he read. When he finished, he read it over again, then folded the letter and stuck it back in the envelope. "Thank you for bringing this to my attention, Lila. I was taken off the Denise Sutton case, but this I can help with."

"You were taken off the case?" I asked. "I thought you left voluntarily?"

He rubbed the back of his head. "Technically, I stepped away. But it was mostly because of Sheriff Lamb. He made some comment about me giving your family preferential treatment, and that he'd crack down extra hard if he sensed I was doing the same for Ronnie. I didn't want to mess things up for your son, but I can help while in the backseat, so to speak. That's why Detective Nowak got promoted ahead of schedule. Since I'm familiar with everyone concerned, I can show him around and introduce him to the people of interest without the sheriff breathing down my neck. I can help him out if he has questions, but I'm not directly involved in the case."

"You don't think these letters are connected to the case?"

"Tangentially, yes. I can't ignore the suspicious timing of the letters. Actually, when did the first one arrive?"

We all looked to Tita Rosie, who admitted, "Either the day of or the day before Denise died. I can't remember exactly, but I know it's why we first visited Ronnie at the winery."

Detective Park stared at her. "And you didn't think to tell me until now?"

She kneaded her hands together. "Ronnie's had trouble before, particularly with Sheriff Lamb, and I didn't want to bring unnecessary attention to him. I was hoping it was just a malicious prank, and Isabel said she'd investigate the emails for us."

"Ms. Ramos-Garcia knew about these? And was looking into them?"

My aunt nodded. "She said to leave everything to her. She knows more about computers than I do, and the letters involve her more than me, so it seemed like a good idea."

Detective Park sighed. "I wish you had told me earlier so we could've nipped this in the bud, but I understand your instinct to protect your son. Do you know if she found anything?"

Tita Rosie shook her head, so I added, "I also had Terrence look into this. He was able to trace it to a computer at the Shady Palms Public Library, but the trail goes cold from there."

Detective Park nodded. "I'll get started on this. At least now I have a reason to get involved with the Denise Sutton case. Detective Nowak will understand as long as it's a parallel investigation, and we don't have to get Sheriff Lamb involved since he only cares about wrapping up the murder anyway."

He glanced at me, then fixed his gaze on his brother, who'd been taking everything in silently. "Keep an eye on them, OK? This letter is postmarked in Wisconsin, but that doesn't mean the sender isn't close by."

"You think we should be worried the blackmailer will approach us in person?" I asked.

"At this point, we don't have enough information on the blackmailer, so we can't rule anything out. I'll assign some officers to watch your house, but I feel better knowing Jae is nearby. It may be chauvinistic, but please indulge me on this."

Jae put a hand on my shoulder and smiled down at me. "I know you can take care of yourself, but I'm going to make myself a bit of a nuisance till this is over. Hope that's OK."

I snuggled under his arm and hugged his side. "Thank you both for taking this seriously."

At that, Tita Rosie acknowledged what the Park brothers were doing. "Yes, thank you so much, Jonathan. Jae. I'm sorry I wasn't more forthcoming about this. I appreciate everything you do for us."

Detective Park smiled down at her, the expression on his face so similar to Jae's it made me smile as well. "Of course. Now let's have breakfast. We all have a long day ahead of us."

So the four of us ate, carefully avoiding saying anything that would upset Tita Rosie more, despite the specter of the blackmail letter and Ronnie and how our town was caught up in another murder hanging over the table. It wasn't until Detective Park finished his third cup of coffee and announced he had to get going that Tita Rosie found the courage to ask what it was she really needed from him.

"Keep Ronnie out of trouble," she begged, plucking at the sleeve of Detective Park's coat. "Please?"

He put his hand on hers and looked into her eyes. "I promise to do what I can to keep him safe. I hope that's enough."

Tita Rosie took his hand and laid her cheek against his palm, closing her eyes momentarily as she leaned into his touch. Then she straightened herself up and let go of his hand.

"Thank you," she said. "Now let's get to work."

• • •

Shortly after my breakfast with Detective Park and Jae, Ronnie stormed into the cafe.

"Why is your detective friend all up in my business? I told you to drop it!"

I was chatting with a customer about a catering order for their holiday party and did not appreciate the interruption or his tone. I called Elena over and addressed my customer. "I'm so sorry, could you excuse me for a moment? Elena will hammer out the details with you."

I glared at my cousin. "In my office. Now."

He narrowed his eyes but followed me quietly. Once I'd closed the door, I rounded on him. "You do not come into my place of business and talk to me like that. You especially don't do that when you see I'm talking to a customer, and especially *especially* do not get to take that tone with me when you broke Tita Rosie's heart and the rest of us are left trying to fix things, as usual. Maybe if you don't want Detective Park in your business, you should stop doing shady BS, how about that? How about you stop lying to us and tell us what's been going on?"

"I didn't ask for you to fix anything! In fact, I asked you to do the very opposite. Don't try to pin this on me when you've just got a savior complex." He leaned forward, the ferocity of his words and tone matching my own. "Anyway, you've got a lot of nerve acting all high and mighty with me when you also left the family. I wasn't the only one who ran away."

I flinched, not able to deny that last statement but not ready to back down. "That was a completely different situation and you know it. I may have abandoned the restaurant at that time, but never the family! I still kept in touch and came back when your mom needed me. But you, you just up and disappeared on us. We didn't even know if you were dead or alive! Do you have any idea what that did to Tita Rosie?"

The haunted look I'd seen on occasion returned to his eyes. "You ever think that I left home because I didn't want my screw-ups to keep affecting her? I was sick of it. Sick of this town, sick of the way people always looked down on her because of me, sick of the way Lola Flor compared me to my dad."

"Look, I get it, Ronnie, but—"

"No, you don't get it. And you never will." He shook his head. "Just let it go, Lila. I can handle my business."

I had been all ready to empathize with him, but his dismissive tone set me off. "It's not just your business when it affects the family, Ronnie! How has your selfish ass not figured that out by now? Your mother gets another blackmail letter, a physical letter, by the way, and the only thing you can think to do is come yell at me? How is that 'handling your business'?"

I kept my voice low, my tone as mocking and biting as possible, knowing that—even more than my words—would be the thing to set him off. For all his apparent confidence and swagger, he'd always had an inferiority complex and lashed out whenever he thought people were looking down on him.

But I must've pushed too far. He reared back and I flinched, thinking he was going to hit me, but instead he punched the wall. The wall was fine, but Longganisa had been napping beneath the desk and the loud noise must've frightened her because she shot out from underneath it and started barking her head off.

I scooped her up and held her close, soothing her. "Get out. Now."

He slammed the door open and rushed out without a word. Adeena and Elena ran into my office to check on me.

"Are you OK? He didn't hurt you, did he?" Elena asked, looking me over.

I told them what happened and both Elena and I had to restrain Adeena to keep her from chasing after Ronnie and showing him what she thought about him and his attitude.

"Stop, Adeena, it's fine." I let her go and rolled my eyes, showing that Ronnie wasn't to be taken seriously. "It was all macho posturing, totally not worth it. But I do know my next move."

Adeena stopped rubbing her fist and perked up at my tone. "Ooh, I know that face. You've got something wild planned, don't you?"

I grinned at her. "Since he thought he could invade my workplace like that, maybe I should do the same. Time for some nighttime reconnaissance."

I didn't care that he was my cousin—Ronnie had been acting too shady for too long for me to ignore the possibility that he was involved in some way. If not with Denise's murder, then with the blackmail letters that hadn't stopped. In fact, they'd escalated, if the blackmailer knew our actual address. No, they knew our restaurant's address, I reassured myself. Just like with Tita Rosie's email, they probably looked us up online and used the restaurant's website to get this information. They didn't really know how to get to us.

Though, I was just avoiding the obvious, wasn't I? Terrence said the emails were sent from Shady Palms based on the IP address. But the envelope was postmarked in Wisconsin. Was there more than one person involved in the blackmail? Or did the blackmailer not realize we'd be able to trace them to Shady Palms and had gone out of their way to throw us off track by mailing it somewhere out of state? If there was only one blackmailer, I couldn't ignore the obvious: the only people who had been in Shady Palms when the first email arrived and were also in Wisconsin recently were Ronnie, Izzy, and Pete.

Izzy was from Wisconsin and the trio met in college there. It couldn't just be a coincidence, could it? They had to be in on it. I had no idea if they'd worked this out together, some sick plan where Ronnie extorted money from his mother, or if his partners were plotting against him. Either way, I needed to put a stop to this.

"Follow the money" was advice you saw all the time in detective shows and novels, and that was as good a place to start as any. Remembering that Ninang Mae's son, Marcus, was the security guard for Shady Palms Winery, I convinced him to let me in and keep an eye out to make sure no one found me in Ronnie's office.

"Look, Lila, I risked my neck for you last time and I ended up out of a job. Why should I do this again?"

"First of all, you quit the last job since you have an actual conscience. Second, if I don't find out what really happened here that night, you'll be out of a job again. And finally," I held up the box of assorted cookies I'd brought for him, "you think I'd come without something for you? I made sure to include your favorite ube crinkles."

His eyes lit up at the treat. "Hell, I don't even like Ronnie, so go ahead. If this helps you and Tita Rosie, that's good enough for me. I'll keep an eye out for you. If you hear me singing 'Jingle Bells,' that means you need to get out."

"Won't that make the other person suspicious?"

"Nah, I sing to myself to pass the time most nights. I'll sing other Christmas carols so nobody thinks it's weird. Just listen for that particular song, OK?"

I nodded and made my way up to the office Ronnie, Izzy, and Pete shared. All three of them needed to be looked into, but I figured I'd start with Ronnie first. His computer required a login but his desk drawers were unlocked, so I flipped through various folders to see if I could find any incriminating documents. I didn't see anything unusual, but there was a sticky note with Ronnie's login and password on it: *RFlores, Is@iah0327!*. Rather lax security, but it worked for me.

Briefly wondering what the "Isaiah" in his password was in reference to (a Bible verse, maybe? I didn't remember him being any more religious than me, but Tita Rosie was a strong influence), I logged on to his account and started to click around, hoping he had all his passwords saved to the computer. A bank website was on his list of recently opened sites, so I navigated to it, and yes, his username and password were indeed saved to his account. I only had enough time to worry about how easy it was (and how my own computer was set up to remember all of my passwords since I could never remember them all) before the activity in Ronnie's account made me almost rub my eyes because I couldn't believe what I was seeing (I stopped myself in time, since I remembered I was wearing eye makeup).

The actual amount in his account was nothing special, but when I scrolled through his account history, I noticed a sudden influx over the past month. Thousands of dollars into his account every week that would then be transferred to a couple of outside accounts.

Was Ronnie involved in money laundering? That's how it worked, right? I made a note to research that later. I clicked to see his payment history and saw a monthly sum of $3,000 being sent to Penny Garcia. Hmm, so he was paying off the mysterious Penny for something. Was she part of this money-laundering scheme? Or maybe . . . Was I wrong about the winery crew? Could this Penny be our blackmailer? I took a picture of the webpage and started to delve deeper into his accounts when I heard a pause in Marcus's singing. Was he talking to someone? Or just taking a break from singing? No wait, there was the signal song!

I quickly logged out and wiped down everything I remembered touching. I cracked the door and peeked into the hallway, but the coast was clear. Marcus's voice was some distance away, but I could still hear him clearly. Which meant that whoever was with him would be close enough to hear me if I wasn't careful. Time to enter stealth mode.

"Marcus, I get that you're bored, but can you actually hear if an intruder's around with the racket you're making?"

Pete's unmistakably annoyed voice drew me up short. What was he doing here at this time? If he was up to something shady, should I stick around and try to spy on him? Or would that be pushing my luck too much?

"Also, are you eating on the job? You know you have to be careful about food out here. We can't afford to have a pest problem because you're dropping cookie crumbs everywhere." Now Izzy's voice joined the conversation.

"Sorry, boss. Lila gave them to me because she knows how hungry I get on duty."

Oh Marcus, you fool. Why even bring me into this?

"She was here?" Izzy's voice was sharp. "Why?"

"Oh, no, what I meant was . . . I stopped by the cafe before my shift, and she packed me a special bag of my favorite cookies. That's all," Marcus said, fumbling the delivery but sounding believable enough.

"That better be all. We have enough problems without an unauthorized person wandering the premises. You find anyone here after hours, arrest them for trespassing. And let us know about it ASAP. You hear me?" Pete snapped.

"Um, you know I can't actually arrest anyone, right?"

"Then detain them and have them arrested!"

"Yes, sir," Marcus responded.

"Good. And one more thing . . ."

But I didn't hear the last of Pete's demands. Figuring I'd pushed my luck enough, and having no interest in getting arrested for trespassing, I slipped out the back way and hurried home.

• • •

Safely at home, with my nighttime skincare routine done, I was now cuddled up in bed with Nisa. I looked over the pictures I'd taken and stared at the money that Ronnie was sending every month to this Penny woman. I suddenly remembered the day we went to clear out Denise's belongings, Ronnie got a call from her and he ran away from Lola Flor and his mom to go answer it. Who was she?

As I was thinking it through, I opened up the Brew-ha chat and sent the pics to Adeena and Elena. They were my family even more than Ronnie was—maybe they could help me figure out what was going on.

Adeena: Whoa what is this

Lila: I hacked into Ronnies work pc. That's his bank account

Elena: Who's Penny?

Lila: Idk. I was hoping you two would brainstorm with me

Adeena: I think she might be your blackmailer

Elena: Yeah, I agree. Same amount, every month? Def sus

I sighed. That's what I thought too, but I was hoping they'd come up with an alternative and told them so.

Elena: Sorry chica. But your cousin got your family involved in some messed-up stuff

Lila: Tell me about it. Random q: you know anything about money laundering?

Elena: Long story, but yeah. You think that's what this is?

Lila: Hard for me to say w/o knowing how money laundering works

Elena: I'll give you a rundown tomorrow

Adeena: You gonna confront him?

I thought about it. In the past, I'd rushed in without a plan, going off the heat of the moment. Or ignored the clues in front of me until it was almost too late. With this, I finally had the upper hand and needed time to formulate a plan.

Lila: Not yet. We got the winter bash this weekend & I need to plan my attack

Elena: Yeah, plus she doesn't have enough info yet. Maybe she could ask Izzy? About that Penny person. She probably knows everyone in Ronnie's life

Elena was right. I'd need all, or at least most, pieces of the puzzle before I confronted my cousin. Tita Rosie would automatically defend him, so I'd need concrete proof before I made my move.

Adeena: Great idea, babe! Lila, you should also try to steal his phone and see if you can find texts from her

Lila: I knew you two wouldn't let me down. I'll def talk to Izzy but how do I get his phone w/o him noticing?

Adeena: Can we talk about this tomorrow? I just dropped my phone on my face and I think I broke my nose

Count on Adeena to make me laugh at a time like this.

Lila: Kk battle plan meeting tomorrow

Adeena: Sounds good. And stop laughing at me

Elena: We would never. Good night, everyone 😘

I smiled and set my phone to silent before plugging it in to charge.

"Good night, Nisa," I said, as I snuggled close to her. "We got a couple of busy days ahead of us."

She responded by farting on me, and after I got up to crack a window (I didn't care that it was freezing out; this tiny dog's farts were *toxic*), we nuzzled together and fell asleep, eager to tackle a new day.

Chapter Twenty-one

"So, what do you think this Penny chick has on your cousin? That's a pretty large amount to be sending her every month. And how long has he been doing it?"

Elena had briefed us on money laundering and then I'd launched into my story about what went down the previous night. While we talked, Adeena prepared our morning drinks. I'd just finished my wrap-up when Adeena set a mug of peppermint tsokolate in front of me, her newest experiment. We'd found a great Philippines-based bean-to-bar chocolate company and were testing out their products to see if we wanted to permanently stock them in the shop. A deep inhale brought the comforting scent of peppermint, both sweet and sharp, as well as the bitter sweetness of good quality chocolate. My first sip had me wondering how many cases was too many for an initial order.

"I almost don't care who Penny is anymore, this is so good," I said, taking a deep gulp. The hot liquid coursed down my throat, burning away the morning chill, and I almost melted in my seat from pleasure. "Think you could make a mocha version as well? I'm going to need some caffeine soon."

Elena smiled at me. "Yeah, I had the same reaction, though I prefer a non-caffeinated beverage. I'm happy that we could meet our customers' expectations on holiday drinks yet put our own spin on it. And from a great company, too. Now I just need Adeena to come up with her take on eggnog and the holiday drinks are complete. I told her to start doing research on rompope, so here's hoping she comes up with a good version."

"You know I love a challenge, babe," Adeena said, making a note in her phone. "But getting back on topic, is this something we should tell my brother? If he's going to be representing your cousin, he needs to have all the facts. I don't like that Ronnie is holding out on him."

"You're right, but I'm hoping we can get Ronnie to confess without me admitting that I essentially broke into the winery and hacked into his computer. To be fair, he left the password lying around, but I doubt that's going to help me much. You two and Marcus are the only ones who can know about this."

Oh sugar, that reminded me, I needed to tell Marcus to keep his mouth shut about last night. You'd think something like that was common sense, but I'd learned that common sense wasn't as common as you'd think. Especially when your mom had a nose for tsismis the way Ninang Mae did. No way I could trust him to not say something to her when pressed. I sent him a couple of texts thanking him for his help and warning him not to say a word to anyone about last night.

ok but my mom saw the last text you sent and thinks you're cheating on Dr. Jae with me

Oh, that's just great.

she's asking so many questions what do I tell her

I looked at Adeena and Elena. "Ninang Mae saw my text saying to not tell anyone about last night and now she thinks I'm dating her son."

The two of them started cracking up and I groaned. "Not funny! What can he tell her that won't make this worse?"

omg she hasn't stopped talking

LILA WHAT DO I TELL HER

They stopped laughing when they saw his escalating texts. "He's not great when put on the spot, is he?" Adeena asked. "You'd think he'd have learned to lie better by now."

"In his defense, Ninang Mae can sniff out tsismis from fifty yards away. Though I do wish he was better at thinking on his feet," I said, staring at his frantic texts. "Ugh, why didn't I ask his brother to help me instead? Joseph is their accountant; I could've gotten their financial info from him. And he's way more level-headed than Marcus."

Then again, he was a big rule follower and likely not cool with illegally passing on his clients' confidential information. Admirable, but not what I needed for this case. Marcus's growing lack of respect for authority had made him seem like the perfect partner in crime, but even he would forever respect and fear his mother.

"Say that the cafe and winery are doing a special collaboration for the winter bash and no one's supposed to know. And he can't tell her anything because he doesn't want to lose his job," Elena said, sipping her drink calmly. Considering she was the nice one of our group, she really did have a devious mind sometimes.

I passed along that excuse and he replied with a thumbs-up emoji.

"It worked! Though now we might actually have to do a collab with the winery so the aunties don't get suspicious."

"That's not a bad idea, actually. We still need to learn more about them and this gives them a chance to advertise the winery, even if they're not open yet," Adeena said. "We can invite them over for a brainstorm, maybe get Terrence in on the branding. This might be good for both of our businesses."

"Are you sure? You're not worried that being associated with the winery would reflect negatively on us?" I asked. As much as I needed a break in the investigation, I didn't want to drag Adeena and Elena (and the Brew-ha Cafe) down because of my family drama.

Elena offered me a gentle smile. "I appreciate you thinking of us, but the town already knows about your family's connection to the winery. Distancing ourselves now wouldn't do much, and the Shady Palms News already reported that the winery's products were tested and cleared. We shouldn't waste an opportunity just because we're worried what people might think."

"Good point. I'll message Ronnie to see if they're free later. He owes me one after his last visit, so here's hoping he doesn't make this difficult." I stood up and held out my mug for another refill. "You know, that thing with Marcus just jogged my memory. So much has happened since we cleaned out Denise's stuff that I forgot to tell you I found a love letter that was *not* from Xander hidden in her shoe closet."

I'd put the note in my bag, thinking to examine it more closely, but had forgotten about it till now. I fetched it and set it in front of my partners. "Whoever wrote it seemed to know them both pretty well. Do you think she was cheating on Xander, or were they on a break or something?"

Adeena spread the letter in front of herself so that she and Elena could read it together. "Hmm, it mentions Puerto Rico. You think they had a romantic getaway or was this someone she met while she happened to be there? I mean, Xander's Puerto Rican, isn't he?" Adeena asked.

Before I could answer, a knock at the door drew our attention. Olivia and Quentin, along with a very excited Poe, who was pushing at the door to get in, stood in front of the cafe waving at us to let them in. Well, this was a surprise. A glance at the clock told me it was opening time anyway, so I shoved the note in my apron pocket and rushed to let them in while Adeena took her place behind the counter and Elena headed to the kitchen.

"Hey, good morning! Welcome to the Brew-ha Cafe, can I get you anything?"

The two of them entered the cafe and scrutinized the interior, taking in the full effect of Elena's plants, Adeena's artwork, and the delicious smell of my baked goods. I gestured toward the counter, and they moved to scan the menu while I introduced the day's specials (ube scones, buko pandan chia pudding, and my holiday cookies), and Adeena talked up her new holiday drink menu.

"An actual coffee shop that offers more than poor quality drip coffee? I could kiss you right now," Quentin said as he lovingly caressed the laminated menu on the counter.

"Thanks, but I don't really swing that way and I'm sure she'd have something to say about that," Adeena said, jerking her thumb back toward Elena, who was emerging from the kitchen with more dog biscuits.

"You know you're always free to explore a different path," Elena said with a grin. "Poe, baila."

At her command, Poe sat up on his haunches and did a little wiggly dance, which Elena rewarded with a sweet potato biscuit.

"I can't believe you were able to teach him to do that," I said. "Do Nisa next and I bet Katie could help us make them internet stars, the Dancing Doggie Duo or something."

Elena laughed, but her attention slid toward the twins and her sweet yet sharky smile suddenly spread across her face. "Hey! I'm so glad you two finally stopped by. Quentin, you have the most beautiful skin, and I've got something you might be interested in . . ."

Adeena and I watched as she led the twins away from the drinks and over to her side of the shop, which had herbal teas, bath goods, and beauty potions.

"How much you want to bet they walk out with no less than fifty dollars' worth of beauty products?" I asked.

Adeena laughed. "You think I'd bet against my girlfriend? Even if we weren't together, I've seen her sales skills too many times to ever doubt her abilities. I bet they also walk out with, like, a ficus, or something totally impractical."

It was an orchid, actually, but close enough.

"Our room is so boring and flat, but this should brighten things up. Isn't that right, Phyllis?" Quentin cooed at the flower.

"Did you just name that orchid 'Phyllis'?" Adeena asked.

"All plants need names. Isn't that right, Elena?"

"Of course, Quentin. Plants are alive, after all, and grow best under loving attention." Elena smiled indulgently. "Since you two are already here, would you mind bringing this tin of yerba buena to Xander? I promised him some of my latest batch."

Quentin made a face, so Olivia stepped in. "I've got it, don't worry. He sent us here to pick up some coffee and treats anyway, so it's not like it's out of our way." She gave her brother a look. "He's paying for us, so we might as well take advantage of it."

Quentin perked up at that. "That's true! Give us one of everything in your pastry case and I'll take your largest peppermint mocha."

"Do you have oat milk?" At Adeena's nod, Olivia said, "Then I'll have a medium latte with oat milk, no sugar, extra hot. And whatever Xander's usual is, but could you wait till we're about to leave to make it? Thanks."

While Adeena made the drinks, I brought over the tray of goodies. "Mind if I join you for a minute? I haven't had a chance to eat yet and would love to chat before it gets busy."

Quentin pulled out a chair for me, as well as Adeena and Elena, and Olivia said, "Of course. Now, these all look wonderful. Which would you recommend we try first?"

"Scones are always best fresh, so I suggest you start there. Here's a dish of my grandmother's coconut jam to enjoy with it as well."

I waited until Quentin helped himself to a scone and Olivia grabbed the buko pandan chia pudding before grabbing an ube scone for myself. Adeena and Elena helped themselves to their faves from the pastry case and joined us. I watched the two of them chatting with the twins and found myself wondering what Quentin's deal was. He may have been slightly snobby, but from what I'd seen, he was quite friendly unless you brought up Xander. I fingered the note in my pocket. Could it be . . .

"Quentin, were you having an affair with Denise?" I blurted out.

Poor Olivia was sitting across from him and got the full brunt of his spit take. Adeena and Elena helped her clean off the mess and I apologized to Quentin, who was having a coughing fit.

When he could breathe again, he asked, "What in the hell would make you think I was having an affair with Denise?"

"I don't know, I just . . ." In for a penny, in for a pound, Lila. Put your cards on the table and let's see what you get. "I found a letter in Denise's shoe closet. A love letter that wasn't from Xander."

"And you thought *he* sent it? Why?" Olivia tried to hold back her laughter and failed.

My confidence went down quite a few notches at that reaction. "I was trying to figure out why he's so hostile to Xander but decent to everyone else, and well, I thought maybe . . ."

"That I was in love with Denise? My own stepmother?" Quentin threw his head back and cackled, him and Olivia laughing it up like a bunch of witches around a cauldron. "Sorry to burst your bubble, hon, but this is not a Lifetime movie and your gaydar is absolutely awful."

"I mean, you could've been bi or pan..." was my pathetic response, and even Adeena and Elena joined in the laughter at that.

"Anyway, can I see this love letter? I'm pretty sure I know who it's from, but I would be absolutely gagged if she had another secret lover!" Quentin said.

I looked at Adeena and Elena to see what they thought, and they both shrugged. Why not. I pulled the note out of my pocket and took a quick picture of it, in case the twins thought to destroy it or take it back to Xander or something.

Quentin snatched the letter out of my hand, and Olivia moved to his side to read it. They looked at each other and Quentin let out a little scream. "I can't believe she kept this! I told you she was having second thoughts, I told you!"

Not the reaction I was expecting. "Wait, you know who sent this?"

Olivia said, "Nope" at the same time Quentin said, "Denise was messing around with Xander's cousin."

"His cousin?!" I said.

Olivia glared at her twin. "Quentin! Not their business!"

He pouted. "What's the point of having such hot tea if I can't spill it?"

"This is getting good!" Adeena grabbed another pastry and leaned in. "How do you know all this?"

Quentin shrugged. "Denise and Xander were on a break, so I convinced her to have a little fun. His cousin is way hotter and less smarmy and hadn't cheated on her, so I thought it was a no-brainer."

"That's why Xander doesn't like you, isn't it?" Elena asked. "I noticed that he treats you differently than Olivia."

He smiled. "Yep. I was the one who caught him cheating, and I let him know I did not appreciate him treating Denise like that. So I told her."

I raised an eyebrow. "Did you just want to stir up trouble or were you protecting Denise?"

Quentin looked wounded. "Olivia and I may have had a rather awkward relationship with Denise due to the circumstances, but honestly, she treated me way better than my father did. And since she couldn't go against his will, she was doing what she could to help us out. She had her troubles, but she was a better person than most people in our lives—though that's not saying much."

He tore up the scone on his plate, his anger reducing the poor delicious pastry to inedible crumbs. "And after all that, he gets to be the one who benefits from her will."

"You know what's in her will?" I asked. Dang, I should've asked Detective Park or Amir if they could've gotten that information for me.

"The lawyer told us while we were in Chicago the other day. Half goes to her favorite charities, the other half to her and Xander's company." Quentin grabbed another scone and started crumbling that one, too. "So it goes into his business account instead of his personal one. Big deal. He's still the one benefitting from her death. She deserved better than that, and we did, too."

His sister put a hand on his arm. "I think you've shared more than enough, Quentin. Despite your feelings about him, Xander is still our employer and he's doing what he can to carry out Denise's wishes." She turned to Adeena and me. "We've stayed far too long. Could you pack up Xander's order and ring us up, please? And throw in a few biscuits for Poe."

Adeena and I moved to complete their order and Elena went to grab the special dog biscuits she'd been experimenting with from the back. Olivia stood at the register, rooting around in her purse for her wallet with Poe's leash around her wrist. When Poe saw Elena returning with the tray of treats, he leaped toward her, knocking Olivia off balance. Her purse dropped to the floor and the contents tumbled out: cosmetics, vegan breath mints, her iPad, and two bottles that rolled halfway across the cafe before I could grab them.

One was a bottle of perfume (nice, but a bit too flowery for me) and the other seemed to be medicine. I glanced at it as I handed it back to her. "Vitamin B12? Is that part of your beauty regimen?"

I was just trying to make conversation—it seemed like a natural assumption to make since Olivia clearly took good care of her appearance. Her skin was flawless, hair glossy, nails perfectly polished, etc. But she didn't appreciate the question.

Olivia snatched the vial out of my hand and shoved it back in her purse. "I have anemia, not that it's any of your business. And for the record, that was pretty rude."

Before I could apologize, she grabbed Xander's things and swept out with Poe, Quentin hurrying behind them.

"Not your best moment, buddy," Adeena said.

"I realize that now, thanks. I'll make sure to apologize next time I see her. Honestly, what was I thinking?" I shook my head at my foot-in-mouth moment.

"Well, other than your invasive question into Olivia's medication, I thought it was a pretty fruitful conversation. We learned quite a bit, didn't we?" Elena asked as she cleaned the table we'd just used.

"Yeah, but where does this new info leave us?" Adeena asked, leaning her hip against the counter to look at me.

I had no freakin' clue, and my head ached trying to slot in all the new pieces. But whenever I had a tough time working things out, there was one surefire way to clear my mind.

It was time to bake.

Chapter Twenty-two

There was nothing like rubbing butter into flour to ground your-self and clear your head. By the time I prepped several pastries for the cafe, dozens of cookies for the cookie decorating event in a few hours, dozens more for the winter bash, and perfected my bibingka cupcakes, I'd come up with a plan. The info I got from the twins didn't change the order of things that needed to be done—I still needed to talk to Ronnie and his partners to convince them to do a collaboration with us and press for more details on this mysterious Penny he was paying off. I'd let the aunties know what I'd learned about Xander and see if they could get more out of him. And then once I'd gathered everything I needed to know, I'd present it all to Detective Park, who could nudge the new detective in the right direction.

My plan in place and day's baking finally done, I washed my hands and popped into the restaurant next door for a much-needed break. I'd eaten nothing but pastries and the sweets I'd been sampling while baking and needed real food to balance all that sugar. I still had a lot of work to do and had planned on just grabbing something to go, but I spotted Jae sitting with Ronnie, Pete, and Izzy, and went to join them.

"Hey, didn't expect to see you here," I said to Jae, giving him a quick kiss on the cheek before sitting next to him.

Ronnie waggled his eyebrows at me, which made me blush. And then I got mad because I was a grown woman, why was I blushing about this? And that made me blush even more, which made me even angrier.

"I texted you earlier, Ronnie. Why didn't you answer me?" I asked, my voice harsher than I meant it to be. I had every reason to still be angry with him, but I didn't need to cause a scene in my family's restaurant. Which he technically wasn't even supposed to be in since Lola Flor had banned him for mouthing off, but of course Tita Rosie wouldn't enforce it. I wondered if he'd apologized to her, or if she had reached out to him to welcome him back. Knowing him, it was probably the latter.

Jae rubbed my back, slowly and unobtrusively, and my shoulders tensed before relaxing into his touch. His hands moved up to knead my neck as he said, "I figured you were busy getting ready for your event tonight, so I came here to grab some food for you when I ran into them. Your aunt insisted I sit down for a 'proper meal' and that she'd pack something for you later. She also said your grandmother has a special dessert prepared, which I'm really looking forward to. It sounds delicious."

Was there anyone or anything more delicious than this man right here? As Jae's strong, callused fingers worked out the kinks in my neck, all the stress and irritation of the day melted away as I relaxed into him.

Ronnie, probably figuring it was safe to speak now that Jae had calmed me, put down his spoon and fork and picked up his phone. "Oh sorry, it was on silent. I'm free after this, if you still want to talk."

"I wanted to talk to all of you, actually, since it involves Shady Palms Winery. I don't have time right now since I need to get back for my cookie decorating workshop, but maybe—"

"Ooh, cookie decorating! Your high school helper came up with that idea, right? Glad you're going forward with it. I used to do it all the time with my family for Christmas, but it's been years now." Izzy smiled, likely reminiscing about those happy times. "When is it? Do I have to register in advance?"

"It's in an hour, actually, and we have some spots open. Happy to waive registration fees if you all come and chat with me about my collaboration idea."

"Izzy's right, that sounds like a lot of fun and I'd love to hear your proposal. If we're talking about the winery though, Xander needs to be there, too," Ronnie said as he cleared his plate and reached for more rice.

That made sense, so I sent Xander a quick text about the meeting and workshop.

Will Nisa be there? Poe and I def need to get out of the house, was his response.

I hadn't planned on bringing her since the workshop would be messy, and with young kids around, it'd be too easy for her to accidentally eat something bad for her. But if Poe came by, he'd be good company for her, and they could do a quick walk around the pet-friendly area of the cafe to greet our customers.

I texted that the two could hang out in my office and he replied with a thumbs-up emoji.

"All right, he's in." I glanced at the time on my phone. "I have to pick up Longganisa and finish getting ready, so I'll just grab some food from the kitchen and head out. See you all soon!"

• • •

O h sugar, I should've reminded you to wear something you don't
       mind getting messy."

Xander, Izzy, Ronnie, and even Pete showed up to participate in
my cookie decorating class. Xander was dressed in a simple dark green
sweatshirt and Izzy and Ronnie wore their matching funky holiday
sweaters, but Pete was rocking a very white and very expensive-looking
(was that cashmere?) sweater.

"Oh darn. Guess I'll have to sit this one out," Pete said. "Sorry,
honey."

"Good thing we have that spare holiday sweater in the car, *honey*,"
Izzy said, the steely glint in her eyes matching the coldness in her
voice.

Izzy was usually all sweetness and light, so unless everything I'd
seen of her was an act, Pete must've done something to piss her off
earlier. I knew all too well what it sounded like when a couple was
continuing an argument that had started earlier and was now spilling
over into a seemingly harmless conversation. I looked over at Ronnie
to see if his expression would give anything away, but he was too busy
pretending he hadn't heard anything to be of use.

"I suppose I can work in a T-shirt. Is there a place I can hang this
where it won't get dirty?" Pete pulled off his sweater to reveal a simple
yet flattering white tee. He wasn't exactly a fashionable or snappy
dresser, the way Xander was, but everything I'd seen him in had been
quality—my mom had taught me to spot things like that from a
young age, and I knew the difference between a Walmart white tee
and a designer one. The one he was wearing was definitely the latter.
I wondered about Pete's upbringing and made a note to ask Ronnie
more about him later.

"I can put it in my office while we work. You're not allergic to dogs, are you? Because Nisa's there now and Poe is going to join her in a bit."

Hearing me say his name, Poe barked happily and stood on his back legs to put his paws on my knees. I scratched him firmly behind the ears and cooed at him. "That's right, you and Longganisa get to play together again! And I have some special biscuits and a nice bandana set aside for you."

Katie, the social media whiz that she was, had posted pictures of Nisa and Poe on our profile and we had requests for more photos and dog merch pouring in, including from people outside of Shady Palms. The dogs had gotten such a great reception wearing the Brew-ha Cafe tees that Naoko designed that we decided to commission her for a whole pet clothing line. We figured with the holiday season, our customers would be more willing to spend on cute knickknacks, so she created screen-printed clothes, bandanas, and bow ties in various patterns, all with the Brew-ha Cafe logo on them, and we were working with Terrence to set up an online shop on our website as well.

I told Xander to choose whatever gear he wanted for Poe and went to get Nisa from my office. Terrence had gifted me the perfect cookie cutters (a dachshund wearing a Santa hat) to supplement the ones I got for the event, so I made sure Nisa had a tiny Santa hat strapped on, along with a jaunty little scarf. The combo had the exact effect I was going for—when I trotted her out, everyone crowded around to coo over her and take pictures.

"I have special Longganisa cookie cutters at each station, and a challenge for all of you. Create the best-decorated Longganisa you can during our workshop tonight. We'll take pictures of all the designs and post them on our social media to let people vote for their favorites. The one that gets the most votes by the end of the winter bash gets a free holiday cookie sampler box and twenty-five-dollar Brew-ha Cafe gift card!"

The kids in the room all cheered and grabbed their adults' hands to drag them over to a decorating station. I motioned to Elena to help the kids while I wrangled the dogs back to my office. When I returned, the PTA Squad, who mostly had tweens and teens, had waved their kids off to have fun while they circled around Pete and Xander.

"I can't believe we haven't been introduced yet!" the head of the PTA Squad said, her head tilted and what she probably thought was an alluring smile tilting her lips. "I'm Mary Ann Randall, and I wanted to welcome you to our lovely town."

Xander smiled and politely shook the hand she offered, but he struggled to keep the smile on his face as she refused to let go of his hand and continued holding it with both hands as she spoke. "We heard that you're fixing up the old winery. What a wonderful idea!"

"We absolutely love wine," one of her underlings said, batting her eyelashes at Pete. "When will you be open to tours? Do you plan on offering events and tastings like they do down in Galena?"

Pete looked at Xander, who shrugged. He wasn't involved in the day-to-day operations, so I guess it wasn't on him to answer. Pete smiled at the woman, a real dazzler that seemed to stun the group of women into silence.

"That's a great idea. I'll make sure to note that for our summer plans, but right now we're focusing on turning out the most delicious wines possible. I'm afraid you may have to wait a while to tour the winery, but I promise it's worth the wait."

He winked at the woman, and I thought I was going to have to install a fainting couch, so many women started swooning. Pete may bore the crap out of me, but I finally understood what Izzy saw in him. He wasn't charming the way Ronnie and Izzy were, but I guess he could turn it on and off when he wanted to.

The PTA Squad member stared into his blue eyes and blurted out, "And we absolutely do not believe anything the *Shady Palms News* says about you, so don't worry! We'll be the first ones lining up once this is all over."

Ronnie, standing off to the side with Izzy, watched the sharks circling his business partners with a bemused expression on his face. "Not that I want their attention or anything, but I'm here, too. Do I not count as a handsome, eligible man?"

"You're OK, I guess. You don't count as a handsome, eligible, *rich* man though, and I'm sure that's what's attracting them. A man with money is like blood in the water for some of those women," I said.

"That better be it because Pete is definitely *not* eligible considering he's engaged to *me*," Izzy said, raising her voice just enough for the PTA Squad to hear.

They all turned to look at her and I groaned. "Girl, no. It is not worth the headache, I promise you."

But it was too late. They left Xander and Pete's side and began to circle us this time.

"So, you're the other winery owners?" The woman who'd been eyeing Pete now looked Ronnie and Izzy up and down and snorted.

Mary Ann Randall narrowed her eyes at Ronnie. "I remember you. Weren't you the guy who stole my car radio back when you were in high school? And tried to sell it back to me when I tried to find a replacement?"

He was.

Ronnie's big brown eyes widened, the very picture of innocence. "I'm sorry, but I have no idea what you're talking about. I remember you, though. Weren't you captain of the cheerleading team? You were a few years ahead of me and I remember how cool you were."

Mary Ann Randall was at least ten years older than Ronnie and they had definitely *not* been in school together, but he knew exactly how to butter her up.

Mary Ann preened a bit. "Well, yes, I was. I was Miss Teen Shady Palms too, you know."

Ronnie grinned. "I'm not surprised. The absolute picture of beauty and grace."

Izzy had been shooting daggers at the women around Pete, but now she turned her sharp gaze toward Ronnie. "Oh?"

Before he could answer, Mary Ann's youngest stomped over. "When are we going to get started? We've been waiting forever!"

Bless you, kid. I made a big show of looking at the clock and being shocked. "Oh, would you look at the time? Let's decorate some cookies!"

Katie definitely needed to be added to the payroll—not only was the cookie decorating workshop such a huge hit that the adults paid me double what I'd originally charged so that we could keep the event going longer, our customers splurged on drinks, pet attire, and our herbal products as well. I was just delivering the latest round of cookies when the sound of our door chimes had me automatically turning toward our entrance.

"Sorry, we're closed for a private—Oh, hey Olivia! What are you doing here?"

I headed to the front where Olivia stood shivering near the door and asked if she wanted to join us. "No, thanks. I'm just here because Xander wanted me to take the dogs for a walk. Something about them being stuck in an office all day?"

Well, that was good of him to include Nisa in this. I hadn't been as diligent about her walks as I used to be since I was so busy now, and I knew she'd been extra antsy because of that.

"Oh, that's nice of you. Is Quentin waiting for you outside? Tell him he can come in and warm up for a bit while I get the dogs ready."

She tilted her head and studied me for a moment. "You haven't heard?"

"Heard what?"

"Xander caught my idiot brother stealing. I guess he picked the lock to Denise's room and was trying to make off with her jewelry. That was the last straw, so Xander finally sent him packing. Knowing Quentin, he's holed up in our hotel room making his way through the last of the wine he took from the winery."

Ignoring that last bit, I said, "You don't sound particularly worried about him. If he fired your brother, why do you still work for Xander?"

She gave me an *Are you serious?* look. "I only receive my allowance if I stay employed, and working for Xander is easy. He's not a diva like Denise was, and even Denise wasn't all that bad considering how I've seen other people treat their assistants. All Quentin had to do was keep his mouth shut and his hands off other people's possessions and he had it easy. I mean, if you're going to screw over rich people, the least you could do is not get caught." She flicked her hand out to emphasize her last statement, as if it were obvious. Which I guess it was.

She continued, "Besides, it's not like he's totally hopeless. We've got some friends who can take him in, and he'll be happier working at their boutiques in Chicago than following Xander around the Midwest. This was a dumb move on his part, but probably for the best. I was getting *so* tired of his sniping."

She sighed, though whether she was bored of the subject or talking to me, I wasn't sure, and moved to chat with Pete and Ronnie.

I sought out Xander, who was surrounded by the PTA Squad. They were all fawning over him and he was drinking in the attention, though I caught the embarrassed smile he threw me when he realized I was watching them.

He excused himself from the crowd and made his way over to me. "Hey Lila, what's up?"

I glanced over at his group of middle-aged admirers to make sure they weren't listening in. Other than an occasional dirty look, they weren't paying us any attention, so I dragged him to my office and blurted out, "Is it true you fired Quentin because he was stealing from you?"

Xander blew out a breath and ran his hand through his hair. "Wow, good news travels fast, huh? Let me guess, Olivia just told you?"

I pursed my lips and stared at him, not wanting to confirm or deny anything.

"I caught him in Denise's room. He claimed he just went in real quick to find his mom's ring, but you know I always lock that door. It's one thing to look for something that should belong to him anyway. You and your aunt were right about that. And I told him that. But for him to be in that room . . . it meant he either picked the lock or stole the key from me and made a copy. Either of those options were unacceptable, so I terminated his employment, effective immediately. I feel bad doing it right before the holidays, but I can't trust someone like that in my house or around my dog."

"I'm sorry you were forced to do that. How are you doing? How did he take it?"

Xander hesitated, his eyes sweeping the room to make sure nobody was listening in. "We got into it. I asked him how long this had been going on. I didn't believe this was the first time he stole from us. He . . . he laughed at me. Said I had a lot of nerve accusing him of theft when everyone knew I had only gotten with Denise for her money. That she knew I'd been cheating on her with Mercedes. Her astrologer," he explained when he saw my confused look.

His eyes begged me to understand. "It was before we were engaged. I stopped as soon as I realized it was Denise I wanted to spend my life with, and it had nothing to do with her money. Denise and I had both made mistakes, but we forgave each other. But Quentin said such ugly things about Denise, such lies . . . I hit him." A look of shame washed over his face, but there was still a hint of anger there, too. "I know I shouldn't have. That was inviting a lawsuit, if nothing else, and he was just lashing out since he'd lost his job. But after I hit him . . ." Xander frowned. "He returned my keys but promised this wasn't the last I'd see of him. Any other day, I'd laugh off a threat from him because what could he do to me? But that look he gave me . . ."

"Did you report him? For both the theft and the threat?"

Xander scratched the back of his head. "I don't really want the police getting mixed up in this. It got really personal, you know?"

"But what if he had something to do with Denise's death?"

His expression wavered. "The thought has crossed my mind, of course. That's partly why I kept him on, after all. Keep your friends close, enemies closer, and all that. But no. There's no way he'd have gone that far. He actually got on quite well with Denise. He talks big, but there's no fight in him."

"Then why are you afraid of him?"

He bristled. "I'm not *afraid* of him. But he's not smart enough to have come up with a plan like that. Someone had not only taken advantage of the fact that Denise had a drinking problem, but also tampered with the wine in a way that she could've been poisoned at any time without the poisoner being around. What if she hadn't drunk those bottles in front of everyone at the winery? What if she'd taken them home and drank them by herself there?" He shook his head again. "But what if someone else had drunk some, too? Who's to say we wouldn't have shared the bottle together? Whoever did this didn't care how many people they could've hurt. Quentin is greedy and petty, but he isn't vicious."

"Then who do you think did it? You must have a suspicion, at least," I said.

Unless we were way off base and Denise's killer was some random person who wasn't connected to the winery at all, the only viable suspects were his assistants and his clients. Well, and him, of course. But he just shook his head. "No idea."

Either he was keeping his cards extremely close to his chest or he really was clueless when it came to this case.

Xander was so sure about Quentin's innocence (at least in Denise's murder), but I still had some questions for him. Maybe he wasn't a murderer, but he could easily be a blackmailer. I thought it was time to let Detective Park know what I'd just learned.

Chapter Twenty-three

I know you want to come with, but there's nothing I can say or do that would justify bringing you with me. Both to the department and to your family. If anything happened to you, your aunt would never forgive me. I don't even want to think about what your grandmother and godmothers would do to me. So again, just please stay where you are and I'll let you know what I find out. OK?"

I'd called Detective Park as soon as Xander left my office and let him know what I'd learned about Quentin and his possible connection to Denise's death and the blackmail letters we'd been receiving. I'd tried to convince him to take me with him so I could find out if Quentin was the scumbag threatening my aunt, but Detective Park shut that down quick. So now I had to continue with the cookie-decorating workshop as if it were even possible for me to concentrate on anything else.

I took a moment to adjust my hair and makeup in the mirror I had hanging in the office so I'd hopefully look casually put together and not like a hot mess about to fall apart any minute because Detective Park had no compassion for my poor nerves.

I exited my office and wandered around the cafe, making sure to stop at each station to provide assistance, instruction, and/or praise, depending on what each participant needed. I thought I was doing a pretty good job of keeping up appearances, but Adeena pulled me into the kitchen on the pretense of needing to bake more cookies.

"What's going on?" Adeena demanded, as she watched me pop the premade cookie trays in the oven. "You're walking around with your fake-ass 'everything's OK' smile, and it's weirding out Elena and me."

As if her girlfriend saying her name summoned her, Elena came in to grab the cookies that had been sitting on the cooling rack. "I bet it has to do with whatever you and Xander were talking about. Was it something Olivia said? She's the one who seemed to set you off."

Dang that girl was observant.

I checked the color on the cookies before responding. "She told me, and Xander confirmed, that Quentin got fired earlier today for trying to steal Denise's jewelry. I mean, he might've been trying to steal other stuff too, but Xander caught him in Denise's room with her jewelry." When they'd reached the perfect shade of brown, I took the cookies out and let them set for a moment before transferring them to the cooling racks. "I called Detective Park to let him know what had happened. He's off to talk to Quentin now."

Elena grabbed the last tray we'd prepared and put them in the oven. After setting the timer, she said, "Do you think he had something to do with Denise's death?"

"Possibly. He definitely had a motive, what with his feelings about her marrying his dad and getting the full inheritance. But the theft also made me think he was greedy or hurting for money, so I wondered if he was the one behind the blackmail letters." I hoped he was.

Having this unknown specter threatening my family was bad enough but knowing what it was doing to my aunt . . . I didn't care what sob story he had about why he needed the money. If he was the one blackmailing Tita Rosie, I'd never forgive him.

Adeena let out a low whistle. "I knew your cousin was a messy bench, Lila, but who knew every single person he surrounded himself with would be, too? Even Izzy has a jealous side I hadn't expected, and I can usually spot the jealous ones a mile away."

Elena nodded. "Pete is the possessive type as well, which is weird considering he must know your cousin's in love with his fiancée."

The timer went off for the cookies, so Elena removed them and turned off the oven. "This is the last batch, right? We still haven't talked to the group about the collaboration we're supposedly doing with them, so maybe now's the time."

"Good idea. How should we handle this?"

"They're all at the same big table, so we can just join them and tell them about the collab idea for the winter bash. And if it goes well, we could talk about an official partnership outside of the wine we said we'd carry in the shop," Elena said. "In fact, would you mind if I took the lead on this? I have a genuine proposition for them, something I've been wanting to do for a while."

Adeena and I exchanged glances—it was rare for Elena to involve herself directly with our shenanigans. She was usually the idea person and backup. Guess that showed how serious she was about this business proposal.

I smiled at her. "Absolutely. Adeena and I will wait for your cues if you want us to jump in at any point, but I trust you on this."

The three of us huddled together and did a quick elbow bump to pump ourselves up, then headed back out to join the Shady Palms Winery table. Xander held up the Longganisa Santa cookie he'd been decorating in the colors of the Chicago Bulls. He'd even iced on a little basketball jersey and decorated one of the plain circle cookies to look like a basketball.

"Longganisa about to break some ankles!" he said with a laugh. He moved the cookies as if Nisa were dribbling the basketball around me.

I squealed with delight. "Oh my gulay, that's so cute! Let me get a picture for the contest."

After snapping the picture and sending it to Katie, Adeena, Elena, and I sat down with everyone. Ronnie was busier eating his cookies than decorating them, but Izzy was hard at work creating intricate parol designs using the star-shaped cookies and various icings we'd prepared.

"These are gorgeous!" I said, carefully picking up a finished cookie. It looked just like a parol, or star lantern. They were a traditional Christmas decoration in the Philippines, and my aunt and grandmother had a bunch they'd brought over with them hanging around the restaurant and our house. The Brew-ha Cafe had one as well, a giant eye-catching ornament that Tita Rosie had special ordered for us as a gift and which we'd hung in the front window of the shop. Parol patterns were colorful and intricate, and I was amazed Izzy had managed such precision on such a small surface.

Adeena must've been equally impressed. "You need a weekend gig? Lila needs help decorating the cookies for the winter bash, and your skills far exceed anyone else's here."

"Oh, is that why you invited us over? To ask for help for the winter bash? Because I'd be happy to help, no payment needed," Izzy said, as she brushed a strand of hair out of her face with the back of her hand. The action streaked some icing across her forehead and Ronnie chuckled.

"You're such a mess. Here, let me—"

He was reaching out to wipe away the icing with his bare hand when Pete swooped in out of nowhere with a napkin. "Here, love, hold still for a moment."

Izzy stilled and Pete wiped away the icing with a slight smile before handing her a glass. "Here's the water you asked for."

"Thanks, babe!" Izzy said, stretching up for a quick kiss.

It was a really cute moment, but my eyes were drawn to Ronnie. He usually sported a blasé or cocky expression to hide how he was feeling, but because I happened to have been looking at him that exact moment, I could pinpoint the second his heart broke.

His eyes iced over the moment his gaze met mine, but there was no going back. He knew I knew. Ronnie cleared his throat. "We can help you with the winter bash if that's what you want, but I feel like there was more you wanted from us. Something about a collaboration?"

Elena leaned forward. "Yes, we have a proposition for you. Two actually; one short-term and one a long-term partnership. For the winter bash, we'd be happy to use your products in our food and drinks to help you advertise your winery."

"Izzy already said yes, so what's this long-term partnership about?" Ronnie asked.

Elena studied him, then turned her attention to Xander. "Right now, you've got some bad press. On the one hand, wine takes a long time to ferment and distill, so by the time you're ready with your new product, the town will probably have forgotten all about this and moved on to the next new scandal."

"But?" Xander prompted.

"But how are you going to make money in the meantime? You need something that ferments faster than wine and that you can churn out quickly and reliably while waiting on your primary product. This is where we come in." Elena, while not exactly soft-spoken, was definitely more laid-back than Adeena and me. However, when it came to sales, the woman was a shark. "I've been wanting to brew my own beer for a while now, but haven't had the time, space, or equipment. I do, however, have the knowledge as well as the license necessary to both prepare and sell liquor."

"Wait, you want us to become a brewery?" Ronnie asked. "I'm sorry, but that's not part of our vision. Our vision is—"

"Completely worthless if we run out of money and have to shut down operations," Pete said. "Let her talk. This might be the saving grace we were looking for."

Xander stroked his beard, nodding slowly. "Pete's right. You've piqued my interest, Elena. Let's hear your pitch."

My respect for Xander grew. He was a businessman, through and through, but he acknowledged and appreciated Elena's intelligence and entrepreneurial instincts.

"Beer is not where your heart is, so it wouldn't make sense for you to invest a ton of time and money into it. But a microbrewery, or in this case, a micro microbrewery since we wouldn't be looking for wide distribution, is entirely doable. My uncle has equipment he's been trying to sell and my cousins and I all know how to work it. We keep distribution purely local, and work on a handful of beers that complement both what we offer at the Brew-ha Cafe and what you'll be offering at Shady Palms Winery."

Pete and Xander looked convinced, but Ronnie and Izzy were having a conversation with their eyes. Elena, sensing there were still holdouts, added, "And unlike with fruit-based alcohol, beer doesn't have a season. You don't have to worry about fresh produce having a bad year or deal with high shipping or import prices. You can just brew all year round during your wine downtime. And of course, once produce is in season, we can experiment with more interesting flavors. Didn't you say you wanted to put Filipino-inspired alcohol on the map? I love a good coconut ale, and it'd complement your coconut wine nicely. And I had an interesting ube IPA once. Wouldn't that be a fun experiment?"

Izzy's eyes widened and she leaned forward. "Ooh, was it the Ube Milkshake IPA? It was interesting, but I kept thinking that it could be even better. I'd love to get involved in something like that, wouldn't you, Ronnie?"

Ronnie could fight Pete and Xander on this all he wanted, but if Izzy was in, then he was a goner. "Absolutely. Sounds like a good way to supplement our offerings. But it's still going to take some money up front to get that equipment and set everything up. Not to mention ingredients, bottling supplies, labeling . . . and are we even allowed to house the beer and wine equipment together in the same space?"

Xander waved his hand. "Let me handle that. I'll put up the capital and there's a building on the winery grounds that's perfect for a small-scale brewery. Elena and I can work out the details; you three don't have to worry about a thing."

Elena grinned and stuck out her hand. "So we've got a deal?"

"Absolutely," Xander said, shaking her hand. "We'll set up a meeting later to make this more official, and you can have your lawyer look over the terms. But I'm excited about our new business venture."

"New business venture? What's going on, Xander?" Olivia appeared beside us, her cheeks tinged pink from the cold and Longganisa and Poe on their leashes beside her. Their tongues were hanging out and they looked like they were having the time of their lives. I had been so into Elena's pitch, I must've missed the sound of the door chimes announcing her arrival.

"An exciting partnership with the fantastic Brew-ha Cafe. Elena here had a great idea on how to expand the winery, and we were just—"

"But what about my idea?" Olivia said, interrupting him. "You've been holding out on this for months, but you've accepted a total stranger's pitch in five minutes?"

"Olivia, let's talk about this later. I told you, your idea isn't fully formed yet. You still need—"

This time, I did hear the door chimes and they announced an un-expected guest: Detective Park. I'd almost forgotten that he'd gone to question Quentin, but if he had taken the trouble to come to the cafe and not just wait until our usual breakfast at Tita Rosie's Kitchen to-morrow, something must be up.

He came up to our table and greeted us quietly before saying, "I have some news that concerns all of you. Lila, is there somewhere we can talk? And Ms. March, I'd like to speak to you first. Privately."

Adeena and Elena said they'd finish up the workshop for me, so I let Detective Park and Olivia into my office, then led the rest of the group to the kitchen, being careful not to make eye contact with the PTA Squad or anyone else who didn't bother pretending they weren't watching our procession. Pete demanded the detective explain why he needed to talk to them, but Detective Park just repeated that it was a private matter.

Once we reached the kitchen, the group huddled together near the oven, everyone too tense to sit down. We didn't have to wait long for Detective Park and Olivia to return, the latter's eyes red and her face tear-streaked. Detective Park cut to the chase.

"Quentin March is currently in a coma. We found him in his hotel room with an empty syringe in his hand. We're not sure if this was an accidental overdose or a suicide attempt, but since you're his only family and friends in town, I wanted to let you know ASAP. Detective Nowak will be coming to talk to you all individually. I'm sorry to say that he feels this might be connected to the Denise Sutton case, so only family is allowed to visit him and he will be under 24/7 police surveillance."

"Wait, connected how? As in, he might be the murderer? Or the murderer thought Quentin knew something and tried to silence him?" Xander asked.

"I'm afraid I'm not privy to Detective Nowak's thought process on his investigation. He just wanted me to give you all a heads-up and ask you not to leave town anytime soon."

"But—" Xander cut his rebuttal short when he saw the tears coursing down Olivia's cheeks, her hand clutching Pete's arm. Pete and Ronnie were awkwardly patting her hand and shoulder, respectively, but Xander swept them aside and wrapped her in a hug. "I'm so sorry, Olivia. Do you want me to drop you off at the hospital?"

She pushed him away. "This is all your fault. If you hadn't fired him, he wouldn't have . . ." She stopped, choking on her tears, and this time when Xander tried to hug her, she let him. "He's all I have left, you know?"

She leaned into Xander's hug for a moment before pulling back with a sniffle. "Wait, you said he was found in our hotel room? Is it considered a crime scene now?"

Detective Park glanced at his watch. "I believe they've finished examining it, but it hasn't been released yet. Unfortunately, there aren't any other vacancies at the hotel. Do you have a place to stay?"

"No, I don't know anyone here." She glared at Xander. "Not anyone I can trust, anyway."

Xander started to protest, then stopped himself. "I'm sorry you feel that way, Olivia. The priority is that you feel safe and comfortable, so it's fine. Take all the time you need. And I really am sorry about your brother."

There was an awkward silence after this, where we could all see Izzy, Ronnie, and Pete having a silent argument with their eyes. I wasn't quite sure who the winner was, but Izzy eventually said, "Hey,

Olivia . . . why don't you stay with us for a bit? Just until you can get back in your room."

If Izzy's less than enthusiastic invitation deterred her, Olivia made no comment. "Thanks so much! Can we stop and pick up a few things I'll need? I really appreciate this."

And with that, the group turned around and filed out of the kitchen in a protective huddle around Olivia. I hung back with Detective Park because I knew him well enough by now to know that he was holding back. "What didn't you want to say in front of them?"

"They're all still suspects, so I didn't want to tip them off, but unless this is all an elaborate setup, I think Quentin was your black-mailer. We found unmailed letters addressed to your aunt's restaurant in his room. That's partially why Detective Nowak thinks this might've been a suicide attempt tied to the Denise Sutton case. He was already caught stealing by Xander and it was only a matter of time before his other crimes caught up with him. That's his reasoning, anyway."

"And what do you think?"

Detective Park sighed, the most bone-weary sound I'd ever heard. "I think the department is going to choose whatever theory is most convenient. Detective Nowak is a good guy and I don't doubt he's genuine in his reasoning. But he doesn't know how the sheriff oper-ates, and if this allows him to wrap up a sticky case quickly and cleanly, not to mention his very first case as a detective, I don't think he's going to question the sheriff's motives all that much."

He paused, noting the dismay on my face. "Though I do agree that Quentin was likely your family's blackmailer. Considering his con-nection to your cousin's investors and that he was always around the group, it wouldn't be too hard for him to learn about your cousin's previous . . . well, not quite indiscretions, but his connection to poor business practices. So cheer up. Whether or not the case is solved is beside the point, at least regarding your involvement. We found the blackmailer, so your aunt is safe. You can rest easy now and enjoy the holidays."

"Rest easy and enjoy the holidays." That's the sentiment we repeated to Adeena and Elena as we were cleaning and locking up the cafe, and again when Detective Park followed me home to talk to Tita Rosie and Lola Flor.

But I couldn't ignore the growing sense of unease building in me. Was Detective Park right? Or was the worst yet to come?

Chapter Twenty-four

After the bombshell Detective Park dropped, I tried my best to relax, I really did. I slipped into my favorite comfy onesie, made a big bowl of popcorn, and snuggled on the couch with Longganisa to watch the latest holiday romance on Netflix. But I just couldn't turn off my brain.

Was my family really safe, or was there still a blackmailer/killer out there? My gut told me that Quentin might be one of those things, but he wasn't both. I didn't know why I felt that way—was it because Xander was so sure? Or was I just stubborn and refused to accept the simplest answer?—I just knew that I couldn't let it go.

Giving up on my relaxing night in, I turned off the TV and shuffled to the kitchen to see what I could throw together. Olivia could probably use some comfort food right now and I had enough ingredients to attempt the ube brownie recipe I'd been working on. The ube base came together quickly and I folded in some white chocolate chunks for extra richness and sweetness. While they baked, I came up with a plan. I'd take the brownies over to Ronnie's apartment, saying I wanted to do my part to comfort Olivia. I wasn't quite sure what I'd do or say once I got there, but I hoped inspiration would strike or they'd give me an opening I could use to delve deeper into the case.

I texted Tita Rosie for Ronnie's address (I wanted to surprise him so he wouldn't have a chance to pretend he was out or hide anything incriminating) and had to laugh at myself for my usual super well-thought-out investigation plan:

Step 1: Bake brownies

Step 2: ???

Step 3: Solve mystery

Well, it had worked twice before, and if it ain't broke, don't fix it, right?

I pulled up to the condo that Ronnie shared with Pete and Izzy, a newer development in the "up and coming" area of Shady Palms. Tita Rosie and Lola Flor had been trying to get him to invite us over for ages, but he'd put it off, saying they were still unpacking and not ready for visitors yet. He couldn't turn me away when I was already here though, right?

Crossing my fingers that his Midwestern hospitality would kick in, I grabbed the bag with my ube white chocolate brownies, rice, and a container of Tita Rosie's vegan ginisang munggo, left over from a previous dinner party, then headed to the door. I scanned the names listed and pressed the button next to their name plate. Waited for a moment. Pressed again. I'd reached my hand up to press for a third time when Pete's voice crackled over the speaker.

"Who is it?"

"Hey Pete, it's Lila. Sorry to just drop in on you all, but I wanted to bring some food for everybody. I know it's been a rough night."

Silence greeted my response and for a minute I thought he was just going to leave me to freeze out there on his doorstep when he finally answered.

"Hold on, Ronnie will be right down."

He'd be right down? Why couldn't they buzz me up?

I asked Pete that but this time he really did just leave me waiting out in the cold. I stamped my feet to warm up (and to let out some frustration) while I waited for Ronnie to come down, wondering what the heck was going on. I was busy texting the Brew-ha group chat about this when Ronnie finally opened the lobby door.

"Hey Cuz, thanks for the food. That was really sweet of you." He stood in the doorway, blocking the entrance, a clear indicator that he wasn't going to invite me inside. "You didn't have to come all this way though, I could've picked it up from the restaurant."

"Yeah well, I figured you'd all be tired and I still haven't seen your place yet, so I could kill two birds with one stone." I held up the bag. "So, are you going to let me in or . . . ?"

"Oh, I'm sorry, man, but we just got back from picking up some of Olivia's things and she's getting settled in right now. I don't think it's a good time for visitors. But hey, I'll make sure to let her know you were thinking of her."

He reached for the bag, but I kept it just out of reach. "You sure I can't come up really quick? I kind of have to use the bathroom . . ."

I did an awkward dance, as if I had to pee and was trying really hard to hold it in. Not my best work, but I tried to sell it as best as I could.

"It's not that far a drive back, I'm sure you could—" Ronnie's refusal was cut off when Izzy squeezed past him to hurry outside.

"Sorry about that!" she called out. "Hi, Lila, bye, Lila! Don't wait up for me."

Ronnie and I watched her hustle over to her car—considering how fast she'd moved, I expected her to peel out immediately, but she sat there for a bit, possibly waiting for the car to heat up.

"What's that about?" I asked.

"Wish I knew," he said, looking just as perplexed as I felt. "She's been disappearing like that a lot lately. I thought Pete was just being overprotective when he first complained about it, but even I've noticed that she's been acting weird the last few weeks."

So Izzy was keeping secrets from her roommates and business partners, huh? Everyone's entitled to their privacy, but considering we were all involved in blackmail, murder, and a (supposed) suicide attempt, I couldn't pass up the chance to find out what she was hiding.

As soon as Izzy pulled out of her spot, I shoved the bag at Ronnie. "Here, enjoy. You're right, I can just go at home."

Trying to move quickly without being obvious, I made my way back to my car and counted out thirty seconds before following Izzy out of the lot. It was only eight o'clock, but it was already pitch-black out and the brightness of my headlights made it hard to hide the fact that I was tailing her. I called Adeena and Elena on speakerphone to see if they had any suggestions on how to follow someone without getting caught and to let them know what I was doing in case this turned dangerous.

Luckily, both of them picked up and I was able to fill them in on what was happening. "So, any bright ideas? I'm also not sure what I'm doing once we get to wherever her destination is."

"What direction are you heading? That might help you figure out where she's going in case you lose her," Elena said.

I took a moment to study the area we were passing through. "It looks like she's going to Shelbyville. Oh good, there's more cars here, so I can stay a few spots behind her."

"Perfect," Adeena said. "Keep your distance and we'll stay on the phone with you. We can't really make a plan till we know where she's going and if she's going to meet someone. Fingers crossed that whatever she's doing, you can watch safely from far away."

The two of them kept me company as I followed Izzy to the neighboring town of Shelbyville and down their main strip. She parked in front of a bar that I wasn't familiar with but must've been popular considering the noise level and number of people I could see hanging out in front smoking and chatting despite the wintry weather. I watched her duck her head and scurry past the smokers to enter the bar.

"Izzy just went inside a place called Wily Cow Emporium. Should I follow her in?"

"Ooh, I've been meaning to check that place out!" Elena said. "My cousins told me they have some awesome house brews and their own microbrewery. The food's supposed to be good, too."

"Want us to come up and meet you? You can pretend that we're having a girls' night out and just happened to be there. Don't want to make her suspicious," Adeena said.

"That's my Plan B. I have no idea how long she'll be staying here and don't want to make you come all the way here for nothing. The place is packed, so I'm sure it's safe and you both know where I am." I parked my car and looked around to see if there was anyone suspicious skulking about. Negative.

"If you don't hear from me in an hour, alert Detective Park and my family. And I just shared my location with you both," I added before hanging up. Bless smartphones for making amateur sleuthing easier and safer.

I pulled my hat down and grabbed my purse before heading into the crowded bar. As I scanned the space, I noted that every table had ordered a burger, the amazing stack of patties and condiments towering so high, I was amazed people could bite into it without unhinging their jaws. They looked pretty darn good, is what I was trying to say. I should check to see if they had veggie burgers since Adeena and Elena were already interested in the place.

After I found Izzy, of course. My momentary burger-induced lapse made me lose sight of her, and I cursed the fact that my brain was controlled by my stomach.

"Excuse me, how many in your party?"

I was so in my head, I didn't realize the seating hostess was talking to me until she repeated herself at a louder pitch.

"Excuse me! Miss? Are you waiting for somebody? Or are you putting your name down for a table?" She gestured to the tablet in her hand.

"Oh sorry! Um, I'm waiting for someone. Is it OK if I grab a seat at the bar until they arrive?" That would be a decent vantage point to spot Izzy.

The hostess said it was all right and gave her recommendation from the pub's extensive list of draft beers. I thanked her and headed to the bar area, which extended along the entire back wall. I managed to find a seat near the edge of the bar and hopped up on a stool to get a better look at the menu. No offense to the friendly hostess, but I wasn't really a beer person—at least they had a selection of ciders to tempt me. Maybe I should bring Jae here, too.

Figuring I'd look odd sitting by myself without a drink, especially since I kept staring at random tables trying to find Izzy, I waved a hand to flag down the bartender.

"What can I get—Lila? What're you doing here?"

Izzy nearly dropped the glass she'd been cleaning as she came to take my order. She had on a tight black T-shirt emblazoned with the name of the pub, cutoffs, and cowboy boots, similar to what the other female servers were wearing. My super sleuthing skills (as well as the fact that, you know, she was behind the bar wearing the same outfit as the rest of the staff) told me she worked here. Had she been wearing this getup under her giant winter coat? She must've to get here so fast, but why all the cloak and dagger? If a side gig as a bartender was her big secret, talk about anticlimactic. Which made me wonder: Why hide this from Ronnie and Pete?

I wanted to ask her straight out, but didn't want her to get defensive, so I stuck with my original plan. "Izzy! What a surprise! Adeena and Elena are supposed to meet me in a little bit. Elena's cousins told her this was a great beer spot and we wanted to check it out, see if the pub would stock the brews Elena plans on making with you all."

She gave a tight smile. "That's a great idea. People come from all around to sample the beer flights here. Can I get you anything?"

"To be honest, I don't really like beer. Can you recommend a cider that's not too dry?"

She winked at me. "I've got just the thing. Want me to open a tab for you?"

I didn't, but I needed an excuse for her to continue checking in on me. "Sure, why not? I told them the drinks would be on me for handling closing tonight."

She moved to get my drink and I texted the other two about what I'd just learned. I put my phone facedown on the bar and it vibrated immediately. Dang, they were fast.

Hey, where are you? I know it's late but I feel like I never see you

Aww, Jae. He was right, we hadn't had any alone time since Ronnie arrived. A date night sounded good and might prove to be the perfect opening with Izzy. I told him where I was and begged him to join me, attaching a photo of the impressive cider list to tempt him.

Haha I would've come even without the draw of a cider but good to know 😉

Heading over now, see you in 20

I responded with a kissy face emoji and put my phone down just as Izzy returned with my drink.

"That's a pretty big smile you've got right now. Were you chatting with your guy?" she said, setting the glass down on a coaster in front of me.

I tried to hide it, but that just led to a bigger grin. "Jae's coming to meet me here. We haven't been spending enough time together with everything that's been going on lately, and—Oh shoot, I should ask Adeena and Elena for a rain check. Hopefully they haven't left yet."

I texted the girls about the change of plans and they both sent me thumbs-up emojis to let me know they got the message. Adeena also sent a bunch of kissy faces, which I rolled my eyes at.

"He's a sweet guy. You two look good together," Izzy said, leaning her arms on the bar.

"Thanks. You and Pete are cute together, too," I said. Picking up my glass, I added, "Does he also work here?"

Izzy had been wiping up a spill from another customer, but she stilled at that question. "Uh, no, he doesn't. He also doesn't know I work here, so please don't say anything."

"He doesn't? How about Ronnie?"

She shook her head.

I took a sip of the cider as I thought about how I wanted to frame the next question. Dang, it was really good. Sweet and tart and not the least bit bitter.

"Well, first of all, you are excellent at your job because this is easily the best cider I've ever had." She smiled at that, so I pressed on. "Second, I won't say anything if you don't want me to, but why are you keeping it a secret from them? It's not like you're doing anything wrong."

She held up her hand to tell me to wait a moment and took the order of the person next to me. As she pulled the draft, she said, "I don't want to embarrass Pete."

She handed over the beer with a big smile and thanked the customer when they slid her a big tip, which she stuffed in her back pocket. She helped a few more customers, moving swiftly and smoothly to fulfill their drink orders, and each time was greeted with what seemed to be a sizeable tip, based on the grin on her face when she took back their receipts or slid the cash in her pocket.

"Wow, your customer base are really generous tippers," I said, with more than a little envy. Service workers often lived and died by their tips.

"Which is why I took on this gig. The three of us ate here when we first arrived, and I noticed the overall great vibes of the place and its customers." Izzy fiddled with her engagement ring, looking like she had more to say. This was a woman who needed to get something off her chest, and with a bit of patience, I'd get what I came here for. I took another sip of my cider and waited it out.

"Remember when you asked me about my wedding? To tell you the truth, I really do want a grand wedding. I want the fancy dress and huge reception and beautiful photos. I want a spread people will be talking about for days. I want my parents to be able to brag about it to all their friends. I want it all. But our funds are all tied up in the winery, and it wasn't a problem before, but recently Pete stopped putting money in our shared wedding account."

She seemed so ashamed to admit this, she couldn't even look at me. "He comes from money and he assured me that I'd have the wedding of my dreams once the winery was up and running. But when I checked the account a few weeks ago, I noticed that the amount hadn't changed in a while. He used to deposit the check his father sent him every week, so I don't know what happened."

"You didn't ask him?"

She shook her head. "He's been fighting with his dad lately, and I thought it might be a sore subject. Besides, I'm an adult, not some kept woman. I figured I could work a few extra shifts and deposit the money myself as a surprise when it was time to wedding plan."

She didn't come out and say it, but there was something in her tone and demeanor that made me think Pete had a lot of pride. If she thought she had to keep her job a secret, he likely considered himself a provider and put a lot of his self-worth into that idea. I knew the type—my ex-fiancé was the same way. I just hoped Pete appreciated all this extra work Izzy was putting in.

"I guess that makes sense. But why hide it from Ronnie?"

She laughed. "Are you kidding? You think that big mouth could keep a secret? Anyway, I don't plan on working here much longer. Our names have been cleared and we can get back to production soon."

Before I could press her on that, my phone vibrated with a message from Jae letting me know he'd arrived. I told him to put our names down for a table and I'd be there in a minute.

Izzy slid over my card and receipt when I finished. "I figured that was Jae, so I closed out your tab. Thanks for listening, Lila. I really appreciate it."

I signed the slip and left her a good tip to thank her for the info. "Anytime. I hope it all works out for you, Izzy. And don't worry, your secret's safe with me."

Well, and with Jae and Adeena and Elena, too. But she didn't need to know that.

Chapter Twenty-five

Fairy lights twinkled all around the community center party room, giving a lovely otherworldly vibe to the usually plain, utilitarian space. The room looked like a tinsel bomb had gone off because every surface was strewn with lights, silver and gold starry tinsel, and paper streamers. And I mean every surface. The decorating committee had tried to wrap lights around our electric kettle and only backed off when I pointed out the very clear fire hazard. They let us wrap tinsel around the handle and called it a day.

Classical covers of modern pop songs piped out of the speakers, a nice cultural and generational compromise for all, and served as a festive backdrop to all the laughter and banter as people wandered from table to table, enjoying free samples and lessons while also buying food and products from local Shady Palms businesses. I was familiar with the town's restaurants and had already planned on doing a food tour once it was my turn for a break, visiting my friends at Big Bishop's BBQ, Sushi-ya, Stan's Diner, and El Gato Negro. However, this was a good chance for me to get to know the other small business owners. I'd spoken to most of them at chamber of commerce meetings but had only ever spent time with Sana and Yuki. I scanned the room until I found Sana leading a jazzercise class (which had become strangely popular in our town) in the corner, Amir sweating along to the oldies with her and looking like he was having the time of his life.

Jae was sitting next to me, helping me run the Brew-ha Cafe table instead of enjoying the Shady Palms Winter Bash like everyone else. His dental practice kept him busy most of the week, so the fact that he was spending his limited free time working meant everything to me.

Though the way he was looking at me, fondly and without a hint of judgment, was making me uncomfortable. I wasn't used to such open affection, not without the fear of a backhanded compliment directly behind it.

"Adeena and Elena will be back soon. You can go have fun, you know. Pretty sure Tita Rosie has a plate set aside for you." I gestured to my family's table, trying to ignore the fact that Ronnie was there. I still wasn't sure what to do with the information I'd found on his computer and how best to approach him about it. Other than the cookie-decorating workshop from the other day (which was absolutely *not* the right time or place for a confrontation), he'd been keeping a low profile and I hadn't had a chance for a one-on-one chat.

Detective Park should've been at my family's table, but he was the perfect example of how even a good cop was subject to department bureaucracy—our town's sheriff was both lazy and vindictive and Detective Park was all too familiar with what happened when he pushed too hard (which he'd been doing pretty much since he first arrived in our town).

Such as Winter Bash security being foisted on him, despite being the department's most experienced member and one of only two detectives. He was currently on duty, but I could see his eyes straying over to my aunt's table every now and then. He was on the outs with her, thanks to a recent argument they had over Ronnie, and it hurt to see how badly he wanted to be with her.

A hand waved in front of my face, jolting me out of my thoughts. Jae laughed and held out a cup of coffee and plate of cookies. "You realize you asked me a question and then promptly spaced out, right? Here, eat something. You look like you could use something sweet."

There was nothing sweeter than him, this gorgeous cinnamon roll of a man, but I didn't say that. "Thanks. I didn't want to eat from our table in case I didn't make enough, but a few cookies wouldn't hurt, right?"

Jae, who'd just dug into one of my mason jar trifles, froze, a spoonful of cake halfway to his mouth. "I'm so sorry, I didn't think of that! And there are so few trifles. I should've saved them for your customers."

He gazed forlornly at the few jars left on the table, looking like Longganisa when I denied her a treat. OK, maybe I shouldn't be comparing him to my dachshund, but they both had the same big brown eyes that melted my heart whenever they looked at me. Who wouldn't want to be favorably compared to the cutest dog in the world? I reached out to touch his cheek when—

"Hey Cuz! The table looks great."

Ronnie, Izzy, Pete, and Xander were all grinning at Jae and me as they helped themselves to the sweets on the table. Well, Ronnie and Izzy were grinning at us. Pete wore his usual politely bland expression, and Xander's sad attempt at a smile had me worried. It had only been a couple of days since Quentin was hospitalized and according to both Detective Park and Bernadette (who I of course pumped for info), there was no change in his condition. Despite everything Quentin had done to him, the dark circles under Xander's eyes had me wondering if he cared more about the twins than he'd let on.

The Calendar Crew, who could sense drama brewing way before any of us were even aware there was an issue, left my aunt and grandmother's table to come join us.

"Here Xander, you look so tired. This will fortify you," Ninang Mae said, shoving a whole bibingka and cup of tsokolate at him.

"I also have a bowl of champorado for you when you're ready," Ninang June said, holding up her offering.

"Ay, you two, he needs more than sweets. Here Xander, eat this siopao first. I got you one asado and one bola-bola since I wasn't sure which was your favorite," Ninang April said, handing over two steamed, meat-filled buns.

Bernadette came over and greeted us all before handing Xander a bottle of water. "Sorry about the onslaught, but you've spent enough time with them to know how they are."

He smiled at Bernadette and the Calendar Crew, a real smile, and the women all let out a sigh of contentment. "Thank you, ladies. I feel bad making you all fuss over me, but I appreciate it. Let's grab a table so we can enjoy our food together. Any of you want to join us?"

The rest of us shook our heads, indicating we had to stay with our table, and they left chattering happily, though Ninang June threw a few suspicious looks Ronnie's way.

"Why does that woman keep glaring at us?" Pete asked, his blond eyebrows furrowing as he studied Ninang June.

Ronnie sighed. "Probably 'cause I'm here. You're just getting it through association."

Pete snorted. "Yeah, we have to deal with a lot being associated with you. You could've prepared us better about what it'd be like living here."

Izzy put her hand on Pete's arm and gave him a look. Pete shrugged and helped himself to more of Adeena's house blend, purposely not meeting anyone's eyes.

Despite all their talk about them being best friends, I always got the sense Izzy and Ronnie were the ones who were BFFs and Pete was the boyfriend who pretended to be open-minded but was really keeping watch to make sure nothing happened between his girlfriend and this dude that was always hanging around. I knew the type. My high school boyfriend, Derek, was that type. I'd become friends with Terrence through Derek since they were best buds from the football team, but Terrence and I had quickly grown close because we had an immediate connection. I'd thought the reason Derek had always pushed for the four of us to hang out, him and Terrence with me and Adeena, was because he was trying to get Adeena and Terrence together. But even after Adeena came out and Terrence had started dating other people, he still insisted on group activities. I was too young and in love to understand that he was watching me and Terrence for signs that we were fooling around behind his back. It wasn't until after we'd broken up and both Adeena and Terrence pointed it out that I'd realized.

So I knew what to look out for.

"Do you need us to take over for you, Lila?" Izzy asked, breaking into my thoughts.

"No, thanks, Adeena and Elena should be here soon. Maybe you could take some coffee over to Tita Rosie and Lola Flor though? They look exhausted."

Izzy agreed, pouring mugs of the house blend and doctoring the brew with cream and sugar according to my specifications. She then made her way over to my family's table, Ronnie trailing behind her with a plate of cookies for his mom. Pete stayed behind, pouring himself another cup of coffee and grabbing a chai gingerbread biscuit to dunk.

As I watched him study our table, deciding what snack to grab next, I realized I knew next to nothing about him. Based on some things Izzy had said and his fashion choices, he probably came from money. Not necessarily big money like Denise and Xander, but he was definitely no stranger to country club living, despite the work he'd done with Izzy and Ronnie after college. He seemed dull, but that could just be because he was always with Ronnie and Izzy, whose larger personalities could easily overshadow a quieter presence. This was my chance to speak to him one-on-one and learn more about him, but I had no clue where to start. Luckily, I had someone with me who was excellent at small talk and could get the ball rolling. I nudged Jae and nodded my head toward Pete, sending a silent signal to start a conversation.

Picking up my cue, Jae turned to Pete and said, "Hey man, you're really enjoying that coffee, huh? Let me get you a refill." Jae topped off his cup from the box on the table, and Pete thanked him with a small smile. Jae filled a cup for himself before saying, "You know, we've never had a chance to really talk before. How are you doing? Other than all the, you know. Are you settling in OK?"

Pete snorted. "You know, you're the first person to ask me that? Everyone here fawns all over Ronnie and Xander and even Izzy, but no one else has thought to pay any attention to me."

I frowned. "You had the entire PTA Squad drooling over you at the workshop. We've invited you to our house, which you turned down, and our restaurant is always open to you."

"Yes, but I haven't exactly felt welcome." Pete studied me. "I bet you're hoping Izzy breaks off the engagement so she can be with your cousin. I see how close she's been getting to your family."

I'd been sipping atole and nearly did a spit take when he said this. After my coughing fit, I said, "Excuse me? I wouldn't wish that on anyone. A broken engagement or my cousin, for that matter. Not if she's happy, anyway."

Pete's eyebrows shot up. "Really? That's a surprise. Most people seem to prefer Ronnie over me."

Now it was my turn for my eyebrows to shoot up. "I don't know you, but I do know Ronnie and, well . . . you seem like the practical one of the trio."

His eyes darkened. "You mean the boring one."

"No, the one who keeps the lights on and the ship running smoothly."

Pete lit up. "So you do get it! Ronnie may be the charming one, but that's not enough to get the girl."

Was this a typical guy thing? To always be in competition with each other, even your best friend? Some major Derek flashbacks were going on right now. But then I caught Jae's eye and thought, no, not all guys were like this. But it let me know exactly what buttons to push . . .

I leaned against the table, careful to keep my tone nonchalant. "The way you're talking makes it seem like Ronnie's in love with your fiancée."

Pete rolled his eyes. "Of course Ronnie's in love with her. But I don't care. She'd never leave me. Izzy's the type of girl who craves security. She doesn't want to be like her family, living paycheck to paycheck, relying on their oldest daughter for everything. That's one of the things that drew her to me. I'm stable. I'm secure. She needs me. If she were to leave, it wouldn't be for someone like Ronnie, who can barely take care of his kid, let alone support a whole family."

The table slid away as I put too much pressure on it, and I stumbled before Jae caught my arm and righted me. "I'm sorry, what? His kid?"

Pete, for all that he was ranting about Ronnie, must've still considered him a friend because he realized his mistake and clammed up. "Uh sorry, I'm getting a call, I've gotta take this." And just like that, he walked away holding a fake phone conversation.

There's no way. There was no way Ronnie had a child and didn't tell us. Unless . . . maybe that's what those payments were about? Ronnie was getting calls from a woman named Penny, and she had to be the same person that those monthly payments were going to. Could it be those weren't blackmail payments, but child support?

On the one hand, good on him for not being a deadbeat dad, at least regarding monetary support. On the other hand, why was he keeping this a secret? Didn't he know how much Tita Rosie would love having a grandchild? Didn't he know how much love she had to give? The more I thought about it, the angrier I got. As I watched him talking and laughing with his mom, knowing he was keeping this huge secret from her, something in me snapped.

I marched over to Ronnie, not even bothering to tell Adeena, Elena, or Jae what I was about to do, and shoved him while he was mid-sentence.

"So then I was like, what the—! What was that for?" Ronnie, not anticipating my sudden attack, had been knocked completely off-balance and had fallen to the floor.

"Who's Penny?" I demanded.

His face went white, a surprising feat considering the amount of melanin he had. "Who—who told you about Penny?"

"Who is she and why are you sending her so much money? *How* are you able to send her so much money?"

Detective Park strode over to us, probably not anticipating having to do any actual security work for this function and certainly not with my family. "What's going on here?"

"Anak?" Tita Rosie came over to help her son up and glanced between the two of us. I wasn't sure who she was addressing with that endearment, but I needed her to see who Ronnie really was.

"Ronnie, tell her. You can't hide something like this from her; she is your mother and she loves you, though Lord knows why." By this point, I was so frustrated I was speaking like every word was in italics, and it was all I could do to stop myself from clapping my hands to emphasize my words even more.

Izzy put her hand on Ronnie's arm. "You still haven't told her? You promised me you were going to talk to them. What's going on, Ronnie?"

Ronnie's eyes swept the array of faces in front of him, me angry, Izzy disappointed, and Tita Rosie confused but encouraging. He kept his gaze on his mother's face when he said, "I have a son. Penny is his mother. I've been sending them money every month as child support, and for the last few months, I've been taking money from the winery accounts to afford it."

"You *what*?!" Izzy screeched.

"I'm sorry, but you know how rough these last few months have been. The winery hasn't been raking in enough money and all those hospital visits aren't cheap. I swear I was going to put the money back once we were back on our feet," Ronnie said. He reached out a hand to Izzy, but she slapped it away.

Tita Rosie stared at him, her mouth moving but no words coming out. Finally, she managed to choke out, "How old? How old is my grandson?"

Ronnie finally had the decency to drop his gaze. "He turns three in March."

"You've kept my grandson from me for almost three years? Did you really hate me so much that you couldn't even tell me about the birth of my first grandchild?" Tita Rosie choked on a sob. Detective Park, not caring that he was on duty, wrapped her in his arms.

Lola Flor stepped out from around the table, a wooden spoon clutched in her hand. "I have a great-grandchild? And you were keeping them from me? Bakit?"

"Yes, Ronnie. Why? Why all the secrets?" I crossed my arms and glared at him.

Ronnie threw up his hands. "Because I'm tired of always being seen as a screwup! I couldn't hack it here, I couldn't make my relationship with Penny work, I couldn't take over the winery in Florida . . . becoming a dad was the best thing that ever happened to me and I didn't want you all to know in case I screwed that up, too."

Tita Rosie said, "Why would you think that? I would never—"

"Well, it's not like I had a real father to show me what to do. I had to figure it all out myself, didn't I? Because you had such poor choice in men and were too weak to leave him until he finally left you. You—"

Faster than you could believe, Lola Flor whacked him across the face with her wooden spoon. "You dare to speak to your own mother like that? You dare to . . ."

Here she stopped and moved to pull off her shoe, presumably to throw it at him. Detective Park stepped in to de-escalate the situation, but there was nothing else to do or say.

"I think you should leave," I said.

Ronnie looked at his crying mother, wrapped in Detective Park's protective arms. At the steel in mine and Lola Flor's eyes as we stood in front of them, shielding Tita Rosie from her thoughtless son. At the Calendar Crew and Bernadette, the expressions on their faces letting him know they'd been expecting him to mess up and that they were right to treat him like a screwup this whole time. And finally, at Izzy, who was staring at him in shock and disappointment and hurt.

Annoyingly, it seemed like the fact that he'd hurt Izzy was what finally got through to him. He muttered an apology and left, his head hanging low, and almost bumped into Pete, who was returning to join us.

"Hey man, what's going on?" Pete asked.

But Ronnie kept walking away, not bothering to look up or even acknowledge his partner. Izzy pulled Pete aside and whispered to him about everything that happened.

After a few beats, Pete said, "I'm gonna go check on him. Make sure he doesn't do anything stupid."

Izzy tried to follow him, but he put a hand on her shoulder. "I think it's best if it's just me. He might be a little more open that way—he knows he hurt you. You should stay here and try to have fun. You've been looking forward to this party since we arrived."

Izzy forced a smile and nodded, and Pete dropped a quick kiss on her head before taking off after Ronnie. The rest of us tried to go about our business and pretend like nothing was wrong—Tita Rosie and Lola Flor went back behind their table to greet people and dish out food while Izzy tagged along with Jae and me as we visited some of the other tables at the bash. I tried to network with the other business owners like I'd originally planned, but my heart wasn't in it and Jae could tell.

He put a hand on the small of my back and leaned close. "Why don't we hang out with your aunt and grandmother? Or maybe we could take over for them so they could enjoy the party?"

I was about to agree when he glanced over my shoulder and stiffened. Before I could ask what happened, he grabbed my hand and dragged me over to my family's table, where Mayor Gunderson and Detective Park were getting into it.

"You're out of line, Detective. Maybe if you spent more time keeping an eye on the Winter Bash like you were supposed to instead of making eyes at your girl, we wouldn't have this problem." Mayor

Gunderson, dressed in the silvery-blue, snowflake-patterned blazer he wore every Winter Bash, stood in front of our table with his chest puffed out, staring down Detective Park.

I slid behind the table to be next to Tita Rosie. "What's going on?"

She shook her head, her face reflecting the bone weariness she must be feeling. "Mayor Gunderson came over to complain about the scene Ronnie caused earlier. He said Detective Park should've done a better job of preventing it."

I rolled my eyes. "Mayor Gunderson, this is ridiculous. There's no way Detective Park could've prevented the argument, and it's not like it hurt the bash in any way, so what's the big deal?"

The mayor whirled around to glare at me. "The big deal is that your family already ruined the Founder's Day Festival. I don't need you mucking up the Winter Bash as well!"

"They did not ruin the Founder's Day Festival, they saved it! Lila caught the murderer that you and Sheriff Lamb insisted wasn't around anymore. Your need to keep up appearances is what nearly ruined the festival." Detective Park leaned closer and closer to Mayor Gunderson as he delivered this tirade. He must've noticed that he'd backed the mayor into our table because he stepped away suddenly, shaking his head. "Neither you nor the sheriff give a damn about anybody in this town. And I'm tired of having to clean up after your messes. I'm done."

With nothing more than a quick glance at my aunt and an "I'll call you later, Rosie," Detective Park marched out of the room.

Mayor Gunderson looked shaken up, but when he noticed us all staring at him, he made a big show of adjusting his blazer and letting out a *harrumph*. "I never expected the good detective to act so common. I really must speak with Sheriff Lamb about him."

"What a sad man," Ninang April said as we watched him storm off.

The Calendar Crew had arrived during all the excitement and were now staring daggers into the back of Shady Palms's mayor.

"Rosie, why don't you head on home? We can take over for you if you need to rest," Ninang June said. "You too, Tita Flor."

"No thank you. I'd rather keep working, but you can go if you want, Nay," my aunt said.

"If you're staying then I'm staying," Lola Flor said.

"No, it's fine, really. You've been cooking all morning, you can go home."

"You've cooked just as much as I have and your son is adding to your gray hairs again. You should go home."

While this back and forth between a grown woman and her mother went on, Izzy got a text. It wouldn't have caught my attention if she hadn't studied the message for a moment before gasping.

"What is it?" I asked.

"I got a message from Ronnie."

"And?"

"I'm . . . not sure actually." She showed me her screen, which showed a text from Ronnie that was just an ellipsis.

"Dot dot dot?" I asked. "Does that mean anything to you?"

"Sort of? Back in college, we'd devised a secret code that we would text each other if we ever needed help getting out of something. This was before Pete and I were together, and they worried about me every time I went on a date. The deal was that if I texted '. . . ' to either of them, they were to call immediately and pretend that something happened and they needed me to come back. Ronnie actually used it more than me since he went on so many bad dates and was too chicken to be honest with the girl." She tilted her head, her eyes on her screen. "We haven't used this code in years."

"Maybe you should call him back?" I suggested.

"Yeah . . . yeah, you're right. I'm just, I'm still so angry at him, you

know? But we promised to only use the code if we needed to, so . . ."
She took a deep breath and called Ronnie.

His phone went straight to voicemail.

"That's odd," she said, and tried again. And again.

Each time the call went to voicemail, and each time the uneasy feeling in the pit of my stomach grew.

"Lila, I can't reach him," Izzy said, her eyes wide. Did she also sense that something was wrong?

I grabbed her hand. "Let's go."

And hand-in-hand, we rushed off to find my cousin.

Chapter Twenty-six

Pete had driven them to the Winter Bash, so we took my car to the apartment they shared on the edge of town. Izzy unlocked the door and ran in, calling Ronnie's name.

No answer.

While Izzy called Pete to see if he was with Ronnie, I wandered around the space. It was a two-bedroom apartment, but it looked like someone had slept on the couch the other night. Several pillows and blankets were piled on the couch and a stack of suitcases was lined up next to it. The coffee table in front of the couch held a plate with a slice of half-eaten toast and the congealed leftovers of scrambled eggs next to an empty glass. A small glass bottle and open box of syringes sat next to it. I picked up the bottle and studied it. Vitamin B12. This must be Olivia's stuff. Remembering how upset she got last time I touched her medicine, I set the bottle back on the table and moved on to Ronnie's room.

The room was neater than I expected, with the bed made and his dirty clothes inside a hamper rather than the floor, the way it used to be when he lived with us. On top of his dresser were several framed baby and toddler photos of the same kid—Ronnie's kid. I wondered if those photos were part of the reason my aunt, grandmother, and I had never been invited to his apartment. Honestly, what was with this town and secret babies?

I picked up the one that looked the most recent, a picture of the kid playing with a child-size basketball and hoop. He was adorable, dressed in a comic book shirt, gym shorts, and red, black, and white Jordans as he attempted to dribble the ball. My nephew.

Izzy came up behind me while I was still studying the photo. "That's Isaiah," she said. "He's the best. I really hope you get a chance to meet him."

I put the photo back on top of the dresser. "What did Pete say?"

Her brow creased. "He didn't answer. Neither did Olivia. She said she was going to have a lazy day here, so I thought maybe she'd seen the guys, but I guess not. I wonder if she had to meet Xander for something."

"Is there anywhere else Pete and Ronnie would go? Like maybe a bar they liked to hang out at after work?"

Izzy shook her head. "We were all pinching pennies, so we didn't go out much. We'd usually just grab food from your aunt's place and drink the old wine stock here at the apartment. If they're not here, the only other place I can think of is the winery."

I couldn't think of a good reason why they'd head there, but she was probably right. My gut was telling me we'd find quite a few answers at the winery.

W e drove the twenty minutes there in near silence until Izzy got another text.

"Oh, it's from Olivia!" She frowned down at her phone, which buzzed several times. "She said Xander had sent her on an errand to the winery and she saw the two of them there, but they left a few minutes ago and said they were heading back to the apartment." She glanced over at me. "Should we turn back and wait for them?"

My hands gripped the steering wheel as things started to fall into place. I was pretty sure I was right, but I had little evidence to back it up other than a gut feeling and what could possibly just be a coincidence. What to do? I thought back to Izzy getting Ronnie's emergency message and then his phone suddenly getting shut off. I was close, I knew it. And the choice I made could mean life or death for my cousin.

"No, we're almost at the winery. We might as well stop by. I've got some questions for Olivia."

I pulled into the parking lot of Shady Palms Winery and noted the cars there. Just as I thought.

Izzy stared at her fiancé's car. "I don't understand. Olivia said he already left."

I put my hand on Izzy's arm. "I'm going to send a quick message to Detective Park letting him know where we are and then we'll head inside. But you need to stay absolutely silent and follow my lead. Do you understand me?"

Her eyes filled with fear, but she nodded her head and squared her shoulders. She was ready to face the truth. The two of us entered the silent factory portion of the winery and made our way to the offices. We tried to be as stealthy as possible, but the heavy snow boots we were both wearing practically echoed in the open space around us with every footfall. We resorted to walking on exaggerated tiptoes like a bunch of cartoon characters trying to sneak around. Still, it worked. As we got closer to the office, we could hear familiar voices inside.

Izzy and I huddled behind the stacked crates of wine bottles next to the open door and tried to peer into the office without being seen or heard—it was not as easy as they made it seem on *Scooby-Doo*. Pete's broad back was blocking something at the desk, and when he stepped away, I saw Ronnie slumped in his desk chair and Olivia trying to position his unconscious form behind the desk.

"What did you do to him?" Izzy burst into the room and ran over to them.

I groaned. So much for having a plan instead of rushing in like I usually did. Well, just because Izzy blew her cover didn't mean I had to just yet. I stayed in my hiding spot by the door—maybe if they didn't know I was here, I'd still have the element of surprise if it came down to a fight. If I peeked around the stack carefully, I could make out part of the scene through the doorway. I made sure to put my phone on silent and texted Detective Park to get to the winery ASAP. At the last minute, I turned on the voice recorder on my phone and put it on top of the crate closest to the door. Who knew how long it'd take for backup to arrive, and not only did we need evidence of what happened, but Izzy might need me to get in there.

"Babe, what are you doing here?" Pete looked furious, like he wanted to shake her, but then his eyes slid over to Olivia, who was looking Izzy over carefully, almost clinically, and his expression changed to fear.

Izzy must've realized her outburst had put the two of us in danger because not only did she not mention my presence, but she came up with a great cover story. "I was worried about what Ronnie said. And, well, I got to thinking, if he was stealing from us, who's to say he wasn't involved in Denise's death? I wanted to confront him, see what he had to say for himself."

"I'm sorry. I know you always thought the best of him, but I think you're right. He insisted on coming here so he could show me how he'd been stealing from the company and to clear out his desk, but then he suddenly attacked me! If Olivia hadn't been here, who knows what would've happened."

Izzy looked at the other woman, who was still studying her. "So, what, you were able to warn him or something? Or did you help him fight off Ronnie?"

"I heard her yell and turned around in time to see that Ronnie had a wine bottle in his hand, raised to hit me, and I managed to dodge it. I was able to wrestle the bottle away and knock him out with it. See?" Pete pointed to a lone bottle of wine lying on its side on the floor. "I didn't want to do it, but I had no choice."

Izzy stooped to look at the wine bottle, and then went back over to Ronnie to examine his head. "There's no blood."

"I tried not to hit him too hard, so there's probably no marks or anything."

Izzy, who'd had to go behind Ronnie's desk to check on him, was now staring at his computer. "What is this? A suicide note?"

Pete sputtered. "Oh, uh, well that's—"

"Oh Pete, drop it already. Can't you tell she knows exactly what's going on?" Olivia finally spoke and went to stand next to Pete.

I tensed, sensing the Big Bad had finally entered the scene. Olivia had been way too calm while Pete stepped on all the conversational rakes that Izzy had laid out. So she either thought they still had the upper hand in the situation, or they were going to shut Izzy up to make sure she stayed quiet.

When she pulled out a vial and instructed Pete to grab the syringe they'd used on Ronnie, I knew it was the latter. Luckily, Pete didn't seem too happy with this turn of events and refused. Maybe there'd be enough time for Detective Park to get here after all.

Pete turned to Olivia. "You said you wouldn't hurt her!"

"And you promised to love and protect her, and all the while you were sleeping with me. So I don't see where you get off acting all wounded," Olivia said, searching through her purse. "Where is it . . . I know I packed an extra, just in case. Ah, here it is!"

"You were cheating on me? After all this time . . . even though I'd chosen you and had stayed faithful to you despite everything . . . you were going to leave me for her?" Izzy said, her eyes filling with tears.

I thought she was going to break down sobbing just when I needed her to fight, but she surprised me yet again, launching herself at Pete and scratching up his face.

"Ten years! I gave you over ten years of my life and you were going to leave me for a blackmailing murderer?"

Pete was too busy dodging her attacks to answer, but Olivia burst out laughing. "You think infidelity is his worst crime? Who do you think gave us the idea for all of this? Who suggested setting aside special bottles just for Denise and Xander? Who gave us access to everything? Who not only knew about what had happened in Florida, but also knew how to contact Ronnie's family? He's been planning this with Quentin and me for months."

That brought Izzy's furious attacks to a halt. "Months?" she whispered. "This has been your plan from the very beginning? Kill our investors and extort Ronnie's family, for what? Money?"

"Babe, it's not like that. I swear, I was doing this all for you. Every choice I've made for the last few years has been to make you happy. We can work this out."

"How could this possibly make me happy, Pete?" Tears glistened in Izzy's eyes as she confronted her fiancé. "How could this have been your only choice?"

"My family cut me off," he admitted. "They wanted me to marry the daughter of my father's partner at the firm, but I told them I only wanted you. So they said if I was going to make selfish decisions, I'd better learn to live with the consequences. Ronnie wasn't the only one who had to dip into the company's finances to pay off debt."

"Oh Pete," Izzy said, her voice barely above a whisper. I had to strain to hear her. "Why didn't you say anything?"

"I knew you only chose me over Ronnie because of my family's money. Because of the stability it provided. When I met Olivia and Quentin and heard them complaining about Denise and their inheritance, it seemed like the answer to all our problems. Ronnie had been bragging about how successful his family was, so I figured they could afford to take the hit. At least until the provisions in the will were met."

"What provisions?" Izzy asked. The look on her face told me she didn't want to know but couldn't stop herself from asking.

Pete dropped his gaze. "Olivia's father's will states that if Denise dies without an heir, his fortune would revert back to Olivia and Quentin. I had my dad's firm look at it and they confirmed that it would supersede Denise's will. We can't touch any of her assets, but anything that came from the March patriarch would go to the twins."

"So you had to murder her before she married Xander and produced an heir?" Izzy guessed.

Pete had the nerve to look at her and say, "It was the only way I knew to keep you from leaving me."

"Don't act like you were doing this all for her. It wasn't that you wanted to keep her, you just didn't want to lose her to Ronnie. You've always thought you were better than them since you were born into money. He even said he refused to live paycheck to paycheck the way you and Ronnie used to," Olivia said, pouring oil on the raging fire.

Those details were too specific for Olivia to know unless she was telling the truth—these were things Pete had said to her. The fight left Izzy's body and she crumpled into a sobbing heap on the floor.

Olivia looked down at her in distaste. "Pete, hold her down." When he hesitated, she made an exasperated sound. "She knows too much. You think she won't tell that detective who's always hanging around everything she heard here? *Hold her down*."

Resignation followed quickly by resolve flashed across Pete's face as he followed his lover's orders.

Izzy, seeing Olivia advance with the needle in her hand, began screaming her head off and bucking to get away from Pete.

To his credit, Pete had tears streaming down his face as he held her down. But it wasn't enough for him to change his mind. "I'm sorry, Izzy. I'm so sorry. Do it fast, Olivia."

It didn't look like the cops were going to arrive in time to stop them, so with Pete and Olivia finally turning their backs to the door, I was able to make my move. They were too far away for me to strike directly, so the best I could hope for was a distraction, which would allow Izzy to fight back. I hefted a wine bottle from the crate in front of me, feeling the weight of it in my hand, and, calling on all the powers of my softball-playing childhood, I chucked the bottle across the room, nailing Olivia on the shoulder.

She screamed and dropped the syringe, and Izzy, not hesitating for a second, grabbed the bottle that landed on the carpet next to her and smashed it across the side of Pete's head. He collapsed in a heap next to her. She sat there staring at him a moment, and raised the bottle again.

"Izzy, don't!"

I'd run into the room to make sure Olivia wouldn't go for the syringe again, but it seemed she'd rather escape than fight, as she slammed into me as she ran out. I fell to the floor, reaching out to stop Izzy, but she seemed to come to her senses and dropped the bottle. She continued staring at her unconscious fiancé for a few moments before scrambling to her feet to check on Ronnie.

"Call for help! I don't know what they did to him, but he still has a pulse."

My phone was still recording out in the hallway, so I used Ronnie's desk phone to call 911 and let them know what had happened and that it was likely he'd been injected with methanol. Somewhere outside the office, I heard shouting, but I ignored it until I conveyed all the information the EMTs would need when they arrived. Once I was assured help was on the way, I ran out to see what was going on.

Olivia was laid out on the floor with Bernadette on top of her, knee in her back, and they stayed like that until Detective Park cuffed Olivia and passed her off to the officers with him. Bernadette must've followed Detective Park here after he got my message and stopped Olivia from escaping.

I had never been so happy to see her. "Ate Bernie, Ronnie's been poisoned! We need you in here!"

Without hesitating for a second, Bernadette sprang up and ran past me into the room to start administering first aid to her ex-boyfriend. Bernadette was a lot of things, but first and foremost, she was a heck of a nurse.

As she got to work, I went to Ronnie's side, opposite Izzy, grabbed his hand, and did something I hadn't done in a long time.

I prayed.

Chapter Twenty-seven

Christmas Eve

Simbang Gabi went off without a hitch, and I'd used the time to
catch up with our priest and friend, Father Santiago. He'd chided
me gently for not keeping up with our weekly runs, and in turn I told
him everything that had been going on. Once the dust had settled
from everything, Xander had returned to Chicago to be with his family for the holidays, but he'd promised Ronnie and Izzy he'd be back
soon to help with the daily operations of the Shady Palms Winery and
possible expansions.

Pete and Olivia were awaiting trial for Denise's murder, Quentin's
attempted murder, theft, and blackmail—Olivia's father's lawyers
agreed to represent the twins individually but refused to post bail.
Pete's family disowned him entirely.

Quentin had recovered and was also being held for the same
charges, but he swore he'd only been part of the blackmail scheme.
Olivia and Pete had tried to kill him after he found out what they'd
done to Denise and flipped out. Last I heard, he'd entered a plea bar-

gain: considering that his dear sister tried to kill him, he was only too happy to give evidence against the other two. Amir had been giving us the updates, but I didn't want to hear any more about it. For the other two cases I'd been involved in, I could at least understand the killers' reasoning behind their crimes even if I didn't condone their methods. But these three? It was greed and jealousy, pure and simple. And I didn't want that bit of human ugliness to taint what was to be a special, magical time. So I turned my attention to the things that were important to me.

Like getting to know my nephew. Penny and Isaiah had come down from Wisconsin for Simbang Gabi to get to know our family and were leaving Christmas Day to be with Penny's family. Penny was smart, straightforward, and knew exactly how to put my cousin in his place. It turned out she was Izzy's distant cousin (Izzy introduced them) and Isaiah's asthma led to frequent hospital visits. That's what the call he'd received the day we cleaned out Denise's belongings was about, and why the winery crew had all disappeared to Wisconsin shortly after it. I wished Ronnie had been able to work it out with her, but Penny assured me they were much better coparents and people if they lived apart without romantic entanglements.

"For all his faults, Ronnie's a great parent and a good guy, and I'm sure sooner or later he'll become a good man. He just needs time to grow up. And I hope he realizes that it's not any woman's job to do that for him, because there's a certain someone who's been waiting a long time for him to figure it out." Penny smiled and raised her eyebrows meaningfully in Izzy's direction.

Izzy was in the karaoke corner of the restaurant dancing and singing with Longganisa (who was decked out in a full Mrs. Claus outfit) and Isaiah to a song that he'd had on a constant loop since he first arrived, and Ronnie stood to the side watching the two with a softness in his eyes I'd never seen before. Penny was right—he still had a ways to go, but maybe for her, for the two people in front of him that he cared about the most, maybe he'd get there in the end.

My conversation with Penny was interrupted by the tinkling of the door chimes and Nisa's barking as she greeted our guests who arrived for our Noche Buena celebration: the Calendar Crew with Marcus and Bernadette, Amir and Adeena, Elena and her mom, and finally, Detective Park and Jae with their parents.

Eating and drinking and talking all began in earnest, and we even fit in a few Christmas carols (of course Adeena sang the Mariah Carey song even though she absolutely did not have the range). As things began to wind down, Detective Park stood up and said he had a few important things to announce.

"First of all, I thought you should know that, effective immediately, I am officially retired. This means no consulting work for the Shady Palms Police Department, no emergency fill-ins, no security guard posts, nothing. I am done with having to clean up after Sheriff Lamb, and can only hope I've trained Detective Nowak well enough to take my place."

"That's great, man," Ronnie said, though he was probably just happy to not have a cop so close to our family. "But what are you going to do now?"

His eyes strayed toward his mom, and so did Detective Park's. Detective Park cleared his throat. "Take it day by day, like everyone else. And hopefully, spend more time with the people I love." He raised a glass in my aunt's direction. "Merry Christmas, Rosie."

My aunt, eyes wide, made her way slowly over to Detective Park (dang, what was I supposed to call him now?) and put her hands in his. As the two shared their very first kiss, everyone cheered and laughed as Longganisa danced around the couple, barking her approval. I wiped the tears streaming from my eyes and leaned into Jae, who wrapped an arm around my shoulder. I needed to remember that: Take it day by day and spend time with the people I love.

I raised my glass to the new couple. "Merry Christmas, everyone!"

What a beautiful end to a heck of a year. I wondered what the next one would bring.

Acknowledgments

What an absolutely wild ride these last couple years have been! When I first signed my contract with Berkley, it was for three books in the Tita Rosie's Kitchen Mystery series. And now here we are at Book 3, and Lila and I have learned and changed and grown so much in that short time. I was extremely emotional when I turned in the original draft of this story to my editors, not knowing if this was the end for Lila and her crew. But thanks to all of you who've bought my books, we get another three books in the series! So first and foremost, I'd like to thank my readers. I honestly couldn't have made it this far without your support.

I of course need to thank the team that makes this all possible: my wonderful agent, Jill Marsal; my editors, Angela Kim and Michelle Vega; and the rest of my Berkley team—Dache' Rogers, Daniela Riedlova, Jessica Mangicaro, Kristin del Rosario, and Jennifer Lynes—as well as Vi-An Nguyen for continually killing it when it comes to my covers. It's kinda like choosing your favorite child, but I think this cover is the best one yet. I'd also like to thank Ann-Marie Nieves and the rest of the Get Red PR crew for all their amazing help.

Shout out to the Berkletes who've been there with me since the beginning of this pub journey, as well as to the new crew—you've made these last few years not just bearable, but unbelievably fun.

Much love to my IRL besties, who keep me grounded and remind me there's a world outside of writing: the Winners Circle (Kim, Jumi, Linna, and Robbie), Amber and Aria (and Matt, I guess), and Ivan aka Snookums. And big thanks to my buddy Oni for letting me use his coquito recipe! So sad that Bacardi 151 was discontinued because it was absolute fire.

Huge thanks to my family, who have always supported me and are the best street team.

And to James: I lied in the dedication, we both know I'm the funny one. Sorry, babe! <3

Recipes

Tita Rosie's Champorado Recipe

Champorado is a sweet rice porridge made with cocoa powder (or tablea, if you're making the traditional version) and glutinous rice, topped with evaporated and/or condensed milk. I'm not usually into sweet breakfasts, but Filipinos love the sweet and salty combination, and I'm no exception. This breakfast treat is traditionally served with tuyo, or dried, salted fish. However, I didn't grow up with that combination, so I prefer serving my champorado with a side of bacon. It has the same salty, crispy smokiness of the fish without smelling up my kitchen so early in the morning (I actually really like tuyo, but frying the fish creates a rather pungent smell that's not for everyone).

SERVES 4

Ingredients:

4 cups water
1 cup glutinous rice

½ cup cocoa powder or 4–5 pieces tablea chocolate,
    chopped
½ cup sugar (I prefer brown, but granulated works
    just fine)
Evaporated milk, condensed milk, and additional
    sugar/sugar substitute for serving

NOTE: You can make this dish vegan by substituting coconut milk or your favorite nondairy milk.

DIRECTIONS:

1. Boil the water and add the rice. Cook for about 5 minutes, stirring often.

2. Add the cocoa powder or chopped tablea and lower the heat to medium-low. Cook, stirring often, until the mixture starts to thicken and the cocoa powder is fully incorporated with no lumps or the tablea is fully melted and incorporated.

3. Add the sugar and cook for 5 to 10 minutes, stirring occasionally so the rice doesn't stick to the bottom of the pot.

4. Turn off the heat once you've achieved your desired doneness and consistency—some people prefer soft rice while others prefer it more al dente. The mixture will thicken as it cools, so you can add more water if you prefer a looser porridge.

5. Serve in bowls and let each diner top their champorado as desired with the assorted milks and sweeteners.

Lola Flor's Bibingka

These soft, spongy rice cakes are traditionally eaten around Christmastime, but are also a yummy snack enjoyed year-round. To get the most authentic flavor, similar to what you'd get from a street vendor in the Philippines, you'd want to grill this over charcoal. That's what Lola Flor does, but she's hardcore. For us lesser mortals, the oven works just fine. The banana leaves that line the molds are optional but *highly* recommended because the flavor they impart in these rice cakes is incomparable.

SERVES 12

Ingredients:

Banana leaves, cut to fit your molds (optional)

2 tablespoons butter, melted

1 cup granulated sugar

¾ cup (6 fluid ounces) coconut milk

¼ cup (2 fluid ounces) whole or evaporated milk

1 ½ cups rice flour (NOT glutinous rice flour)

1 teaspoon baking powder

¼ teaspoon salt

Toppings (optional):

1–2 salted duck eggs, thinly sliced

Unsweetened coconut, shredded
Cheddar cheese or Velveeta, grated
Butter, melted
Granulated sugar

DIRECTIONS:

1. Preheat the oven to 400°F.

2. Clean the banana leaves under running water, making sure not to rip them. If your banana leaves are tough, pass them briefly over an open flame on your stove or microwave them in 30-second intervals. Once the leaves are soft and pliable, line a 12-cup cupcake/muffin tin or brioche mold with the banana leaves. You can also make it in one 8-inch round pan, but you may need to adjust the cooking time. Use scissors to cut off the excess banana leaves around the edges, since they burn easily.

3. In a large bowl, mix the melted butter and sugar until combined.

4. Add the coconut milk and whole milk to the bowl and whisk until combined.

5. Sift the rice flour, baking powder, and salt into the wet ingredients. Whisk together the ingredients until there are no lumps.

6. Pour ¼ cup of batter into each mold. Top with one to two slices of duck egg, if using.

7. Put the molds on a sheet pan to help stabilize the bibingka. Put the molds and sheet pan into the oven.

8. After 10 minutes, rotate the pans 180 degrees to promote even baking. Sprinkle with coconut, if using, and return the pans to the oven.

9. Bake for another 10 to 15 minutes. Check for doneness by pushing a chopstick or thin knife into the center of the bibingka. If it comes out clean, it's done.

10. Brush the tops of the bibingka with melted butter and sprinkle with sugar and grated cheese, if desired. Let cool slightly and enjoy warm or at room temperature.

Lila's Salabat Snickerdoodle Squares

As delicious as the traditional snickerdoodle, but so much easier to make! This is another recipe for you ginger fiends out there, though the spiciness can easily be adjusted up or down by how much crystallized ginger you choose to include. If you omit it completely, you might want to add a bit more sugar to compensate for the extra sweetness the crystallized ginger supplied. This is one of Lila's new favorite recipes, and mine, too!

YIELD: 12 SQUARES

Ingredients:

Cookie bar:

1 stick of butter, melted
1 egg
½ cup granulated sugar

⅓ cup brown sugar, packed

1 teaspoon vanilla extract

1 cup flour

¼ teaspoon cream of tartar

¼ teaspoon salt

¼ cup crystallized ginger, chopped (optional)

Salabat topping:

¼ cup granulated sugar

2 teaspoons cinnamon

1–2 teaspoons ground ginger

⅛–¼ teaspoon cayenne (optional)

DIRECTIONS:

1. Preheat oven to 350°F. Prepare an 8-x-8-inch baking pan by lining it with foil and/or spraying it with oil or nonstick baking spray.

2. In a large bowl or stand mixer fitted with paddle attachment, mix the melted butter (cooled to the point it's no longer hot) with the egg, sugars, and vanilla extract. Mix until smooth.

3. Add the flour, cream of tartar, salt, and crystallized ginger (if using) and stir until just combined. Don't overmix it!

4. Pour the batter into the prepared pan, smoothing the top lightly with a spatula.

5. In a bowl, combine all the ingredients for the topping and whisk until combined.

6. Evenly sprinkle the salabat topping mixture over the batter. Use all of it! It may look like a lot but it soaks in while baking.

7. Bake for about 25 minutes, or until done. A knife or chopstick inserted in the center should come out clean or with a few moist crumbs, but no wet batter. Cool before slicing and serving.

Xander's Coquito

Coquito, which many people think of as Puerto Rican coconut eggnog, is a rich, delicious treat served around the holidays. Like Xander, this recipe is loud and packs a punch. Drink responsibly! (Credit goes to my friend Onix Orellano for his recipe!)

YIELD: A LOT; ROUGHLY TWO 750-MILLILITER BOTTLES

Ingredients:

4 cinnamon sticks

3 cups water

3 egg yolks

2 12-ounce cans evaporated milk

2 14-ounce cans sweetened condensed milk

2 15-ounce cans cream of coconut

1 tablespoon vanilla extract

1 750-milliliter bottle Malibu black rum

½ cup Bacardi rum

DIRECTIONS:

1. Place cinnamon sticks and water in a small pot and turn heat to

high. Boil for 4 to 5 minutes or until the water is very brown and the cinnamon flavor is infused in the water.

2. In a large bowl, whisk the egg yolks, then mix in the evaporated and condensed milks, cream of coconut, and vanilla.

3. Slowly mix in 2 cups of boiled cinnamon water.

4. Add the Bacardi rum.

5. Add Malibu to taste.

6. Pour into large pitcher(s) or bottles and chill in fridge or freezer before serving.

NOTE: After chilling, coquito makes a solid layer of coconut cream. That layer can be skimmed off and discarded or whisked in before serving.

Keep reading for a special preview of

Murder and Mamon

Coming soon from Berkley Prime Crime!

"Y ou do realize we're a cafe, not a plant shop, right?"

I stared at the array of blooms and greenery filling the front of the Brew-ha Cafe, all lovingly grown and arranged by Elena Torres, the cafe's resident green witch. Her plants, dried herbs, and teas had always been an important part of our business, but they usually had their own corner, which she carefully tended. Today, they spilled out over almost every surface in the shop: our floating shelves held potted spring flowers, adding a riot of color that popped against our brick accent wall. Long tendrils of lush greenery trailed down our pastry cases. And the invigorating aroma of fresh herbs wafted around the cafe from their placement at each table, the fragrance of basil, rosemary, mint, and lavender providing a wonderful antidote for those getting over the winter blahs. You'd think it'd be overwhelming combined with the cafe scents of coffee, tea, and pastries, but they somehow worked in harmony and created our own version of Brew-ha Cafe aromatherapy.

Elena just grinned at me. "We are a business that likes to make money, and I guarantee you that all the plant parents and aspiring plant parents that come here will snatch these up in no time. Besides, spring is so beautiful and fleeting, we should really take advantage of it. Our customers love our seasonal offerings."

Spring had most definitely sprung in my little hometown of Shady Palms, Illinois, and all the residents were preparing for the Big Spring Clean next week, an annual monthlong event when local business owners offered discounts to entice customers out after a long winter. It was also the perfect time to clear out old stock and start advertising our new seasonal offerings.

My best friend and other business partner, Adeena Awan, was embracing spring's floral vibes by pushing her signature lavender chai latte as well as her new seasonal creations, including a lavender honey latte (the honey sourced from Elena's uncle's local apiary), lavender calamansi-ade, and a wildflower matcha (I didn't really like floral flavors, but even I had to admit the matcha drink was stunning). Adeena's begging led to me developing lavender-salted honey shortbread and lavender-calamansi shortbread to pair with her drinks, both of which were absolutely divine. In exchange, she came up with two "Filipino cream soda" recipes for me: pandan and calamansi, the flavors and bright colors as unexpected as they were delicious and refreshing.

As for me, I was leaning into "spring means green" and had prepared pandan-pistachio shortbread and brownies with a pandan cheesecake swirl. I also came up with a red bean brownie recipe, which wasn't particularly springlike, but hey, I was in a brownie mood. I finished stocking the pastry case and moved to prop open the cafe door—we weren't due to open for another fifteen minutes, but on a sunny day like today, the gentle breeze and fresh air were more than welcome in the shop.

I stood in front of the cafe for a moment, my face lifted to the sun. My preference for cold weather and dark color palettes aside, there was something about me that absolutely craved a good bit of sunshine. Maybe it was my Filipino heritage, and the love of sunlight ran deep in my islander blood. Or it could just be a vitamin D deficiency, I don't know. Either way, I appreciated this moment of Zen before the morning rush began.

"Hey Lila, get back in here! I made you another iced wildflower matcha!" Adeena called.

Forget Zen, caffeine was calling.

As I picked up my drink from the front counter, the money plant next to the register caught my eye and I remembered that I actually had plant-based business with Elena to take care of. I joined my partners at the table, a tray of my pastries and several dishes of honey waiting for us.

"What's with all the honey?" I asked, as I split open a fresh-baked scone. A curl of steam escaped and I hummed to myself as I dolloped a bit of clotted cream on top and added a drizzle of honey.

Elena studied my face as I took a huge bite. "The honey I've been sourcing from my tio's apiary has been selling really well here, so I thought it'd be fun to play with an infused honey recipe. Something exclusive to the Brew-ha Cafe. So what we've got here is—"

Elena pointed at the dish of honey I'd just used, but before she could tell me what was in it, Adeena interrupted her. "Wait, don't tell her! We wanted to test her palate, remember? See if she can guess what you used to infuse each honey."

I had a pretty good, though untrained, palate and sense of smell, and Adeena was forever coming up with little tests to see if I could determine what was in certain foods and drinks. I didn't mind— these tastings had fast become a ritual with us, a fun way to start the day and keep my senses sharp. Plus I did enjoy showing off a bit.

I was pretty sure I knew what spices were in the honey I'd just sampled, but just in case, I took another healthy bite of the honey-topped scone and chewed slowly, letting the contrasting textures and flavors permeate my mouth. The crisp crust of the scone yielded to a soft, fluffy interior that melted in the mouth. The clotted cream added body and richness and perfectly complemented the sweetly spiced honey.

"Star anise, cinnamon, cloves, black pepper, and just a touch of ginger," I pronounced. "Did you take inspiration from Adeena's chai spice mix?"

Adeena applauded and Elena laughed and said, "That's it exactly. I wish I could get a better ginger flavor in there, but too much ground ginger changes the texture of the honey, even when strained. And fresh ginger introduces moisture to the mix, which means it would need to be refrigerated so it wouldn't spoil. I'm working on a salabat honey for you, but it's going to take some time to get that ginger right."

"Yay, looking forward to it. So I'm guessing the chai honey represents Adeena and you're working on the salabat for me, so one of the dishes here is your signature honey?" I asked.

She pointed at the dish in front of her and I broke off a piece of scone to sample this new flavor. One bite and my tongue flared with a powerful, exciting heat. I couldn't decide if I wanted to gulp down an iced latte to cool my mouth or guzzle down the rest of the honey straight—it was a sweet, delicious pain.

"Oh my gulay, is this red chile?" I asked, trying to play it cool as if my nose wasn't running and I didn't have tears threatening to spill over. The heat finally got to me, and I gulped down my wildflower matcha, letting the milk in the tea latte sit on my tongue to stop the burning.

Adeena and Elena cracked up at my reaction, the latter handing me a napkin to dab at my runny nose and watery eyes.

"I'm so sorry, but Adeena insisted that I not tell you to better test your powers. And that's the spicy variation, for people like me and Adeena. I also have a mild variety for people who only want a hint of heat," Elena said, a contrite smile on her face.

Adeena, that jerk, just laughed harder. "She'll be fine. You should've seen her the first time she ate at my house. She started crying after her first few bites, but she wouldn't stop eating. My parents were so weirded out, watching this little kid shoveling biryani in her mouth while tears were running down her face."

My face was already flushed from the spiciness of the honey, and I turned an even deeper shade of red as Adeena relayed that embarrassing childhood story. "I'd never had spicy food before that! Tita Rosie's food is usually on the milder side since Lola Flor's stomach can't tolerate too much spice. I wasn't expecting my food to hurt me."

"So then why did you keep eating it even after it made you cry?"

I dabbed at my watery eyes, careful to only touch them with the napkin in case there was chile residue on my fingers. "It would be rude to not eat the food your family served me. Plus it was super delicious, so the pain was worth it."

There were two other infused honeys on the tray, floral ones if my trusty nose was correct, but I'd have to wait and taste them later—the chile pepper had overwhelmed my taste buds and I would need some time before I could properly taste anything with a more delicate flavor. Once I'd gotten my runny nose under control, I brought up the topic I'd forgotten to ask Elena about earlier.

"Is the money tree for the Calendar Crew ready yet? I want to give it to them before their grand opening on Monday."

My godmothers, Ninang April, Ninang Mae, and Ninang June (or the Calendar Crew, as I privately referred to them), had recently gone into business together, deciding to open a laundromat next door to the dry cleaning service Ninang June had taken over from her deceased husband. Their grand opening was timed to start the same day as the Big Spring Clean, which was rather genius on their part since Shady Palms residents likely had tons of heavy winter bedding and clothing that needed professional cleaning. To congratulate them on their new business, I'd commissioned Elena to grow the biggest, most eye-catching money tree possible. These lovely trees with their ornate braided trunks were symbols of good fortune, and I wanted to show my appreciation to the aunties who'd provided so much help (and stress and judgment, but that's neither here nor there) this past year.

Elena handed me her phone to show me a picture of the plant. "I know you said you wanted the biggest tree possible, but these things can reach eight feet tall, and that seemed a bit much. This one is closer to six feet and really lovely."

After I gave her (and the money tree) my nod of approval, she swiped to the next picture. "I also have a potted orchid I was thinking of giving them. At first, I was going to gift them these gorgeously scented jasmine flowers since you said it was the flower of the Philippines, but I figured the aunties would want something brighter and more eye-catching."

I laughed. "Your instincts were spot-on. Orchids give off a more luxurious feel and the aunties are all about appearances. Thanks for handling this for me, Elena."

As I gave her back her phone, the chimes above the door signaled our first customers of the day. When I saw who they were, I shot out of my chair. "Oh, good morning, ninangs! What brings you here so early?"

All three of my godmothers stood near the register, completely ignoring me as they continued their conversation, talking over each other in rapid-fire Tagalog.

"Honestly, April, this is too much—"

"She's family!"

"I know, but it's so last-minute—"

"We need more help anyway—"

"Exactly, and we don't have the time—"

"We'll figure it out—"

"But does she even know what she's—"

"Of course she knows what she's doing—"

"Yes yes, she's very smart, you keep on saying that, but—"

The three women volleyed these half-finished statements back and forth so quickly, I was getting whiplash trying to keep up with their conversation.

I waved my hand to get their attention. "Um, can I get you all anything? We've just released our seasonal offerings, and—"

"Lila!" Ninang April interrupted me. "Just the person I wanted to see. You're close to her age, you'll be the perfect guide."

Ninang Mae and Ninang June, both wearing grim expressions, brightened up as they studied me. "You might be right, April," Ninang Mae said. "We don't have time for this distraction, so it's better for the young people to welcome her."

"Welcome who?" I still had no idea who or what they were talking about, but now that their plan involved me, a sense of dread pooled in my stomach.

"My niece just arrived from the Philippines, and she'll be staying with me for a while. She just graduated from college, so she's only a few years younger than you. I thought maybe we could have a welcome dinner for her at your restaurant, and you and your friends can play tour guide," Ninang April said, smiling first at me, then at Adeena and Elena.

Behind her back, Ninang Mae and Ninang June shook their heads vigorously at me but stopped as soon as Ninang April turned to look at them. That definitely didn't bode well for me, but I couldn't think of a way to turn down Ninang April without upsetting her and incurring her wrath.

"Why don't we see if Tita Rosie and Lola Flor are available for that welcome dinner first and we can go from there?" I suggested.

My aunt and grandmother ran Tita Rosie's Kitchen, the small Filipino restaurant next to my shop. Considering my aunt was the kindest, most welcoming person ever—and her nurturing nature meant she was determined to feed the world—I knew this was just me delaying the inevitable. Of course Tita Rosie would host the dinner. But I needed time to talk it over with my crew and figure out what the heck was going on and why my godmothers were so divided over this.

"You're right, I need to go over the menu with them anyway. Divina is rather picky, I have to make sure the food meets her standards," Ninang April said, almost to herself, as she turned away and headed toward the door. Ninang Mae and Ninang June just shook their heads and followed her out.

"Yo, what was that all about?" Adeena asked as she cleared the table we'd been sitting at.

Elena took the tray of dirty dishes from her girlfriend and started back toward the kitchen. "Sorry to say this, Lila, but this is your family we're talking about, so you know what this all means."

I groaned, as the truth of her words sank in. There was no doubting it. A lifetime of dealing with my aunties and all their drama told me one thing:

Ninang April's niece was going to be trouble.